Previously published as *Wonder Woman's Guide to...*
...JULIE ANNE LINDSEY

A MEMBER OF THE SERIES:
...

# A GEEK GIRL'S
# GUIDE TO JUSTICE

# A GEEK GIRL'S GUIDE TO JUSTICE

## JULIE ANNE LINDSEY

**WORLDWIDE.**

TORONTO • NEW YORK • LONDON
AMSTERDAM • PARIS • SYDNEY • HAMBURG
STOCKHOLM • ATHENS • TOKYO • MILAN
MADRID • WARSAW • BUDAPEST • AUCKLAND

Recycling programs
for this product may
not exist in your area.

A Geek Girl's Guide to Justice

A Worldwide Mystery/May 2019

First published by Carina Press

ISBN-13: 978-1-335-45542-0

**Printed in U.S.A.**

# A GEEK GIRL'S
# GUIDE TO JUSTICE

# ONE

"WHAT DO YOU THINK?" I shifted from foot to foot in a plaid A-line skirt and crimson blouse. "Too much?"

My best friend, Nate, dragged his reluctant, unseeing gaze from my big screen to me. His thoughts were obviously elsewhere, more specifically in the online kingdom of REIGN, a role playing game we co-owned. A game in desperate need of a project manager to handle promotion, improvements and scheduled updates. A game he'd recently quit an amazing job to run full time. He jostled the leggy blonde on his lap. "This is all you."

Fifi slid onto the cushion beside him and clapped. She clapped for everything. I'd hired her as tech support at my day job last fall, and she'd accepted the position as Nate's girlfriend shortly thereafter. Normally, her enthusiasm was delightful, but an hour before my big date, the clapping wasn't helping.

I scooped cast-off wardrobe pieces from my enormous leather sectional and held them to my body. "What about something more casual?" I arranged a short-sleeve black sweater against my blouse and tipped back at the waist so it wouldn't fall. "This? You think this is better?" I pressed the waistline of my favorite tan pedal pushers against my hips. "We can concentrate on the key pieces. I'm accessorizing with fear and awkward."

Fifi tilted her head in deep consideration. "I like the skirt. It's very you—smart, sassy, fantastic."

Nate wrinkled his nose while typing madly on a wireless keyboard. "I liked what you had on when we got here."

I closed my eyes and jogged in place. The growl that followed might have been mine. "Please be serious." I'd had on ten-year-old jeans, toe socks and a Chewbacca T-shirt. "I haven't seen Jake in two months. It feels like we're starting all over again, and I can't take this kind of pressure. You know I can't. I should cancel." I turned in search of my cell phone. "We should meet for coffee sometime instead. Ease back into things."

"No!" Nate and Fifi answered in unison.

Jake Archer was a Deputy US Marshal and my sort-of-boyfriend who'd spent the past two months undercover. I'd met him ten months ago when he thought I was a cybercriminal and possible murderess. Eventually, I'd cleared my name, and he asked me out. Lots of lead-up, but the relationship hadn't really taken off. We were too busy.

Nate crossed his legs and looked my way. "Did Fifi tell you, we decided you guys are our OTP."

People who desperately loved a movie, show or book and really wanted two characters to get together called them their OTP. One. True. Pairing. Like Han Solo and Princess Leia or Elizabeth and Mr. Darcy. I'd never been treated like a fictional character before, but I liked it, and I couldn't argue. If real thirty-year-old geek girls could fall in love with men who also weren't fictional, I'd fall hard for Jake. Unfortunately, real-life romance had never been my sweet spot. I excelled more in comic books, technology and trivia.

"Breathe, Mia." Fifi pushed onto her feet and headed my way. "What are you most comfortable wearing?"

"Pajamas."

She traded the pedal pushers in my left hand for a pair of white cuffed and pleated shorts. "Lies. Try these with the sweater."

"Fine." I ran down the hall to my room. "These shorts are kind of short," I hollered through my open door. My newly constructed penthouse apartment was too extravagant for my taste, but I adored the location, so I was adjusting to the super fancy everything. If I could've found a one-bedroom furnished with beanbags and surrounded by twenty-foot walls, I would've probably opted for that, but beggars can't be choosy.

Nate's low chuckle carried over the drone of REIGN's background music.

"What did you say?" I hustled back to my gargantuan living room and struck a no-nonsense pose. A newly setting sun bathed my wall of windows in an array of delightful hues from scarlet to gold. "I heard you laughing."

He lifted his palms as if I might actually whack him. "Nothing. I only pointed out that you're roughly the size of a pixie so nothing can be short on you."

I fussed with the sweater hem and adjusted my tortoiseshell glasses. "I'm almost five foot three and you know it." The price tag on the shorts poked my skin. There was a reason I'd never worn them. They were too short.

Nate held up a peace sign. "Five-two. Accept your fate. It could be worse. You could be a six-foot brainiac ginger, built for boxing." He threw some air punches. Fifi clapped.

"I'm changing the shorts. This whole place smells like pizza rolls and popcorn." I threw in a secondary complaint for good measure. My mood was on a downward spiral.

My playlist cut out and my phone rang. Maybe Jake was canceling.

Nate lunged for my phone before I could reach it. "Mia Connors's phone."

He spoke sweetly for a moment, then pressed the device to his chest. "It's Grandma."

I dropped my head forward and mimed pulling my hair. My family was cuckoo. Extremely codependent, successfully functional, but otherwise bananas. I didn't have time for whatever Grandma wanted at eight o'clock on a Friday night. I'd seen her twice today, once for lunch and again at the Renaissance Faire. I needed time for my own crisis. "Hello, Grandma."

"Mia, can you do me a favor?"

I lifted my eyes to glare at Nate. "Sure."

"Good. Something strange is happening and I want you to check on it for me."

"Of course." I went to my room and kicked off the shorts. I stepped into a pair of vintage gray culottes. "What's going on?"

"Do you remember Dante Weiss?"

"No." I inhaled the calming scents of my room—soft powders, floral sprays and makeup—then headed back into the living area, where the pungent odor of slightly burnt junk food hung in the air.

Fifi stopped me with a grotesque expression. She pointed at the culottes and stuck out her tongue. I went back to my room.

"You remember Dante," Grandma insisted. "He's one of my oldest friends. He and your grandfather were like brothers. We did Civil War reenactments together for years. I was a nurse back then."

"Aww." Sometimes I forgot Grandma had a vibrant and colorful life before she became matriarch of our crew. "I've always wanted to be a soldier in one of those reenactments. We should do that sometime."

"Oh, it's a hoot. You'd love it."

"I'd like to be the drummer. Hey! I think the Battle of Gettysburg is in July. We can make it a getaway week-end, but I don't want to camp unless we take an RV."

"We could rent an RV."

I swapped the culottes for the short shorts and tugged the bottoms, hoping they'd get longer. *Why'd I even buy these?* Eighty-five percent of my thighs were showing. I needed a tan.

I finger-brushed my waist-length hair and swiped gloss over my lips. "You said you needed something, Grandma?"

"Oh! Yes. Dante called. He said it was urgent that he see me. He sounded awful, so I told him to come right over, but he never arrived. Dante was the first person to invest in our company. Without his startup funds and advice, your grandpa and I would never have given our dream a chance."

Slowly, the name jiggled loose a memory. "Okay. I know now. His personal assistant and I are friends on-line."

Dante might have funded Grandma's initial line of Guinevere's Golden Beauty products, but thirty years and the internet had made her semi-famous, at least in the Renaissance Faire world. As the CIO and face of the company, I kept tabs on everything digitally. "Do you think he's okay?"

"I don't know. He sounded frantic when he called. He said he wasn't far and he'd be here in a few minutes, but he never arrived."

"Weird."

"Are you busy right now?"

I pulled handfuls of dark barrel curls over my shoulder and assessed my hopeless wardrobe choice. "I'm getting ready. Jake's coming over." I swapped my tortoiseshell glasses for black frames and reevaluated. I barely knew what to say to my coworkers when they came back from vacation. What was I supposed to say to a guy I'd dated a few months before he disappeared? We'd spent more time together during the murder investigations than after.

Jake was a busy guy. I was no better. Between my responsibilities to Grandma's company, my day job as IT Manager at the gated community where I lived, and acting co-owner of REIGN, my time was spent before I earned it. Add in all my family's emergencies and general drama, and it was easy to understand why I was terminally single. I'd resigned myself to that fate until Jake came along and messed it up. Now I was wearing short shorts and too much eye shadow. "I have to go, Grandma. I don't have anything to wear and I need to freak out."

"Fine, but will you check with Bernie about Dante?"

I made a face at my reflection. "Why not? Maybe by the time I walk to the guard gate and back, I'll be calm."

"Excellent. Let me know what she says."

"Sure." I disconnected and changed back into the plaid skirt and red blouse. I rolled my hair into a classic bun and dusted my palms. If Jake didn't like it, there was nothing I could do.

"Guys?" I called, sliding down the hall to my living room on bobby-socked feet.

Nate laughed when he saw me.

Fifi smiled.

"Grandma wants me to check with Bernie about a guest she's expecting. You want to come with me?"

Nate levered himself off the couch and set the keyboard aside. "Everything okay?"

"Yeah, but I've got nervous energy to burn, so I'm going. While I'm out looking for her friend, I might as well stop by her place and go over some things."

Fifi moved into the foyer. "How many square feet is your place?"

"Twenty-five hundred. Why?"

"Two bedrooms?"

"Three."

She tipped her head side to side, considering the idea. "Or two plus a really nice-sized closet?"

"Basically." I grabbed my keys and slid my feet into black flats. "Let's hurry. I want to get back before Jake gets here. Should we order Thai? Do you think he's eaten? Is it rude that we already ate?"

They followed me onto the elevator and exchanged a look.

Nate shook his head. "We ate junk food two hours ago. That didn't count as dinner. Don't worry about it."

Fifi stroked his arm and shot me a remorseful smile. "We made plans for tonight. We assumed you'd want to be alone with Jake." She leaned into the sharp V of Nate's side and wrapped her thin arms around his middle. Her Tiffany blue sundress was a perfect match for her eyes.

"Oh, yeah, of course. You guys go ahead." I stepped into the evening with enough nervous energy to run a marathon.

Warm summer air kissed my cheeks and settled my

frantic heart. An ethereal lavender dome curved over-head, shocked with lines of apricot and gold. The sweet scent of wildflowers hung in the air. There was no place better than Ohio in June.

I paced my steps toward the guard gate, thankful Bernie had taken the extra hours when one of the part time co-eds quit.

Nate's lanky shadow stretched over mine and Fifi's. He hung long arms over our shoulders and squeezed himself between us on the narrow sidewalk. "Mia, don't forget about the meetings we lined up for REIGN. I've got the evening meetings. You're joining in on breakfast and lunch appointments. Right?"

Six project manager interviews in two weeks. Yuck. "Yep. I've got it all saved in my calendar with remind-ers set."

We stopped at the little cedar shake—covered booth guarding the entrance to our gated community. I hugged them goodbye. "Enjoy your night."

The couple snuggled against one another as they made their way to Nate's SUV in the clubhouse parking lot.

"Mia!" Bernie's happy voice split the quiet night be-fore her smiling face popped into view. The brown park ranger-esque uniform coordinated with the nature re-serve theme of our community. Bernie was one of my favorite people on earth and the singular most efficient resource for all things Horseshoe Falls. "What brings you out tonight?"

"I'm looking for a friend of Grandma's. He called to say he was coming, but he never made it to her place."

"That's odd." Bernie puckered her face. "I let a guest in for your grandmother almost twenty minutes ago. He should be there by now, or he should've come back for better directions."

"Don't worry about it. I'm on my way to her place. I'll flag him down if I see him." It wasn't like he could've gotten far.

Horseshoe Falls was surrounded by twenty-foot ivy-covered walls erected to protect wealthy nature enthusiasts from the dreaded urban sprawl. Personally, I liked the sprawl, but I also liked the walls. I lived in the new condo construction. Grandma lived on the other side of the community, where homes were the size of airports and the age range was roughly fifty-five to dead.

"See you later, Bernie." I stepped onto the street and immediately jumped back.

A pack of joggers in sweat suits and hoodies pounded past me on their evening circuit around the main drag. An overzealous runner bringing up the rear broke free and headed around the guard gate into the wide world outside. Good for him. I glanced admiringly at my new ballet flats and did a mental waltz through my shoe closet. I'd run with the female cross-country team in college, but these days I didn't go farther than I could strut comfortably in my designer collection. Working three jobs earned me the right to aching, well-appointed feet, and it was a perk I wouldn't give up easily.

I pushed the reminder of Jake's impending arrival from my mind. What was I supposed to say when I saw him? What if he'd met someone else while he was under-cover? What if he changed his mind about me? Maybe he'd be happier with a nice country girl who didn't wear costumes and babble when he got too close.

I checked the time on my phone and teetered, decid-ing on a pace. I needed to be home when Jake arrived, so I should hurry, but I didn't want to be sweaty when he got there, so I should slow down. Maybe Dante had made it to Grandma's and I could turn back. I brought up the keypad.

A commotion near the lake caught my attention, and I turned my phone in that direction, using the illuminated screen for a better look. A pair of silhouettes made shrill, unintelligible sounds in the distance. One seemed to be human.

I changed direction and ignited my phone's flashlight app, abandoning the call to Grandma. The setting sun hadn't wasted any time dipping behind the two-story walls and distant hillside, casting our community in shadow. "Hello? Everything okay?"

"Help!" A woman's voice called back. "My Sam is in the lake again!"

*Oh, dear.* I sprinted in her direction, tallying a mental list of men named Sam at Horseshoe Falls. I landed at her side moments later, out of breath, but relieved to see "her Sam" was a dripping wet spaniel and the woman was Grandma's neighbor Polly. Sam was at least twice my age in dog years, but spry as a sprite. He jumped onto the shore upon my arrival.

"Hello, Sam." I dropped to my knees and rubbed his wet head. "What are you doing in the lake? You're getting all wet and upsetting your mama."

Polly handed me his leash. "I'm so glad it's you, Mia. He won't listen to me at all."

I snapped the clip onto his collar and stood to preserve my outfit. "It's no problem." I passed her the leash before I ended up in ten-year-old jeans and a Chewbacca shirt after all.

"Thank you. He saw something in the water and tried

to pull it ashore, but couldn't manage with his arthritis. I can barely see this time of night, which is why we're headed home. We'd be there by now if Sam would stay out of the lake." Her exasperation was palpable. "I hope it's not trash in the water," she fussed. "This isn't that sort of community."

I shined my phone's light across the lake's gently rippled surface. "I'm sure it isn't trash." Hopefully it wasn't a duck Sam had slaughtered. I brushed the hand I'd petted him with against my skirt and gagged. Dead duck cooties were no way to start a date night.

"There. Do you see it? It looks like an oil spill." Polly crept closer to the water's edge.

There was definitely something. I baby-stepped around the perimeter for a better look. It was too large to be a duck. "Oh, no." My pulse hammered between my ears, clogging my throat and sending black dots into my periphery. *It's not real.* I closed my eyes and practiced various versions of the mantra that had kept me mostly sane since my run-in with two killers in ten months. *It's not real. You're safe. It's not real.*

I reopened my eyes to the reality I feared most. The body was real. "Call nine-one-one!" I ran my phone to Polly. "Tell them there's a man in the lake and he's not breathing." I tossed my glasses onto the grass and jumped into the murky water. I immediately lost both shoes to the sticky lake-bottom muck. I curled trembling fingers around the gray trench coat floating on the surface like an oversized lily pad and dragged the body toward me.

I flipped the man over and cradled his head on my shoulder as I swam his lifeless body to shore. "It's going to be okay," I assured myself as much as him. I crawled onto the bank and caught him under both arms to pull him over the fresh-cut grass. The job was nearly impossible without the water's assistance.

Polly's voice hiked into hysterics as I cleared the man's airway and checked his pulse. His soft pale skin was cool, but so was the water. There was no pulse, so I breathed for him as a small crowd formed around us and Sam nudged me with his wet muzzle. I worked the man's chest, ashamed at my relief that I didn't know him. I'd lost two friends in less than a year and my heart couldn't take losing another. Ever. I listened to his silent chest and repeated the pumping and breathing pattern until hot tears stung my frozen cheeks.

Polly knelt beside me and pressed her palm to my back. "It's okay." She rubbed a steady circle over my soaking blouse and repeated the words softly. "It's okay."

A wild sob broke free, and I fell back on my haunches, wiping my mouth with both hands, unable to steady my violently chattering teeth. Polly was wrong.

I hadn't remembered Dante Weiss's face at first, but there was no denying him now. Wide rectangle jaw, hooked prizefighter nose, bushy unkempt brows. The man from the lake was Dante Weiss. He was special to Grandma, and he was gone. That was definitely not okay.

# TWO

I SAT ON the ambulance's bumper as an EMT checked my vitals and shined a penlight into my eyes. My glasses were off balance on my face after I nearly crushed them while searching the grass for them. The beautiful summer night I'd admired an hour before had taken a horrific turn. Everything seemed suddenly ominous and foreboding. Even the wildflowers smelled like sadness. I tugged the itchy sterile blanket tighter around my shoulders and pushed the image of Dante's still face from my mind. I pressed the blanket to my mouth. I could still feel his cold lips on mine. Dad had warned me never to perform CPR without a barrier. What if Dante had been poisoned? My tummy knotted painfully. What if I was poisoned?

"How are you feeling?" the EMT asked for the tenth time.

"I should've kept the CPR going longer." Until the ambulances arrived. Until Dante's heart restarted. Until there was a different outcome.

"You did all you could. Tell me how you feel. Physically."

Physically, I was fine. Mentally, I flailed. My ability to process new information had gotten jammed up on the conundrum of *how is this my life*? I'd found three bodies in a year. It was statistically improbable for someone like me, yet here I was, soaked in fish water and calculating when the next one might appear, so I could be in Fiji instead. I'd also determined the number of deadbolts I could feasibly fit on my fancy nine-foot apartment door. Twenty-five, if I left room between each mechanism for proper installation. The idea of installing twenty-five deadbolts was ridiculous, of course, because they'd run floor to ceiling and I'd need a ladder to reach the top ones. Plus, no pizza deliverer in town would wait for me to get my ladder and open twenty-five locks. So, I'd only buy ten.

"Ms. Connors?" the EMT pressed. "I can give you something to help you rest tonight."

I squinted at the full moon and twisted lake water from my hair and clothes. "No, thank you." I didn't want to sleep. I had too many questions and too few locks.

Why had Dante come here? Why tonight? Why had he called Grandma? What could she do to help him? What was his problem?

Uniformed cops shooed wildlife away from the crime scene and strung a makeshift fence of caution tape around a line of dowel rods. A cluster of geese waddled across the street, honking and balking at the unwelcome disruption. Squirrels and owls complained overhead. Men and women in navy windbreakers appeared. White block letters formed the words Crime Scene across their backs. The group spread out and shined giant flashlights at the ground in search of clues.

Where had Dante come from? How'd he end up in the lake?

"Mia!" A familiar tenor boomed up the street.

I craned my neck in search of Dan Archer, Jake's younger brother and our local homicide detective. Footfalls thundered over the pavement, closing in on me at breakneck speed.

"Mia!" He stopped before me with fear in his eyes. "You're okay?" He gripped my blanketed shoulders and released a long shaky breath. He took a seat at my side. "Praise the Lord." He took long steady pulls of air and tapped his phone screen to life. "You scared the crap out of us."

"Who?"

"Jake and me." He made a crazy face. "We heard the call on our scanners. We couldn't get ahold of you or Mary. No one's at the clubhouse this late and Bernie hasn't updated her blog."

Mary was my grandma's name, but everyone called her Grandma, except the Archers, who were far too polite to impose.

"She's on her way. I didn't know you called. Polly has my cell phone." Shoot. Having my precious device be AWOL made me nervous. I hadn't willingly separated from my cell phone in my life.

"Who's Polly?"

"Grandma's neighbor. She was at the lake when I went in. I gave the phone to her so I could try to help."

"Where's Polly now?"

I pointed. "Grandma called when she heard the sirens, but I was having trouble forming words. Polly was with me, so she took the call. The EMT brought me over here a few minutes later."

Dan put his phone away. "I told Jake you're okay. He's on his way."

"What?" I climbed off the bumper and tossed my blanket into the ambulance. "Why is he still coming? I can't let him see me like this." I raked a shaky hand through wet, knotted hair. "Look at me!"

"He doesn't care what you look like. He cares that

you're safe. You're starting to make a track record for yourself. When Dispatch announces a call in your zip code, we worry."

Grandma appeared several feet away. Her normally jovial expression was gone, changed by fear and anxiety to something heartbreaking.

I swung both arms overhead. "Grandma!" I jogged to her side and stopped short of a hug. "I'm so sorry."

She pulled me to her chest and squeezed. "Here. I brought you something dry." She shoved a quilted bag at my chest. "They're things from your old room. I'm not sure they'll fit, but at least they'll be warm." She looked me over and pressed her soft hands to my cheeks. "Polly told me everything. She said I have a very brave and heroic granddaughter. I told her I've always known."

"Thanks, Grandma." Emotion stung my eyes. "You remember Dan Archer."

"Of course." She marched past me and extended her hand to Dan. "You're going to get to the bottom of this, I hope. Dante Weiss was a dear friend of mine. He didn't deserve this."

I climbed into the ambulance and pulled the doors shut behind me to change clothes. The little area smelled of bleach and bandages. I'd never gotten inside an ambulance willingly.

Dan's voice carried through the closed doors. "I want to help you, but I can't overstep here," he explained to Grandma. "I'm limited to homicide investigations. Trust me. If there's any reason to think this was something other than accidental, I'll make certain Dante gets justice."

I shoved damp legs into low-rise skinny jeans from a time in undergrad when I'd lived briefly with Grandma, and pulled a clingy V-neck Batman T-shirt over my head.

The dry fabric warmed me instantly. The soft cotton top still fit, but I was wider and significantly more endowed than the last time I'd worn it. My twenties had been good to me. Then again, late blooming was a lifelong pattern of mine. I rubbed a scratchy blanket against my hair and eavesdropped on Dan and Grandma's conversation.

Grandma's disposition devolved slowly as I pulled tube socks and gym shoes over my frozen, filthy feet. I couldn't make out her words, but her pitch and tone indicated Dan should agree with her soon or be stoned.

I opened the ambulance doors and rejoined them, taking a seat on the cool metal floor.

Dan whistled long and slow. "Hello, Batman."

I wrung excess water from my discarded clothing and dropped the outfit into Grandma's empty bag. "Let's never speak of this outfit again."

Grandma huffed. "It was that or the denim skirt with all the zippers and that tube top with a bull's-eye."

Cool evening wind whipped through me. I pulled my knees to my chest and traced the marks on my shoe with a frozen fingertip. My gray Converse were covered in doodles from a permanent marker and a busy young mind. "This is fine. Thank you for thinking of it. The tube top doesn't have a bull's-eye, though. It's Captain America's shield."

"You always loved the soldiers."

Truer words were never spoken.

Dan tried to cover a laugh by coughing into his hand. Didn't work. He did, however, regain Grandma's attention.

"Dante couldn't swim," she started again. "He wouldn't have gone into the lake. He wouldn't have gone near the lake. Someone put him in there."

I wasn't convinced. "Maybe he learned to swim since you last discussed it. It has to have been years since you'd have a reason to talk about swimming."

"He was deathly afraid of water." Her voice cracked. She covered her mouth with one hand. "He was terrified."

*Not really the time or place for a swim either.*

Dan stared through the night to the lake. Perhaps her proclamation or despair had gained his interest. "He was fully dressed when he went in?"

"Yes," I answered. "He even had a trench coat on."

Dan swung his gaze back to Grandma. "Any chance he'd been drinking? History of drug use or a medical condition that might have disoriented him?"

"No. I mean, maybe in the sixties, but that was another time. He's an upstanding citizen today."

I shook my head. "Don't say anything else. We don't need another public relations nightmare."

She pulled her long silver braid over one shoulder and fiddled with the ends. "There's nothing to clean up. We stopped hanging with Mary Jane decades ago, if you know what I mean."

"I do. Everyone does. Please stop."

"Life was simpler then."

My life was simpler a year ago, before I faced my first murder victim and shortly thereafter, his murderer. Time made everything more complicated. "I don't understand where he left his car. Bernie said she let him through the gate about twenty minutes before I found him. The only vehicles I see are emergency responders with police chasers."

Dan scanned the area. "Horseshoe Falls isn't that big.

If Bernie saw the car come in, and not go out, we'll find it tonight."

Grandma widened her eyes. "Did you say *we*? You'll help?"

"I'll do what I can, but this won't be assigned to me unless there's reason to assume foul play."

Grandma pursed her lips. She'd already made her case.

Polly and Sam closed the distance between us. She handed me my phone. "I didn't realize I still had this." She hugged Grandma. "I gave my statement to the officers. We're going home. I need hot tea to process this nightmare. Sam needs a bath after swimming in that water. He smells like duck doo-doo."

I turned my head for a sniff of my hair. Gross, so did I.

Polly hugged Grandma goodbye, and offered me a sad smile and tiny wave.

I gave the unfortunate scene another look. Cops and flashlights speckled the night. Freestanding spotlights aimed at the lake. A familiar silhouette stormed its way up the crowded street, dipping around barrier tape and moving with swift authority.

A brick of emotion wedged in my throat. "Jake's here and I'm dressed like a Bratz doll."

Dan shook his head. "You're fine."

"I smell like duck poop."

He laughed.

"Mia." Jake's protective arms were around me in an instant. "What happened?"

"Uh." I sniffled. "I'm fine, but I found him and he's not fine. Grandma knew him." I pulled away. "I stink. I'm so sorry."

Jake's eyes sparkled with a smile that hadn't quite

reached his mouth. He lifted his gaze to his brother. "Got anything to add?"

Dan filled him in while I mentally lined up the questions from here to Cleveland.

Jake crossed his arms. "How'd you get here so fast?"

Dan looked away before answering. "I told you. I heard it on the scanner."

"Yeah. That's not what I asked. I was on my way here when I heard the call. You still beat me, which means you were in the area. Anything going on tonight?"

"No." Dan closed his eyes for a long beat. "I met a woman for dinner. It's new, and it's not a big deal. I don't want to talk about it."

Was everyone dating someone?

Jake relaxed his stance. "Who found the victim?"

"Dante," Grandma corrected. "Polly's dog found him in the water. Polly didn't know it was a man until Mia came along."

"And you went in to save him?" Jake asked me.

"Yeah." Not that I was any help.

He nodded stiffly. "Nice work."

"He's dead."

"You didn't know that."

A little bald man with a navy windbreaker hustled into our growing circle. "Archer?"

"Yeah." Jake and Dan turned to face him.

He smiled. "Well, what do you know? Two Archers." He shook their hands. "We've probably met before. I'm with the medical examiner's office. Which one of you is Homicide?"

Grandma harrumphed. Her version of *I told you so*.

"That's me." Dan stepped forward and shook the

man's hand. "Detective Dan Archer. This is my brother, Deputy US Marshal Jake Archer."

Jake stared, blank-faced, at the man. The ready-for-anything expression was simultaneously sexy and terrifying. "Nice to meet you." Law-enforcement mode was officially activated.

"I've got something for both of you then." The ME waved to a pair of medics wheeling a gurney between them. Dante was zipped into a black coroner bag on top.

He stopped them before they loaded the gurney into a neighboring ambulance. "Just a minute, fellas." He unzipped the bag and motioned the Archers in for a closer look.

I hung back with Grandma.

Dan circled the gurney, making room for Jake. "You got extra gloves?"

The ME handed each Archer a pair of blue surgical gloves. "You see this?" He pushed Dante's coat aside. A red stain marred the white pinstriped dress shirt. "I'll have to run some tests, but at the moment, cause of death is a toss-up. Maybe he drowned. Maybe the stab wound killed him. I'm not sure why someone would throw a dead man in a lake, but that's your jurisdiction, not mine. I'll stick to pathology reports, and let you guys do the rest."

Jake opened Dante's shirt and prodded the broken skin with gloved fingers.

Dan shined a pocket light over the area. "That's a broad wound. What do you think did this? Not a kitchen or pocketknife."

"Machete?" Jake offered.

"Nah." Dan moved the light over Dante's abdomen. "No one stabs with a machete."

The ME zipped the bag. "Like I said. Tests."

I stepped closer. "Maybe the thing he was stabbed with is in his car. We should look for the car. He might've been injured there and made a run for it."

Dan turned serious blue eyes on me. "I'm going to need to take your statement."

"Polly found him. I only hauled him out after the fact." I pointed in the direction Polly had gone a few minutes before. "Last house on the right."

Jake planted giant hands over narrow hips. "I'll get Mia's statement if you want to catch Polly before she puts Sam in the bath."

"Yep." Dan jogged down Grandma's street at a clip.

The ME turned on Jake. "Your turn."

Jake peeled off the gloves. "What do you have?"

The ME dug into his case and retrieved a baggie. "You know this guy?"

Jake turned the baggie over in his fingers. "That's my director. Where'd you find this?"

I peeked around his side. "What's in the baggie?"

"Deputy director's business card."

"Why would Dante have that?" I turned for a look at Grandma, who'd become unusually quiet.

She tented her eyebrows. "Dante was a philanthropist. He supported local charities, schools, politicians, girl scouts."

"Policemen's Ball?" I asked.

Jake frowned. "No." He pulled his phone from his pocket and tapped the screen to life.

The ME snagged the baggie and stuffed it back into his case. "Two Archers on one case. How lucky is this guy?" He hooked a thumb toward Dante's bag.

"Not very," I said. "He was afraid of the water. Some-one stabbed him then threw him into a lake."

Imagine if we all died from our worst fears. I shivered. I'd be suctioned from a spacecraft without a suit.

Grandma wrapped her arms tight across her middle. "Polly said Sam just took off. He pulled his leash right out of her hands. She followed him the best she could, but she didn't see anything unusual."

"Did she hear anything?" Jake asked.

"Just Sam barking and water splashing. He was wet when she got there."

I snaked my arm behind her and pulled her close. "Dan will find out everything he can. These guys will get justice for Dante. Don't worry." I leaned my head against her shoulder.

A cell phone rang and everyone reached for theirs. Jake, Grandma, the ME and I exchanged looks. It wasn't any of ours.

Jake and I had our flashlight apps on in a nanosecond, scanning the ground for gold.

"I'll bet that's Dante's phone," I announced, moving swiftly in the direction of the ringing. "Or the killer's."

The ringing stopped and everyone froze.

We cast our lights in wide arcs over the stubby green grass.

Ding!

I pounced. "Voice mail." A few more steps and "Got it!"

Jake scooped it into a plastic baggie and smiled proudly. "Yes, you do." He worked the phone through the plastic. "Password protected, but this is definitely the vic—Dante's phone." He shot an apologetic look at Grandma. "There's a selfie on the lock screen." The phone went dark a moment later.

I opened and closed my hands in the universal sign for gimmee. "I've got this."

Jake handed me the baggie.

"Grandma?" I swiped the phone to life. "What was Dante's favorite team? Where'd he go to school? Did he have children?" I ran through the list of middle-aged-lazymen passwords as she answered the questions. "It's none of that." I stared at the lock screen wallpaper. A much younger Dante stood on a fishing boat, surrounded by friends. He had a pole in one hand and a massive bigmouth bass hanging from a hook in the other. An aged Jack Russell panted at his side. "What's Dante's dog's name?"

"Barker? He died years ago."

"Perfect." I turned the phone to face Jake. "I'm in."

# THREE

I OPENED DANTE'S recent call log. Whoever he'd spoken with last might give us a clue about what happened. Jake leaned over my shoulder. Dante had an obnoxious amount of calls from two contacts: That Guy and PITA, but the last number he'd dialed was Grandma's.

I handed the phone to Jake. "Any idea who this PITA might be?" I turned for a better look at the area around us. Could the killer be here somewhere? Watching?

Jake examined the phone. "Well, based on these text messages, she's someone who likes to swear and wear low-cut dresses." He turned the display in our direction.

The contact photo on the screen was taken at a fancy event. Her eyes were glassy, probably from the cluster of empty wineglasses behind her, and the curve of her bra was visible in the dip of her clingy red dress. Straight black hair. Big brown eyes. Olive skin.

Grandma poked the evidence-bagged phone. "That's his ex-wife, Angelina, and he's right. She is a PITA."

Jake's cell phone buzzed in his pocket. "Hang on." He handed the evidence baggie to me. "Archer." He strode away, stopping out of earshot.

I dug into Dante's voice messages. The password was simple to crack. *Barker* again. It was disturbing how little people tried to protect their privacy. Of course, at the moment it was also incredibly convenient.

The bulk of Angelina's messages were in angry Mandarin mixed with some choice English names she'd most likely picked up while hanging at the county jail or with sailors on leave.

"Wow." I skipped through the bulk of her calls and paid special attention to the others. Angelina wasn't the only one aggravated with Dante, though the others didn't elaborate so colorfully. Most just left a clipped message and hung up. "He was not a beloved businessman."

"The good ones never are," Grandma said. "They have to make tough choices. People don't like when the chips fall against them."

I worked up an encouraging smile. Grandma was shocked and grieving. I wasn't making this easier. "Sorry. I'm sure you're right." She and Dante had been good friends at one time, and kept in touch over the years, but people changed. "His personal assistant and I are online friends. I see Lara's name pop up from time to time in a forum I frequent. I'll reach out and see what she can tell me. Maybe there was a change in his recent work behavior, or a client who seemed exceptionally unhappy with Dante's services."

"Thank you." Grandma swiped the pad of one thumb under each eye.

Jake sauntered back to us. He'd rearranged his features to something more sympathetic and less cop-like. "Sorry about that. How are you holding up, Mary?" His softer tone and gentler demeanor were incredibly comforting.

I smelled a rat.

"Find anything?" he asked me.

"I reviewed his voice mails. Angelina's a hostile ex. That Guy left a ton of messages, trying to touch base about something non-specific. Mostly every one sounded disgruntled." Lara's insight would help me sort the list into regular people and potential killers.

I followed Jake's gaze over my shoulder to Dan, returning from his trip to see Polly.

"That was quick," Jake called.

Dan shook his head, closing the space between us at a clip. "She was in a hurry to bathe Sam and go to bed. She's a mess. Someone should check with her tomorrow."

"I will," Grandma said.

He nodded and stopped to face off with Jake. "She didn't see anything. She stubbed her toe and nearly tripped a half dozen times on the way up her walk. If I had to guess, I'd say her eyesight isn't too great to start with and her night vision's gone. She said Sam got away from her and headed for the lake. He likes to chase the geese, so she didn't think much of the splashing or commotion. She could've overheard a struggle or it might've been the sounds of Sam jumping in."

Grandma tipped her chin up and squared her shoulders. "I'm going home to make tea."

Her blank expression worried me. "Do you want me to come with you? I can stay tonight, if you want."

"No. Stay and help these boys. I'll initiate the phone tree."

The phone tree was a sad little list of five phone numbers, six if we couldn't reach my sister directly. In that event, we called her husband. The other numbers on our list were Grandma's, Mom's, Dad's and mine. We were a scrawny crew, but we had heart.

Grandma headed home, alternatively illuminated and shadowed by cones of streetlamp light over the sidewalk.

"Do you think she's safe?" I asked. "What if the

killer's looking for her? She was the last person Dante called."

Dan waved to a uniformed cop. "Can you follow that woman to her home and check the perimeter?"

"Yes, sir."

"Then let's get the community canvassed. The killer has to be somewhere and the twenty-foot walls are going to slow him down if he hasn't left yet. What was the victim driving?"

"Late model black town car, sir, according to the woman at the gate." The officer strode down Grandma's sidewalk, easily catching up with her. He spoke into the walkie-talkie on his shoulder as he went. Hopefully, arranging a search team.

The ambulance carrying Dante groaned to life and eased away.

Dan rubbed the back of his neck. "Any idea what your deputy director has to do with this?" he asked Jake.

Jake clenched and released his jaw. He gave me a pointed look. "Yeah. Headquarters called. Dante's been working as a CI."

My mouth fell open. "An informant?" I stage-whispered. "What? Why?"

Jake leveled me with cool blue eyes. "This is confidential information. Understand?"

I nodded.

"Anything you hear or see tonight needs to be kept in this circle." He point to his brother, himself and me. "And keep your grandma out of this investigation. I didn't like the look on her face when she went to make tea." He dragged out the final word.

I'd had the same feeling when she walked away. Hopefully her expression was a look of shock and not conspiracy. "I'll try, but they were friends and the women in my family are…"

"Nuts?" Jake offered.

"Obstinate."

Both Archers laughed.

They weren't wrong. "If she's up to something, I'll find out."

Dan stepped closer and leaned in. "We're not suggesting she's done anything wrong. However, I know personally how tempting it can be to withhold information in the hopes of saving a friend's reputation."

"Right." Jake nodded. "Her dear old friend wasn't the upright man she thought he was. She could be tempted to intentionally overlook something important."

I straightened my spine. "She doesn't know anything."

"Probably not," Jake agreed. "But Dante Weiss laundered money for criminals, most recently for Terrance Horton, a fugitive the marshals have been chasing for years." He paused until I worked my mouth shut. "Going dark takes a lot of cash. We never understood how Horton stayed funded for so long, so we reached out to Dante. He'd been arrested years ago for funding criminals and traded his jail sentence for time serving the marshals. We asked him to get in touch with Horton and offer his services. He did, and Horton took the bait. Dante made an appointment with the deputy director. He had enough information for us to issue an arrest on Horton."

"What kind of fugitive is he?"

Jake gave me a long look. "He's a dirty businessman, not as networked as a mobster, but just as calculating and unsavory. He's wanted for tax evasion, gambling, fraud and unlawful coercion of a minor."

"Gross."

"He's a human leech, but a very wealthy one, but I can't imagine he'd risk coming out of hiding to do this. Not unless the stakes were extremely high."

I scanned the night for someone who looked like a killer. "Could he afford to hire a gun? No. Scratch that. Doesn't matter. Hired guns shoot people, they don't stab and then drown people in quiet community lakes."

Dan shifted at my side. "I'd agree with that."

"So this was personal?" I looked in the direction of Grandma's house.

Jake pulled in a long, audible breath. "We need to locate Dante's car. You came to the lake from your apartment?"

"Yeah. I cut through the field behind the clubhouse when I heard the commotion."

He tipped his head and moved away from the scene. Dan and I followed.

The early summer night grew cooler with each step, struggling to shake the grips of an unusually cool spring. Uniformed officers moved through darkened lawns, shining lights around trees and bushes.

I mentally mapped the fastest way to canvass Horseshoe Falls in search of Dante's car. No one parked on the streets and very few residents left their cars out at night. Unless Dante had left his car in a stranger's driveway, it wouldn't be hard to find. "I'll take the roads east of the clubhouse. If one of you takes the west side and the other walks the parking lots running along the community's center, we can cover the area relatively fast." I ticked off the lots for good measure. "Clubhouse, boathouse, tennis courts, stables."

Jake slid out of his jacket and hung it over my shoulders. "You look miserable. You're pale and your teeth are chattering. We can handle this. I'll walk you home first."

I gripped the jacket on instinct, before it could fall. "Thanks. No. I want to help."

"Your lips are a little blue."

"I'm fine."

"Maybe that outfit cut off your circulation."

Dan snorted. "She is Batman."

I slid my arms into too-long sleeves and snuggled beneath the soft material, pre-warmed by Jake's body heat and scented with his signature fragrance. Shampoo, body wash and cinnamon gum. "We should split up. We'll cover more ground faster."

Dan slowed at the next cross street. "Dante couldn't have run far with a wound like that."

Jake cocked a narrow hip and scanned the night. "Agreed. Question is, which direction was he coming?"

I chewed my lip. "I don't know. From the guard gate, I'd expect him to go this way, but who knows what he was thinking?"

Dan turned in a slow circle. "Think carefully, Mia. Did you see anything out of the ordinary tonight?"

Besides a stabbed man in a lake? "I didn't see anything. Just Polly and Sam, then I pulled Dante from the water." My heart hammered painfully with the memory. "I should talk to Bernie again. The killer might've driven Dante's car out of here. She doesn't stop people on their way out."

Jake widened his eyes slightly, refocusing on Dan. "Did your men secure the gate?"

Dan nodded.

The Archers moved swiftly in the guard gate's direction.

I dialed Bernie. The killer could've been long gone before Dan gave that order. "It's Mia. Have you seen anyone leave in Dante's car?" I stuck two fingers in my mouth and whistled.

The men spun back.

"Bernie said the car hasn't left." The killer was still here. I scurried to Jake's side. Suddenly, staying with him seemed like a really smart idea.

From my new vantage, the parking lights of a town car caught my attention. "Look."

The car was half on the curb, still running, and the driver's door hung open. We were little more than a block from the lake, as Jake predicted.

The men approached with care, each with one hand on their sidearm and eyes vigilant. Wind tussled the limbs of a reaching tree, manipulating shadows over the car.

The brothers circled the vehicle like a pair of sharks. Jake reached into the open door and shut down the engine. He fisted the keys and headed for the trunk. The look on his face sent terror through me.

I swallowed bile. "If there's a body in there, I don't want to see it."

"Worse. Luggage."

Dan snapped on a pair of gloves and opened the back door. "He was running."

Jake slammed the trunk and swore again. He dug the phone from his pocket and dialed. "Weiss was a runner. We've got his car with a trunk full of suitcases. Wherever he was headed, he didn't pack light."

So Dante had made an appointment to meet with the US Marshal Deputy Director, offered to dish the scoop on a fugitive, then changed his mind. Why? He had the director's card in his pocket. Maybe he planned to re-schedule? Something had changed his plans.

*Or someone.*

Panic seized me. I looked for a place to sit before I fell over.

Dan poised his phone and snapped another photo. "Check this out."

Jake leaned over his brother. "What'd you find?"

I crowded in and peered around them. "What is it?"

Dan ran a blue-gloved finger along a tear in the seat's ruined fabric. Blood saturated the leather and pooled at the seam between the seat and back support. "It looks like he was stabbed while he was in the car. The door's open. He probably made a run for it." Dan called some-one on his team for evidence markers, bags and a spare crime scene technician. "It suggests the killer was here."

Jake moved methodically along the street, shining his phone's flashlight app on the asphalt. He followed a sparse trail of blood in the direction we'd come. "He definitely made a run for it. The volume of blood loss increases. His heart was pumping hard."

A young woman jogged to Dan's side with his re-quested supplies. She handed off the bags and set up little numbered plastic teepees beside the blood spots in the street as Jake pointed out the trail.

I wandered ahead, speculating about the final mo-ments of Grandma's dear friend. A man, it seemed, she didn't truly know. He'd been headed in the right direction until he crossed the street toward the lake. Why hadn't he steered clear of the lake if he couldn't swim?

Jake stopped at my side and stared across the field with me. "He was leading the killer away from Mary's house."

I turned my eyes on him. A lump formed in my throat. "Yeah?"

"That's my best guess." He put his arm over my shoulder and tugged me to his side. "We'll figure this out."

I sniffled. "Okay."

"Really." He squeezed me tight before releasing me. "We've got this. You should get some sleep. Check on Mary in the morning. Dan and I will find out who did this."

I nodded, emotion reemerging from nowhere. "I'm sorry about our date." I pulled the coat tighter around my middle. I was a human train wreck. Every time we met after being apart, it was at a crime scene. "I'm glad you're here."

"Dan," Jake called. "I'll be back."

Dan gave him a thumbs-up and kept working his way around the car.

Jake nudged me forward. "I'm walking you home. I'll wait while you shower and change if you want."

"You don't have to."

"I want to."

"Maybe just walk me up."

"Fair enough. I'll come back and check on you before I head home."

As we reached the guard gate, the candy-cane-striped lever rose and fell. Grandma's boyfriend, Marvin, rolled through in his Lincoln.

He powered the window down and stopped. "I heard what happened, Mia. I'm so sorry. Is there anything I can do?"

I shook my head. "Jake's walking me home. Grandma could use some company, I think."

He tipped his hat. "I'm on my way." He powered the window back up and drove away.

Jake smiled. "I like that guy."

Me, too. It helped to know Grandma wasn't alone. I didn't particularly feel like leaving my apartment again tonight, or possibly ever. I imagined sliding into bed and sleeping for a month.

After Jake saw me home, I locked and bolted the door. My brain powered on in the shower and went berserk, tossing questions and wild theories into the abyss. There was a zero percent chance of sleep in my future.

I slipped into my favorite college T-shirt and cotton shorts, then headed for my living room laptop. I opened two windows and typed Dante Weiss into the first search engine and Terrance Horton in the next.

Every search result on Dante suggested Grandma was right. The world had known him as she had. He was a brilliant investor who picked winning projects and supported them until they were on their feet. Dante exchanged startup funds, business contacts and sage advice for a percent of the receiving company's earnings.

He didn't show up on the criminal justice website. Not even a parking ticket.

Terrance, on the other hand, was slick enough to slide off my screen. He'd made off with millions of dollars from unsuspecting people following a number of frauds, and he didn't discriminate. He'd posed as a high-powered broker to the rich, charmed them out of their money for stock investments, then took off with it. He'd also swindled elderly shut-ins out of their retirement by pretending they'd won the lottery. He offered to act as their liaison and collect their winnings for them, *if* they paid him a fee. The fee was small, compared to what he claimed they'd won. The fee was usually the content of their bank account. He'd even posed, briefly, as a scientist holding clinical trials for AIDS research and charged Medicaid for nothing more than saline and vitamin B infusions. He'd transferred those monies to diverse holdings and disappeared when the FBI came calling. When he went dark, he made the fugitive list and became the marshals' problem.

According to Jake, Dante had laundered the money for Terrance that kept him out of the marshals' reach. Terrance knew Dante was trustworthy because Dante had already helped others go to ground, change their identities or flee the United States altogether. How had a lifelong philanthropist gotten in bed with criminals? Was he ever clean? Maybe the person Grandma thought he was had always been a lie. Whatever his deal was, something had spooked him and he was trying to run. Why? My best guess was that Terrance had gotten wind of his CI status and threatened his life. If so, the Archers would figure it out.

Grandma's voice sprang from the speaker of my cell phone. "Hello, hello! Hello, hello!" Marvin had introduced her to the option of voice-recorded ringtones at Christmas. Guess what her gift had been for everyone?

I grabbed my phone and collapsed onto the couch. "Hey, Grandma."

"How are you, pumpkin?" She sounded better than when I'd last seen her. Marvin undoubtedly had a lot to do with that.

"I'm okay."

"Marvin said he saw you with Jake. Is he with you now?"

"No, but I'm fine. He said he'd stop by before he heads home."

"Good." She went quiet for a long beat. "Listen, Marvin and I have done some digging."

I swiveled upright fast enough to blur my vision. "No. Don't do that. Don't dig. Dan and Jake will handle this."

"Dante was my friend. I knew him longer than I've known my daughter. He was your grandfather's best friend."

"I know, but—"

"I want whoever did this to be punished." Her voice broke anew. All pretenses of calm and strength gone. "I just want answers. I have so many questions."

"I know you do, but please promise me you won't look into this yourselves." Horrific memories of being chased through the darkened fairgrounds flashed in my mind's eye. She was over seventy and no match for a lunatic bent on stopping her amateur investigation. I swallowed a painful ball of terror. "You know what happened to me."

The silence filled my heart and lungs.

"Grandma," I pleaded. "I promise to hound Jake for information and give it to you at every turn. I'll dig a little, too, and help in any way I can."

She sniffled and sobbed quietly. "You're excellent at finding dirt."

I liked to think of it as finding truth, but yes. I was. "Let me. Okay? Not you."

"Marvin and I weren't going to beat the pavement." Her voice was suddenly sharp and clear. "I don't want you doing that either. It's dangerous."

"I won't."

"But you'll look online? Where it's safe? And report back what you hear from the Archer boys?"

"Yes." Using the internet to find every minute detail of a person's life was a longtime hobby turned lucrative side business of mine. I could tell Grandma the remaining balance on Dante's high school girlfriend's mortgage in an hour. "It's no problem."

"I still won't be able to sleep tonight."

That made two of us.

# FOUR

I WOKE WITH a headache and a keyboard imprint on my cheek. It was probably fitting I start the day with a pain in my neck. If life had foreshadowing, this was mine. I had lunch plans with Bree, my twin sister and real-life pain in the neck. My muscles were uncooperative in lifting my head from the laptop. My back said I was ten years too old to sleep at my desk when I had a fantastic queen-size bed two rooms away. The rest of me didn't disagree.

"Yeesh." I pushed my roller chair back and willed my body upright with a creak and a groan. Either thirty was the new fifty, or I needed to take better care of myself.

I kneaded the muscles along my shoulders as I puttered into the bathroom for another piping-hot shower. Two steaming cups of coffee later and memories of my evening swim had me back on edge. Someone had murdered a very important person from my grandma's life. And they'd done it inside the walls of Horseshoe Falls, the place I'd moved to feel safer.

I slid bare feet into new kitten heels and grabbed my keys. I'd done enough research last night to know Dante Weiss shouldn't have died like that and Grandma deserved answers. Plus, she'd all but threatened to look into things herself, and that was definitely not happening on my watch.

Early summer sun warmed my cheeks as I emerged from the building and headed toward the scene of the crime. Hard to believe anything bad could happen in a place so beautiful and alive. Wraparound porches overflowed with potted plants and hanging baskets. Emerald-green lawns were outlined in every variety of flower. The air smelled of roses and wisteria. Even the soft blue sky was decorated in dainty white puffs.

The world was deceiving.

I stepped off the perfect cobblestone path leading to the clubhouse and outdoor café and into the pristine field. Fifty yards away, a cluster of people watched the local police drag the community lake. A few residents seemed offended by the unsightly scene. Others snapped photos. The overwhelming majority looked blatantly alarmed.

Darlene Lindsey pulled a red Radio Flyer wagon over the lumpy ground behind her. Trays of lidded paper coffee cups with Dream Bean, her shop's logo, bounced and jostled on the little transport. She handed the cups to onlookers with a smile and a gentle squeeze of her friends' and neighbors' arms.

I jogged to catch her, poking my tiny heels in the ground with every step. "Darlene."

She turned with a bright smile that faded when she recognized me. She dropped the wagon handle and met me with a tight hug. "Oh, sweetie. I'm so sorry. I heard about what happened." She released me and rubbed my arms with her palms. "You must be a mess. Did you sleep?" She wrinkled her nose. Probably at the stubborn imprint marks on my cheek and temple. "Would you like a coffee?"

"Always."

She handed me a cup and looked over the crowd. "It's good you're here. They need to see that you're okay. Everyone's pretty shaken. Things like this don't happen here." She blinked against the sun and plucked wind-blown hair from her eyes. The short dark locks returned to her face faster than she could keep them away. "Coffee makes things better. I have tea, too. Anything to warm us from the inside. You know?"

I blew into the tendrils of steam rising from my drink and curled my fingers around the cup like a security blanket. "Have they found anything?"

"Not yet. Bernie said they're looking for the—" she lowered her voice to a whisper "—murder weapon."

A greasy feeling slid into my gut. *Murder weapon.* The words felt pointed at me. A result, no doubt, of the PTSD I'd struggled with after my most recent run-in with a killer. "I'm going to check on Grandma. She knew the man." I glanced pointedly at the lake.

"Of course."

I hastened past the commotion, unable to smile, not even for the reassurance of my community. I had no idea what really happened. How could I tell anyone that life here would be unaffected? That they had nothing to worry about? I nodded and waved, keeping my brisk pace until arriving on Grandma's doorstep.

I knocked before letting myself in. The entire family had keys to Grandma's and my parents' homes. Almost everyone had keys to Bree's. My key had been revoked following a birthday incident wherein I'd assumed she was at work, when in fact, she and her husband had taken the day off to celebrate in their birthday suits. In my defense, I'd stopped at my Mom's for breakfast to plan the details, and Bree had dropped her daughter off as usual, giving no indication she hadn't planned a normal day at the office. Not one clue she and Tom had planned a day of hide the pickle. When I'd shown up with two enormous balloon bouquets and an armload of bags to decorate her house, the naked party was already in session. I hadn't eaten at her kitchen island since. I'd resented her taking away my key for a long time. I was clearly innocent, but I still worried anytime I entered another person's home unannounced.

"Grandma?" I shuffled along the high polished floor to her kitchen, half holding my breath.

Grandma's home was all masculine lines and wide, inviting woodwork. The super-sized craftsman style matched her personality perfectly. Her kitchen alone was enough to make Frank Lloyd Wright weep with jealousy.

"Good morning, Mia. Come in. Eat." She stood at her large marble island clicking the button on her television remote. The flat screen flipped from station to station. "I thought there'd be something on the news about Dante. Surely they've heard by now. Where's that windbag from Channel Three when there's an actual story to report?"

She posed an excellent question. "The police might be using the walls to their advantage. I can call Bernie and see if she has a directive to stave off reporters."

Grandma tossed the remote onto the island, disgusted. "I plan to take Bernie some lunch and see what she remembers about last night. Tell me you found something."

I'd found lots of information, but I wanted to talk to a human. Someone who'd been with Dante in his last few days. "I took some notes on Dante's recent mergers and acquisitions. I'm thinking of meeting his personal assistant, Lara, for lunch Monday."

"Good. What about his company? How was business going? Anyone out to get him?"

"Nothing stood out as hostile. All the online articles back you up. He was a beloved member of the community. A successful businessman. Maybe the grouchy tones I heard in his voice mails were the natural sounds of stressed-out middle-aged men."

She leaned on her elbows over the island. "You want to say something else. I can see it on your face. What else did you find?"

I pressed my lips together, sorting the words into a direct and nonjudgmental framework. "I uncovered some details that suggest Dante was known to associate with people on the wrong side of the law. Possibly even a fugitive."

She looked away.

"Also, you mentioned his ex-wife was a pain. I looked into her a little bit and it looks like she's his beneficiary on a sizable insurance policy."

Grandma blanched. "Define *sizable*."

"A quarter million dollars."

She tilted a palm left and right, indicating that could go either way as motive for Angelina. "She's loaded from the divorce and probably makes more than that annually."

"True." Angelina Weiss was a leading scientist at Happy Farmer, an organic grain and produce company. "Her finances looked good. No significant debt, healthy account balances. No evidence of gambling problems or anything hinky like that. Even still, a quarter mil is a lot of money."

"Are you going to talk to her?"

"Probably." I dashed the toe of my shoe against the beautiful white bead board wrapping Grandma's island. "Anything I need to know before I do?"

"Besides she's the devil? Not much. Self-important. Status-obsessed. Power-hungry. In love with her shoes and reflection."

I could relate with the shoe thing. "So, she's mouthy and driven, but would she kill him? Even if she hated Dante, they were divorced. She'd already successfully removed him from her life and taken more than her share in the split. Where's her motive?" I narrowed my eyes. "*She's the devil* doesn't count as motive."

Grandma lowered her shoulders.

My phone rang. The standard old-fashioned phone ring, not a caller-specific, advanced-warning ring. I braced myself. Phone calls were the pits and usually bad news or a telemarketer, which also classified as bad news. Why didn't everyone text? No small talk needed. *Bring pizza. 7pm. Easy. Bring bail.* Straight to the point.

I accepted the call, prepared for anything. "Hello?"

"Yeah. This is Trey at Ohio Wiring."

Except that. I'd nearly forgotten about my new project. "Yes?" Ohio Wiring had come in at an amazing price on a bid request I'd sent several companies about network cabling. There was nothing Horseshoe Falls residents liked more than their rustic, parklike setting and Wi-Fi. They'd hated the ugly telephone poles and cables, so those went out long ago in favor of underground utility wiring. My new upgrade was a surprise I couldn't wait to deliver. The whole community was going wireless. In a few days, residents of Horseshoe Falls could enjoy the same high-speed internet access they had at home anywhere within our walls. I could almost see the email praises rolling in. "Everything on schedule for Monday morning?"

"Actually, we finished our job in Shaker Heights early. We can get the process started at your location today if that works for you."

"Well." I wavered. "It's Saturday." I paused. Way to

state the obvious. "I have some things to do this morning. When will you be here? I'd like to talk with you before you begin. Is there any additional charge for weekend hours?"

"No extra charge. We're still in Cleveland, but we'll be in the area after lunch."

I checked my watch. It was already ten. I preferred they didn't arrive before the police finished their work at the lake. How long did it take to drag a lake? That probably depended on the size of the weapon the police were looking for. The muck had eaten my shoes in seconds. It seemed unlikely the murder weapon would be recovered if it was truly in the murky depths of our geese-poop-infested lake. More likely, the killer had taken the weapon with him to dispose of properly.

"Ma'am?" Trey huffed. "Are you there?"

"Sorry. Yes." I shook the windstorm of questions from my mind and concentrated on something I could do. Be here to help make the community smile. "Is after two too late?"

"Nope. We'll see you then." He disconnected.

Four more hours seemed like enough time for the police to finish up. If not, I'd deal with the conflict when it came.

"What's at two?" Grandma asked.

"The guys are coming to start the wireless project today instead of Monday."

"That's wonderful. Did you say you have plans? I'd hoped you'd stay awhile. I can make lunch."

I flipped the hem of my skirt. "Can't. I'm meeting Bree at Le Bouchon at eleven. I put the contractors off awhile so I can be back before they arrive. If the police are still here, I wouldn't want the wiring guys in the way."

"I'll keep an eye on them. In fact, when I take Bernie lunch, I'll tell her about the contractors. I'll find out if there have been any reporters, too."

"Deal."

"Tell Bree I send my love. Anything new with her today?"

I whipped her latest list of demands from my purse. "Not much new. She's lost her blessed mind, but that's been thirty years coming." Bree was my identical twin sister, but our list of commonalities stopped with genetics. She was everything I wasn't, including married and a mother. She also thought sex ran the world and Harley Quinn was a book publishing company.

Grandma took the list and read it silently, making faces every few seconds. She returned the paper to me with a forced smile. "Well, good luck with that. I'm sure the shower will be lovely."

"You can help if you want. We can divide and conquer."

"I would, sweetie, but I don't want to." She followed me to the door. "Would you do me a favor when you have time?"

"What do you need?" I held my breath as she picked polish off her thumbnail.

"Will you look into Marvin for me?"

Today was full of surprises. My muscles tensed. "Why? Is something wrong? Did he do something?"

"No, no, no. Nothing like that." She flapped her hands. "We've been dating for six months, and it's getting serious for me. I don't want to be foolish with my heart." She averted her gaze briefly but shook off the strange vibe with the lift of her chin. "I thought your grandfather was my one true love, but I'm beginning to think Marvin would make a nice long-term companion. As long as he isn't a criminal or hiding a perversion of some sort. I don't deal with perverts. Also make sure his finances are in order. And check for alter-egos and outstanding warrants."

Jeez. "Okay." She partially lost me at *perverts*, but I got the gist.

She opened the door. "No need to tell anyone about this."

"None." I wondered if I should stay and ask more about this "long-term" business, but if I hurried, I'd have time to pay Angelina a visit before lunch with Bree. The Happy Farmer headquarters was right down the street from Le Bouchon.

She nearly shoved me onto the porch, as if she'd read my mind. "Thank you. Call me after you finish."

"After I finish with Bree?"

"No," she guffawed. "With El Diablo."

Oh boy.

I PARKED ON the street outside Happy Farmer and checked my watch. If I hurried, I'd still be late for lunch, but it couldn't be avoided and Bree held me to unreasonable standards where time was concerned. She was born with a stickler gene. Science might not have located the chromosomal predisposition yet, but Bree was evidence it existed. I, on the other hand, couldn't get anywhere on time. I tried. It never worked. Things happened to me. I forgot details. Lost directions. Got sidetracked. Followed combine tractors at eight miles per hour. You name it, it happened. The fact Bree, or anyone, was never late baffled me. I assumed black magic.

I stepped into the revolving door at Happy Farmer and cringed. The jingle from their commercial played on hidden speakers. It was one of those adorable numbers that wormed into my head and made me slowly insane. Not unlike the cheerful children's chorus in the It's a Small World ride at Magic Kingdom. Our parents had taken Bree and me when we were six, and I'd lain flat on the boat's bottom through nine countries and fourteen childhood strokes. That ride was terrifying. I'd filled many journal pages on the topic afterward and actively avoided animatronics to this day.

The revolving door dumped me inside a soaring four-story foyer. I headed for the welcome desk, ignoring the jingle that seemed to come from everywhere. "Hello. Angelina Weiss, please?"

The bright-eyed coed behind the counter beamed. "Sure thing!" She typed on her keyboard. "Looks like she's in her office. Go right up."

"Thanks." I took my time passing the desk and rubbernecked the coed's computer screen. Tiny blue dots moved around a grid. "You track the employees?"

"It's a big campus." She smiled wider, a little manically, but it might've been the damn jingle getting to me.

I scanned the board outside the elevator for Angelina's office number. Fourteenth floor. I climbed onboard and pushed the button.

The shiny doors closed, trapping me with the munchkin sounds of *"Hap-py Far-mer. Hap-py, Hap-py Far-mer. Fruits and veggies, breads and grain, all organic, washed with rain. Hap-py Far-mer..."*

The doors opened and I dove off. Dear Lord. How could people work here?

I hustled down the sterile white hall, lined in framed photos of the Happy Farmer employees and campus, to Angelina's slightly opened door and knocked before swinging it wide.

"Hello." A beautiful woman with olive skin and sleek black hair pushed to her feet behind the desk. "Come in." She motioned to the chair across from hers. "Thank you for coming on such little notice."

Well, that explained how I'd gotten in to see her so easily. She thought I was someone else.

I extended a hand her way. "I'm Mia Connors, but I don't think you are expecting me."

She raised perfectly sculpted brows. "Oh? May I ask why you're here?"

"Of course." I lifted my chin. Could she be any taller? As if being beautiful and shapely enough to model lingerie wasn't enough of a golden ticket to life, she had to be six feet tall, too? Maybe five ten, but still. She probably never had to have her jeans hemmed or ask for help reaching things while shopping.

Her eyebrow inched higher.

Right. Why was I in her office? "I dragged your ex-husband from a lake last night."

She clutched the pendant on her necklace. "What?"

I cursed my inability to make small talk or negotiate tough conversations with grace. I wetted my lips and started again. "Dante Weiss made an appointment to meet with a Horseshoe Falls resident last night, but he never arrived." Cold memories flashed in my mind. I took the chair to settle my stomach. "May I?"

"Yes," she whispered. "Is he...?" She let the notion linger.

"He didn't make it. I'm sorry." I gripped the straps of my handbag for strength. Clearly, I hadn't thought this through. Meeting new people was stressful. Telling a stranger I pulled their murdered ex-husband from a lake was the epitome of awful. Also, why hadn't the police contacted her? Was it because they were divorced?

We stared at one another. I'd plotted a clever line of questioning on my drive into town, but all those thoughts had vanished, eradicated by the obnoxious chorus trilling outside her door.

Angelina looked away first. What did that mean?

*Think, Mia. What would Jake say?*

"Where were you at eight o'clock last night?" I pressed my lips together. She didn't have to answer me and we both knew it.

"Here. Working." She raised glassy eyes and a troubled expression to meet my stare. "Why?"

"Can anyone confirm that?"

Her jaw dropped. She lifted her phone from her desk and wiggled it. "They track us."

I pulled my lips to the side. Why would employees agree to be tracked? "That's an odd practice, isn't it?" Was that the age we lived in? Employers tracked their employees? Why? To verify they stayed on task, or didn't linger over potty breaks? George Orwell might have been a few decades off, but he'd seen this coming.

Angelina dabbed a tissue to her eyes. "It's a big campus."

"So I've heard."

She lowered gracefully into her chair and crossed her too-long legs. "I can't believe he's dead." Sincerity rang in her voice. She was shocked, and I'd delivered the news with the grace and humility of a drunk monkey.

"You left Dante several heated messages recently. Do you have any idea what he was up to last night? When was the last time you saw him?"

Distress turned to anger on her pretty face. "I didn't kill my ex-husband, if that's what you're asking. Though whoever did probably had to fight for position in line."

"Are you saying you know of someone who wanted to hurt Dante?"

"Everyone wanted to hurt Dante. He was a tyrant and a greedy bastard. Ask any of his clients. He made himself sound like their savior with his startup funds, then he cheerfully collected a chunk of their income forever as repayment. He made far more from his clients than he'd ever put up front, and he never stopped taking."

I inched forward on my seat. "I'm sure that was all spelled out in their contracts. They must have known what they were getting into. They agreed to the terms." Everything had to have been done legally or the public would've heard about it. Someone would've sued. I'd checked him out thoroughly. No one had ever filed any complaints against him or his practice.

"Legal doesn't make it ethical."

That was sadly true.

"If there's nothing else, I think it's time you go."

I scanned the room, desperate for a follow-up question before she forced me out. The room was tidy. Inbox clear. Pens lined up like soldiers. Framed photos of gardens and fresh produce adorned the walls. A plaque on her cabinet named her employee of the year three years ago. A manila folder from A-Res Labs mounted a stack of evenly piled papers.

I stood slowly, formulating a parting question. The files brought her accusation back to mind. "Any particular clients of Dante's who might want to hurt him?"

"Yes. All of them."

"Can you narrow that down a little?" I could've found out on my own if every minute of my life wasn't already spoken for, but this was quicker. "If you know something and don't tell, it's considered obstruction."

"Isn't that your job?"

And it hit me. She assumed I was with the police department. Not clearing that mistake up was probably also a crime, but I hadn't introduced myself as a detective and she hadn't asked, so I'd file this away and ask Marvin later. Lucky for me, Grandma's boyfriend was an excellent attorney.

Angelina huffed, seemingly disarmed by my silence. "Regency Antiques. Cornwall Sheets. Maggie's Muffins. Little Timers. Like I said, ask anyone."

A knock fell on the door. "Ms. Weiss?"

"Got it. Thanks." I excused myself, repeating the list mentally as I passed a woman in a pantsuit and boarded the elevator. Inside I made a note on my phone to contact those companies first.

I hastened across the soaring foyer, struggling not to press my hands to my ears, and jogged down the street to Le Bouchon.

In accordance with my life, I was ten minutes late for lunch with Bree.

And certain to hear about it.

# FIVE

I TIPTOE-RAN THROUGH the first set of double doors and nearly toppled the doorman attempting to open the second for me.

"Sorry!" I skittered to a stop at the podium and addressed the man peering down his nose at me. "My sister's expecting me."

"Name?"

"Mia Connors. No. You mean her name. Bree Connors." I shook my head hard, begging my brain to catch up. "Bree Macangus." Four years after their wedding, and I still struggled to think of Bree as anything other than a Connors.

The man snapped his fingers.

A maître d' manifested. He smoothed his lapels and stuck his nose in the air. "This way." He strolled slowly through the crowded room, shoulders back, head high. Overdressed couples and clots of men in golf gear filled the high-backed chairs surrounding tables dressed in black linens and anchored with floating candles in crystal vases.

I longed to push him out of the way. Didn't he realize I was late? I imagined Bree staring at a stopwatch, deciding my punishment. She'd be homicidal if he moved any slower.

We turned a corner, breaching a private area where tables were farther apart and set more finely. Waiters stood along the perimeter, hands folded at their backs, awaiting their next summons.

Delectable aromas of tangy red sauces and buttery rolls tangoed in the air. My tummy sang in excitement, planning my menu. I'd devour a thick slice of lasagna and wipe the empty plate with a fat hunk of garlic bread.

Bree's laugh shocked me still.

The maître d' looked over one shoulder. "Madame?"

"Right." I regained my place at his heel, joy bubbling in my tummy. I was saved. Bree was smiling open-mouthed at Nate. I'd live to see another day thanks to the world's best friend ever.

Bree turned a cold stare my way, as if she'd sensed me coming. She waved dismissive fingers at my escort. "Thank you."

He bowed and left.

I took the chair beside Nate. Sitting next to Bree seemed risky.

He stood until I was situated, then helped me with my chair. His crisp white shirt was rolled at the cuffs and unbuttoned at the neck, revealing freckled skin and matching white undershirt. Both emphasized his green eyes and ginger hair. "How are you feeling? Bree filled me in on all the crazy. I had no idea any of that went on last night or we would've come over to check on you."

Nate was now a "we." If only *he'd* known then *they'd* have come. It was strange. Neither of us had ever been attached to anyone. The dynamic I'd grown comfortable with was changing. I rubbed my arms.

Bree lifted her water glass and swirled the contents. "Welcome to my world, Nate. I wouldn't have heard about it either, if Grandma hadn't started the phone tree last night." Her expression puckered. "Are those cats on your dress?"

"It's vintage." The soft black material was cinched at

the waist and sprinkled with cream-colored feline sil-houettes. It was adorable. "Are those beach balls on your blouse?"

She set her glass on the table with controlled effort. "They're polka dots."

"Oh." I nodded in mock agreement. "Must be the size of the framework that threw me off."

Nate coughed into his fist.

I turned to him. "What are you doing here?"

"I love hanging with you and Bree. You know that." Translation: he liked the way Bree ruffled my feathers. "How's the grant work coming along?" he asked her. "Have you finished the human sexuality study?" Another topic he knew made me wildly uncomfortable, not due to the topic so much as the way she used my identical face and body to research it. Last year, she'd played the role of harlot at Ye Ole Madrigal Craft Faire, and I ended up playing *her* in the burlesque routine she'd volunteered for, after she was poisoned by a lunatic bent on hurting me. Our relationship was complicated.

She swung her gaze to him. "We're just getting started. Actually, the pregnancy came at a perfect time and expanded our thesis. We've had the opportunity to explore and track the impact of my changing body and hormone levels on intimacy."

Nate's smile overtook his face. He glanced my way with pinched eyes and round cheeks. "Well? Do tell. In-quiring minds, you know."

I kicked his giant foot under the table. "Gross."

Bree cocked her head to the side. "It's not gross at all actually, it's science and it's life. You should read the paper when we finish. We hope to get it published in next year's *University Journal*."

Hopefully without pictures.

A waitress arrived with food. She set an avocado and tomato croissant sandwich in front of me. Nate received a steak and Bree had pasta smothered in Alfredo sauce. "Will there be anything else?"

I was tempted to ask her why she thought I'd want this for lunch when Bree was having Alfredo, but I shook my head instead.

The waitress retreated and Bree dug in.

Nate smiled. "Bree ordered for you."

"I wanted lasagna."

She stuffed a bite of thick noodles between her lips. "You were late."

I chopped the croissant in half and took a bite before Bree got started on my tardiness.

She ate smugly for several minutes before launching into the real reason we were there. "I've made an appointment to do a walk-through at the lodge on Congress Lake. They have an opening in about two weeks, but I want to see the place before I settle."

"Congress Lake?" I made a face. "That place is a total nature reserve. It's practically a spa retreat. Don't you think it might be a bit of an overkill for a second baby shower?"

She went rigid. "It's not over the top. It's normal. I considered this place, but apparently they're booked for at least a year. I can't be picky when we've waited until the last minute like this."

I pulled my hands onto my lap and counted silently to ten. "What's wrong with your house? Or Grandma's or Mom's?"

"Or Mia's," Nate added.

"No," I corrected. "No. No."

Bree's face darkened. "Congress Lake is beautiful. What's wrong with beautiful?"

"They have a paddle boat shaped like a swan."

She dropped her fork against her plate with a clatter. "I only said I want to walk through it. What's the big deal?"

For starters, she'd spent three months following her pregnancy announcement insisting she didn't want a baby shower because she already had a shower for her toddler, Gwen. Then, last month, she had a change of heart and suddenly it became my duty to create a massive Noah's Ark shower of biblical proportions in less time than it took me to plan my outfit. I had one month, and she had insanely specific instructions on how she wanted it done. She needed a coordinator but insisted it was more meaningful coming from me.

Frustrated as I was, it comforted me to know her husband had it worse. Tom had to live with her and he was in charge of her smaller gender-reveal party. Which was to say he knew the gender of their new baby and she didn't. Not an easy secret to keep from a hormonal version of my high-strung doppelgänger.

Whatever happened, the shower would be over in two short weeks and I would be free. The thought made me want to spread my arms and twirl.

She grabbed the fork and stabbed it into her meal with a crazed look. "This is probably the last pregnancy I will ever have, so I want to make it special. Is there something wrong with wanting to make big memories?"

"No." Note to self, keep my trap shut until this baby came or Bree was likely to kill me in my sleep and claim insanity due to hormonal imbalance. She'd probably get away with it. Anyone could see she was nuts. Tom could write a paper about the whole thing and they would profit from my untimely death.

She pressed her belly against the table and leaned in. "Good. Now, don't forget my gender-reveal party."

"Your what?" Nate asked.

I'd already ranted about this. Nate was a pot-stirrer.

Bree took the bait. "Tom's throwing me a party with virgin drinks and themed foods. We're going to play games and eat and share memories of my first pregnancy. The bakery is preparing a special cake. When we cut into it, I'll know if it's a boy or a girl by the color of the center. Pink cake for a girl, blue for a boy."

"Blue cake?" As if this might keep him away. "What flavor?"

"Vanilla. They add food coloring."

"How's Tom kept it a secret so long?" he asked. "What about ultrasounds?"

"We've had three ultrasounds. I asked the doctor to hide the screen from me. No big deal."

I marveled. Her doctor must be a wizard because no one else had ever been able to hide anything from Bree.

"Isn't three ultrasounds a lot?" Nate continued. "My sister only got one. I remember because she was pissed they couldn't tell her the gender and she had to buy everything in yellow."

I tensed. "Is everything okay?"

She nodded fiercely. "Tom says the doctor's just being thorough."

Nate mulled it over. "Can Fifi come?"

Bree touched her chest with one set of fingertips and her voice went soft. "Aw. Of course. Tom will get you the information."

Nate went back to sawing his steak into giant pieces.

I took a big bite of the croissant to keep from whacking him with it.

"So." Bree took a small bite of her delicious-smelling lunch. "How are things with Fifi, Nate?"

"Good. She's amazing. Smart. Funny. She looks like Barbie." He smiled obnoxiously wide. "I always loved Barbie."

Bree pointed her fork at me. "Mia hates Barbie."

"Do not." I rubbed my brows to stop a feminine rant about unfair female stereotypes. Besides, "Fifi's much better than Barbie." Fifi was real. She was one of the few people I considered a friend. I didn't have many, so when I found one, I protected them fiercely, if only from accusations of being a brainless impossibly figured toy.

Bree watched me, expectantly.

"What?" I looked to Nate for a clue.

Bree huffed. "I asked how you and Mr. Sexy Marshal Pants are doing."

"Oh. We're fine." I shoved a chunk of croissant into my mouth.

She shook her head at me. "I'm going to need more than that."

I chewed and swallowed slowly. "Like what? We're fine. *Fine* is good."

"No. *Good* is good. *Fine* is lackluster and noncommittal. Are you not committed to him or to your answer? Hopefully the answer because Jake's…"

I wiped my mouth with a soft linen napkin and checked for the nearest exit. I felt a sex lecture coming. As in, *do it. Now.* "Please don't finish that thought."

She rearranged her expression into something reminiscent of the cat who ate the canary. "I was going to say he's a nice catch."

Sure she was. I rubbed one shoulder. My pain in the neck was back. "I haven't caught him. Jake has free will. He's free to go."

"Or stay," she added. "Do you want him to go?"

"No." Heat rose in my cheeks. I answered too quickly and Bree jerked one eyebrow into her hairline. "Can we please talk about you?"

"One more question and I'll stop."

I dropped my head forward.

"How's the sex?"

Nate swung an elbow over the back of his chair and turned to face me. "This is why I crashed your lunch. You two are always so much fun."

"I hate you," I muttered to Nate.

I lifted my head and made my most congenial face for Bree. "Jake's been gone for two months. We only went out a handful of times before he left for his undercover assignment. Nothing's official and we barely see each other. What do you think?"

She shrugged. "I don't know. That's why I'm asking. Besides, it's my job."

I wasn't sure if she thought it was her job as my sister or as a researcher. Probably both.

"You should take him to the family cabin for a getaway weekend. You could both use the break, and it will give you a chance to reconnect emotionally. Be still for five minutes. Maybe you can find your Zen or at least work out some of that tension." She pointed to my shoulder.

I dropped my hand to my lap and bunched the awaiting napkin like a stress ball. A weekend alone with Jake sounded like a fairy tale. Neither of us could walk away from everything for that long. It was hard enough to find a few hours for a date.

Nate wiped his mouth and kicked back, having demolished his steak. "Sounds like a plan, just don't forget about our appointments."

Case in point. I couldn't get away. I had too much to do. "I'm on it. Don't worry."

"What appointments?" Bree asked.

Nate launched into a lengthy explanation while I sucked my water glass dry. "We're interviewing project managers. We have a plan to double our online users in the next eighteen months, but we need more resources than myself and a woman with three jobs."

I set the empty glass back on the table. "We want to check the pulse of our current subscribers, so we're looking for a group to issue surveys for us and analyze the information collected. We're looking at everything from new user adaptability to the interface, color schemes, font—any aspect that could draw a player in or leave them unimpressed. Some test groups are probably in order."

"Interesting." Bree pretended to care.

I appreciated the gesture.

"Aren't those the sorts of things you love to do? You've handled them for Grandma since forever."

I poked my boring sandwich with a fork and regret. "I know. I want to." I desperately wanted to lose myself in making REIGN our own, but, "I don't have the time to give any of those things the attention they deserve, and I don't want to cut the game short because I selfishly insisted on handling everything myself. Now, let's discuss your list of shower demands." I dropped the utensil and dug a printout from my purse. "This is my most current copy." I smoothed the paper on the table.

She dragged it closer with her pointer finger. "This is everything. We just need to confirm the venue."

I rubbed the bridge of my nose beneath my glasses. "I'm not doing all the things on this list."

"Why not?"

"It's too much."

"Money?"

"No. Look." I tapped the line I'd highlighted and written "no way" next to. "I'm not getting you a pair of doves to release or renting fancy china. You're getting whatever plates come with the venue and no wildlife. Also, you need to cut this guest list in half."

"Those are my friends."

"You have one hundred female friends?"

"Mmm-hmm." She nodded, tight-lipped.

"Cut it to thirty, and I need the contact info today so I can get invites in the mail. We'll name Congress Lake as the venue, but you have to cut the list."

"Seventy-five." She pushed the paper back. "And we can change the doves to butterflies. Two for each guest to release."

I sighed. Bree's popularity had only grown since high school. Not only did she keep in touch with all her friends since elementary school, she belonged to women's groups all over town. Book clubs, yoga, historical societies and mommy groups galore. She volunteered everywhere, spent oodles of hours at the college researching with Tom, and the women in his family would want to attend, too. When our family trees combined, we'd had an instant forest.

I planted a palm on the paper before it reached my edge of the table. "Fifty guests. I'll think about the butterflies. I don't even know where I can get one hundred butterflies or how the heck I could distribute them in pairs. Some people won't want bugs on them."

"Sixty guests. You'll need one hundred and twenty

butterflies. I'll poll my friends to see if anyone else is afraid of butterflies."

"I'm not afraid of them, but I don't want them touching me."

"Story of your life." She smiled. "I would've agreed to fifty guests."

"I would've allowed seventy-five."

"Hey," Nate interjected. "You didn't tell us why you were late for lunch."

I took a moment to decide. Truth or a lie? Did I have a reason to lie? Why did the truth feel like I'd done something wrong? "I'll tell you if you look into butterfly vendors for me and forward the pertinent details. I don't have time to research that."

He lifted his little finger for a pinky promise.

I hooked my finger to his. "I went to visit Angelina Weiss. She works up the street at Happy Farmer, so it seemed like the perfect opportunity."

Nate released my pinky and passed a folded ten-dollar bill to Bree.

"Told ya," she gloated.

Nate slumped. "I thought you were hung up at Horseshoe Falls, nosing around the scene of the crime."

"I did that earlier."

Bree laughed. "I told him you'd exhausted that by now. I mean, it's been nearly twelve hours since the murder. I'd wagered you were out harassing friends and family of the deceased. I won."

"Next time," Nate warned.

"Bring it."

I puffed air into side-swept bangs. "I wasn't harassing anyone. I stopped by to see if she'd heard the news and to tell her I was sorry for her loss."

"You said that?" Bree asked. "You told her you were sorry for her loss?"

"Sort of."

She waited.

I squirmed. "I might've asked her where she was last night at the time of the murder."

Nate barked a laugh that startled several women at nearby tables. "What'd she say?"

"She said she was at work."

"Can anyone confirm that?" he asked.

"No, but they track their employees. I could probably hack in and see for myself."

Bree widened her eyes. "Really? Do you think she was lying?"

I had mixed feelings on the topic. "I'm not great at interpreting body language."

"But?"

"But she didn't seem surprised. She said everyone hated him, which goes against everything I've read. I need to talk to more of his acquaintances and business contacts to know if she thinks that because she's projecting her feelings or if the internet is being fed filtered information. Both are plausible."

Nate tapped his thumbs on the table's edge. "Need any help?"

"No. I can probably get the information with a few phone calls or emails. There's always a chance she'd already heard the news and pretended she hadn't, or maybe they've been divorced long enough that she didn't care. Though, she did seem truly sorry to hear he was gone. Then again, there's an insurance policy in her name and that's motive." I worked the napkin in my fingers.

"What else?" Nate prodded.

"She didn't seem surprised to hear he was in a lake. That's weird, right? Drowning when he was afraid of the water? I'd expected that to raise questions from her."

"Maybe she was in shock," Nate said.

Bree leaned in conspiratorially. "Or she was the one who held him under."

The waiter materialized at my side and I nearly wet myself. "Can I get you anything else?"

"Nope." I gasped.

He dropped the check beside my hand and left.

"Thanks for lunch," Bree said.

"You're welcome. I'll deduct it from the cost of your insanity shower."

"Ha."

I covered my half-eaten sandwich with the napkin. "Next time I buy lunch here, I want lasagna."

I slid my credit card from my wallet and placed it inside the folder with our bill. "Now you've done it. I can't think of anything besides what happened last night. Was Dante a hero or a villain?"

Bree slid a gloss stick over her lips. "If you poke around, let Nate help you this time. I'm too close to my due date to get another call telling me you've been abducted. That shtick is getting old. You don't want to be the reason your niece or nephew is born prematurely. Those babies have a much harder time in life. Don't put that on your conscience."

"I'm not getting involved," I repeated. "I might ask a few more questions, but that's all. Grandma needs the closure."

Bree dropped the gloss back into her purse. "Good. Don't forget about my shower."

As if I could.

# SIX

I STOPPED AT home long enough to change into my Queen Guinevere costume and leave for the Renaissance Faire. The early weeks of Ren Faire season were always an exercise in controlled chaos as vendors found their groove, but our family had it down to a science. Grandma had been part of the local Faire for almost fifty years, so she was a pro. Bree and I had followed in Mom's footsteps, growing up at Grandma's ankles, trading her holistic beauty products for cash and enjoying the culture. Basically, Ren Faires were our jam.

We each had our role to play. As the face of Grandma's company, I was Guinevere, Queen of Camelot. Mom and Dad helped wherever they were needed, wore thirty-year-old gypsy costumes, drank pints of rum and disappeared regularly for a bit of light canoodling. Bree played a harlot, and Tom was the pirate who chased her around making off-color comments about booty. They were ridiculous, but they were happy, and happy was nice. Grandma was the saleswoman who enticed shoppers with her chipper presence and air of authority. If anyone knew holistic, it was Grandma. From Memorial Day through Labor Day, the local apple orchard turned Enchanted Forest was my family's home away from home.

I nodded magnanimously to the maidens outside the replica castle gates as I approached. "Good day."

"Good day," they echoed with a curtsy.

The orchard was beautiful this time of year. Strands of twinkle lights wrapped the limbs of most trees, ready to illuminate the evening. Lines of pinwheels and painted fairy statues stood sentinel at vendor booths. Rennies in every form of costume strode merrily along, whistling or humming to the music of a live minstrel band.

"Mia!" Marvin waved to me from several feet away. He carried a giant drumstick half wrapped in grease-soaked butcher paper. "I was fetching Mary a snack. Can I get you anything?"

Until Marvin had come along last fall, Grandma and I had solidarity in our singleness. Alas, he was a gem of a man who loved the Faire and performed seasonally as a magician. There was no competing with that. Plus, he made her happy, so I'd never dare interfere.

I ignored the pang of emotion that bounced in my chest. Whatever that was about, I didn't have time for it. "No, thank you. I had lunch with Nate and Bree."

He frowned. "Ah, yes. The shower details." He fell in step beside me when I reached him. "How's that going?"

"Two weeks until it's over."

He chuckled. "Right. Right. And what about you? How are you doing? I didn't think I'd see you today."

"Life goes on." I cringed at my poor choice of words. "Staying busy helps. I tend to dwell. I think I owned a mirror store in a past life, and destroyed my inventory with a hammer."

We moved in companionable silence to the Guinevere's Golden Beauty booth.

Grandma hustled out to collect her drumstick. She lifted onto her toes and kissed Marvin's cheek. "Thanks, babe." Her long gray braid swung against her hips.

I scooped a sample basket off our counter. "You were

right about Angelina Weiss. She didn't seem to care Dante was gone. She said everyone hated him."

"Shrew," Grandma grumbled against the side of her drumstick. "What else?"

"She has an alibi."

Grandma mulled that over. "That's too bad."

I nodded, unsure if she was disappointed we hadn't solved the case in twenty-four hours or if she'd hoped to see Angelina in jail.

She wiped her mouth on a napkin and gave me a curious look. "Your wiring people made it in okay, and they didn't get in the policemen's way because they finally finished dragging the lake."

Shoot. I'd forgotten about the wiring crew again. My brain couldn't seem to hold a thought that didn't relate to what had happened at the lake. "Really?"

"Yep."

Marvin tipped his hat to a passing group of women with shopping bags.

I handed samples of Buxom Beauty to the group and smiled. "Well? Did you see what they found? When did they find it?"

Grandma waited until the shoppers were out of earshot. "I didn't check the time. All I know is I was taking lunch to Bernie and saw the police wrapping something in plastic. After that, they packed up and rolled out."

"What did it look like?"

She handed me her drumstick and wiped her hands on a napkin. "I got a picture." She dug in her purse and fished out a flip phone. "Here."

I stared at the grainy photo. "Why don't you use the new phone I got you? It has the best camera on the market. This is awful."

"No it's not." She pulled glasses from her apron pocket and squinted at the terrible photo. "The new phone has too many buttons. All I want a phone to do is make and accept calls. It took me years to learn to use this camera. Why can't people just buy a phone anymore?"

I rolled my eyes skyward. "You don't have to use all the apps. Use what you like and ignore the rest. Call. Text. Take pics. There aren't rules obliging you to operate every aspect of the device."

"Then why pay for all those gizmos you don't use? It wastes money."

"It really doesn't."

She guffawed. "Why does my phone have to be an email and a calendar and a flashlight? Why does it have to be my record player and radio and step counter?"

"Grandma," I interrupted. "Never mind. Don't use the other phone. This one is great. I'm glad you got a picture." I rubbed my thumb across the screen. "What's it a picture of? Is that a sword?"

"Too short. Maybe a dagger. There's a lot of mud."

"I was thinking." I softened my voice to cushion the question. "Do you think one of Dante's clients could have killed him as a result of some perceived injustice? He didn't have to have an enemy to die. People attack randomly sometimes. Crime of passion. Nothing preconceived, just a moment of insanity. Sometimes the killers are the only ones who know why they're mad." I wasn't convinced Dante was as lovable as she remembered, but there were lots of things to consider right now.

She stepped away. "Who knows why people do horrible things? What about the criminals he was allegedly involved with? Anyone brought them in for questioning?"

I bit my tongue. Terrance Horton was the only criminal in play that I was aware of, and he couldn't be found, hence the whole fugitive thing. Plus, I'd promised not to discuss him with Grandma. Not that she would've listened.

Dante wasn't the man she thought he was. He had to have been in deep to stay on as an informant with the marshals. It was possible Terrance Horton had gotten wind that Dante was going to narc and followed him to Horseshoe Falls, but the idea fell apart when I remembered the bizarre, overly complicated execution. "I don't know. The whole thing feels more like a crime of convenience. Doesn't it? Or some kind of fluke. He practically ran straight into the lake."

Grandma stacked jars of our new product onto a cedar display. "I'm not sure how convenient a dagger is. Do people even have those anymore?"

"Someone did." I twisted a jar on the display to bring the label forward. "How are these selling?"

She accepted my subject change with a tight smile. "Like a fountain of youth. I can barely keep the Pampered Womb products stocked. Who knew your sister was a genius."

"I've always known she was something." Bree had examined her body head to toe from the beginning of this pregnancy, terrified of stretch marks. She never mentioned the possibility during her first pregnancy, which suggests she learned something last time around. I certainly wasn't asking. It was strange enough to see my body double expand in every direction since Christmas. I didn't want to know what stretch marks could do to it.

Our new Pampered Womb product line evolved from her fear of imperfection. The products started as a conversation. Then Grandma got involved and worked up some recipes. Bree used them and gave feedback until the formulas were perfect. I contacted a company who took it from there. Now Guinevere's Golden Beauty had mommy-centered products, from stretch mark reducers to nipple creams. I was proud of Bree for turning fear into action and secretly prayed she'd never tell me why she needed nipple cream.

Jake's handsome face broke through the crowd.

I smiled immediately, all other thoughts forgotten.

He made long, confident strides in our direction, wearing his casual cowboy apparel. Tight jeans, worn leather boots and his favorite barn coat that was soft from wear and scented by fresh air, earth and campfires.

Grandma slid her gaze to Marvin, who was cheerfully making our product samples appear behind shoppers' ears. "Have you had time to look into the other thing I asked you about?"

"Not yet, but I will."

"I'll let you visit with your beau."

Jake's grouchy face lost its edge when he finally arrived at our booth. "Hello, Mary. Mia."

"Hi," we answered in unison.

"How you doing, Marvin?"

"Never better," Marvin said.

Jake leaned a hip against the booth. "You look nice."

I performed a deep curtsy, embracing my inner queen. "Thank you, good sir."

He gave me a lazy half smile. "Have you heard they found the murder weapon?"

I made a surprise face.

"It looks like a mid-sized dagger. They sent it to the lab for testing. The investigation is moving along nicely. We hope to have answers soon."

"That's good news, right?" I waved at gawking passersby and struck a pose for a woman across the path with a camera aimed at me.

Jake marveled. "Doesn't that get annoying?"

"What?"

"Being stared at all the time?"

I hadn't thought of it like that. Outside the Faire, I wouldn't survive being the center of attention. This place was different. I wasn't me. I was Guinevere, beloved Queen of Camelot.

"You don't even like people."

"Hey." I bristled. "Yes, I do. I don't always know what they mean or what to say to them, but I do like them." Especially from afar, and particularly the ones who weren't trying to hurt me.

A toddler dressed as a knight ran ahead of his parents and bowed to me. I returned a small curtsy and he changed his mouth into a perfect O of childish surprise.

"You're really good at this," Jake said.

"I've had plenty of practice."

"No." He tilted his handsome head. "It's more than that. You love what you do and it shows. I knew it the first time I met you."

I laughed. "Oh, do you mean when you thought I was a cybercriminal and murderess? I loved those jobs."

"Yeah. That worried me."

I laughed again, this time unintentionally. Why did that happen? Were we flirting? Taking compliments made my skin prickle. Tiny spotlights trained on me, and like true spotlights, they were hot on my skin, quickly turning it pink. "I thought you were mean when we first met."

"That's my thinking face."

"Uh-huh. You must have a busy thought life."

His frown deepened and I laughed again.

Grandma and Marvin turned to look at us.

Heat crept over my cheeks and up my throat. Bree's words came back to me in a blast of older-sister sage. Jake and I were too busy for whatever was between us, but I was far too dogged to let it go. I liked him. He had brains and brawn. A rare combination. "Do you want to grab something at the Twisted Mister?" Twisted Mister made their pretzel dough fresh every morning and added something to the mix that tasted like magic. The menu boasted a dozen types of dips from various melted cheeses and sauce to icing and chocolate. My mouth watered despite the lame lunch I'd just eaten.

"Can't. I'm on my way to Parma following a lead on Terrance. The Faire wasn't too far off-route, so I thought I'd catch you while I could."

I did a quick calculation. "Where were you coming from? The Faire had to have taken you off-route by at least half an hour."

He shifted his gaze to the ground and back with a youthful smile. "So?"

I tugged at the neckline of my gown. If I continued having heat flashes like this I'd need early menopausal medication.

Silence swelled between us. How could two people make a go of it these days? Humans were busier than ever. We didn't have time for complicated arrangements. Everything in my analytical mind said to drop this quest and put the wasted time to more fruitful use. "Are you busy tomorrow? You could come to family dinner at my folks' house. Listen to Bree talk about her pregnancy and badger me over baby shower details for two hours."

I had a hard time listening to my analytical mind where Jake was concerned.

"That sounds good."

"Okay."

"Can I pick you up?"

"Yeah."

He patted the counter. "I'd better get to Parma." He leaned forward by an inch, as if he might kiss my cheek, but straightened instead. His arms lifted and dropped as he apparently changed his mind about a hug, too. His brows knitted tighter together.

I extended a hand. "See you tomorrow."

"Tomorrow." He accepted the offering, pumped once and strode away.

Marvin and Grandma spun their faces away the moment I caught them watching again.

"Well, at least we had an audience," I muttered.

"We saw nothing." Grandma explained herself to the air without a glance in my direction.

The Faire grew steadily more crowded as the sun made its circuit left to right over the orchard. By dinnertime, we'd sold out of Bree's creams. Grandma made a note to bring a bigger box of those tomorrow.

Busy as I was playing Queen Guinevere, I couldn't get the muddy dagger from my mind. Death by dagger didn't seem like anything from this century, so why? Was it a crime of passion and convenience? Something spur of the moment? Did it have a deep meaning I didn't yet understand? If so, what could it mean and who on earth had a dagger at the ready? A candlestick, maybe. A leaded glass vase or fireplace poker, those were things people had on hand. Not daggers.

Maybe the killer was one of those weird death-obsessed

people on the edge of climbing a clock tower, and Dante unwittingly pushed him over. The worst part of that theory was the unhinged person could be a resident of Horseshoe Falls. I hadn't thought to ask Dan or Jake how long Dante bled on the seat before running through our community. The seat was torn, so he must've been seated when stabbed. Did the killer flag him down along the street where his car was found and stab him, or was he already injured when he called Grandma to tell her he was coming? And, if not, why had he called Grandma on his way out of town? Did he need money? Didn't he have other rich friends?

I grabbed a stack of company flyers and slipped away from the booth. "I'm going for a walk, Grandma." I scanned the crowd for unseen dangers. Lurking killers or maniacal, dagger-wielding lunatics.

She waved from her perch on a chair, surrounded by fairgoers. She stood tall on the seat, balanced by Marvin's steady hand, and touted the benefits of her products the way I imagined it had been done in the Renaissance. Loud and with pizzazz.

My mind on the biggest clue, the dagger, I went to the local arms expert. Adele, the blacksmith's daughter.

The blacksmith shop was a handcrafted weapons depot situated beside the stables. The walls bowed under the weight of shields and chain mail, battle-axes and good-luck horseshoes. Faint scents of hay, oil and manure peppered the air. A steady clang pointed me in Adele's direction.

She swung a hammer against glowing red metal, pounding it into submission on the giant stone where she worked. Long raven hair hung over one shoulder to her waist. She smiled when she saw me. "Queen Guinevere."

"Good day." I moseyed closer, keeping an eye on nearby shoppers. "I have a question about daggers."

She tented her brows and wrapped strong hands over full hips, discarding her work. "Are ye in need of protection, milady? Point me in the scoundrel's direction and I'll make him sing like a schoolgirl." She made a gripping motion with one hand.

"No." I inched around the giant stone in the small space, closer to her, farther from nosy shoppers. "A dagger was used in a murder near my home last night."

"Mary!" She pressed a palm to her heaving chest and gasped. "Are ye a harbinger of death or are ye simply cursed?"

Well, I should've expected that. Adele and I had met under similar circumstances. "I am neither, fair maiden, I assure you. I'm only curious where I might find a dagger such as this." I slid Grandma's flip phone from my gown pocket. Luckily she wasn't attached enough to the device to notice I'd kept it. I brought the picture up and turned it to face Adele.

She pulled the phone close to her face. "Are you certain this is a dagger and not a stick run over with mud?"

"Yes." I dropped my botched Elizabethan. "That's a dagger pulled from a lake where a man drowned after being stabbed. I don't know why it was left there when we know it was used at another location. Maybe to hide it. Maybe in haste. If I know where the killer found it, maybe I can get a bead on who to question next, or develop a profile for the killer."

I stopped short to reevaluate myself. I didn't sound like a woman *not* getting involved. Then again, I hadn't done anything hugely out of my way. Adele was a friend and Angelina worked across the street from where I had lunch.

Adele pushed the phone away. "It's a terrible photo. I can't see the detail. It could be mass-manufactured rubbish or a true collector's piece. In case of the latter, try antique stores, collectors and eBay. If it's the former, try Walmart."

I let a Cheshire smile slide over my face. Regency Antiques topped Angelina's list of clients who allegedly hated Dante. Perhaps the angry ex had been useful after all.

# SEVEN

I SLIPPED AWAY from the Faire an hour before closing. My parents had shown up after dinner wearing shades of the same lipstick. I assumed the transfer was made behind the privies after a few rounds of rum punch. They'd joined Marvin, taking cash and filling bags while Grandma rallied the shoppers. I'd blown a stream of air kisses and headed for the gate.

I hefted layers of heavy material in both fists as I hurried across the field outside the Enchanted Forest. I trampled the hem of my gown, despite my best efforts, and sank further into soft spring ground with every step through the grass to my car.

Stella was surrounded by a horde of behemoth trucks and psychedelic love buses in the employee area of the lot. The larger, knobby-wheeled, oversized barbarians dwarfed my poor Mini Cooper, but she was my shiny pink princess, the belle of their ball. I took my final step and tossed one hand overhead. "Huzzah!"

"Huzzah!" The soft chorus of those in earshot echoed back.

I beeped her doors unlocked and tossed my handbag in first. I stuffed the bulk of my skirts in next and wedged my body in after, adjusting the mounds of material between my body and the wheel. Cozy.

I reached for the open door and spotted a sad little mouse in the grass below me. My heart broke for the poor little guy, alone in the field. He didn't move. I waved my hand at him. Nothing. "Ugh!" I slammed the door and braced my hands on the wheel. Had I run him over on my way in? I shook off the cold sweat brewing on my neck. Time to go.

I bounced Stella through the lot and onto asphalt with a sigh of relief. She was certain to get her little tires stuck in the mud one day, but blessedly, that day wasn't today. Traffic was light on the freeway. I skipped my usual exit and veered south to Sugar Creek, a little town in nearby Amish Country. If anyone asked where I went after the Faire, I would tell them I had a hankering for home-made fudge and the baby Swiss cheese that melted on my tongue. In reality, I wanted to visit Regency Antiques, a company initially financed by Dante and at the top of Angelina's suspect list. She thought all Dante's clients wanted him dead. Adele believed an antique shop might carry daggers like the murder weapon. If the shop owner wasn't the killer, he or she might still be an expert who could tell me more. Specifically, the type of person who'd have a dagger in their possession for a crime of passion. Either way was worth the trip.

Noise-blocking walls and lines of houses faded into cornfields and red barns with the occasional background John Deere. I exited the highway and took a two-lane road around sweeping curves and through rolling hills and valleys. Shortly, the world became flat and green. Cows speckled the horizon and crows lined pasture fences, craning their shiny black heads at each passing car. Twilight had arrived in its full glory, streaking a lavender sky with the fiery bands of a setting sun.

I chose a parking spot along the curb, close enough to the Amish buggy parking that I could enjoy the beauty of the horses, and far enough away that I wasn't likely to step in any of their road garnish.

I paid the meter and hoped Regency Antiques wasn't closed. Some of the local shops had a tendency to lock up before dinner and call it a night. The warm air was as inviting as the scenery. Scents of hot kettle corn and cinnamon-toasted almonds wafted over me as I passed a vendor. I stared long and hard, begging my feet to stop, while willing them to go. If the antique store was still open, it probably wouldn't be for long and I didn't want to make the trip south again tomorrow. Kettle corn had to wait.

A group of teen girls in muted green and blue dresses covered their mouths and giggled as I passed. A little boy in black overalls and a light blue dress shirt gawked openly. I nodded, dipped a quick curtsy and stayed my course. It would be impossible to keep a low profile in Amish Country dressed as Queen of Camelot.

The sensation of being watched crept over me, and I brushed my palms over goose-pimpled skin.

Regency Antiques was on the next block and all the lights were on inside. I grabbed the doorknob and checked the hours. Thirty minutes until closing. Jackpot.

A cowbell bonged overhead as I let myself inside. Voices carried from the backroom of an empty store. The open area was set up in multiple large displays, each representing a different room in a home. Old artwork lined the walls. White noise and jazz filtered softly from an old turntable near a vintage armchair and floor lamp. Aprons made of slightly yellowed material hung on a coatrack by the gold-speckled kitchen table. A Victorian ensemble and rug anchored the bedroom scene.

I dragged my finger over the dusty spines of novels

on an overflowing bookshelf and stopped short at the corner. Tucked behind the desk holding a cash register and black telephone was a line of weapons. Swords and knives with detailed hilts and ornately carved blades lay on a mat of plastic. The wall above held only hooks and anchors, where I assumed the blades had once hung. I took a step back. Had I found the killer? Was he making a break for it with the rest of his collection? How would he feel to find me here?

"I have to check on my customers," a whiny voice lifted from the back. "Please. I know I heard the bell."

Panic shot up from my feet to my head like a lightning strike. Was I in danger? There was only one way to find out, and I preferred not to. I ducked around a room divider embroidered with an array of brightly colored threads and waited. The faint scent of old books and dry wood reminded me of my parents' attic where Bree and I played hide-and-seek. I squeezed my hands in prayer.

Soft footfalls carried over the floorboards. "I'm afraid it's time for you to lock up for good," a familiar voice said. Relief swept over my muscles. I would live! Unless the man with that familiar voice killed me.

I peered through the wooden slats of the divider.

Dan Archer removed handcuffs from his belt and latched them on the wrists of a man twenty years his senior and thirty pounds his junior. That was the killer? I was nearly as big as that guy.

"I didn't do it," the graying man whined. Desperation crumpled his gentle face into a heap of anguish.

Dan nudged him forward. "Evidence says you did, Mr. Plotz. Your dagger. Your prints." Dan forced the door open with a hip and escorted Mr. Plotz outside.

The man cried. Outright bawled.

My heart broke.

Dan returned a moment later and headed to the backroom. "You get everything you need?"

"Yeah." Jake's voice raised the hair on my arms. That little liar said he was going to Parma. Parma was in the complete opposite direction from Sugar Creek.

"Lock up. I'll meet you at the station."

I hefted my skirts and made a break for it. My toe caught on the corner of the room divider and the structure wobbled. I grabbed it with one hand and my dress took out a knickknack on the nearby shelf. "Crap!" I whispered, compelled to right the knickknack but eager to flee. I pulled in a shallow breath and resolved to execute poor manners, leave the trinket on the floor and save myself a word-lashing from the Archer brothers.

I zoomed through the front door like the Flash, sending Plotz's cowbell into a frenzy. I darted down the quaint brick street toward Stella. Mr. Plotz blinked long and slow as I passed the car where he was locked in the backseat. With any luck, he thought the stress had brought on a hallucination and wouldn't tell the Archers he saw the Queen of Camelot escaping his store in a blast of crazy.

Jake's voice called out nearby. "I'll catch up with you later."

Yikes! I pulled my gown four inches off the ground and pumped my knees, putting distance between myself and that voice. I'd never make it to Stella before he saw me in my big green velvet gown and knickers. I ducked into the next shop door I saw and pressed my back to the interior wall. I closed my eyes to steady my pulse and prayed for invisibility.

Dry scents of grain and alfalfa clogged my throat and

generated a hearty sneeze. Two dozen Amish men stared, mouths agape. I pressed both palms to my massive amount of exposed cleavage, a commonality at the Renaissance Faire but not at an Amish feed and grain store. "Sorry," I whispered. "I won't be long. I just needed…" Another sneeze rocked my body and tilted me forward at the waist. "I'm allergic to everything in here. Not you." I forced a smile. "Hay. Mostly hay."

A young man removed his straw hat. "Gesundheit." No sooner had he spoken than a gray-bearded man dragged him behind his back. To safety, I supposed. From the crazy woman in need of proper clothing and her prescription antihistamine.

The car Dan had locked Mr. Plotz into rolled past the window with Dan at the wheel, Plotz in the back, and no Jake.

I sneezed again, this time so deeply I could've cracked a rib. My skin was on fire and my vision was weird. I forced my body out the door. Into the fresh air. Whatever they kept in the feed store was from the devil. I'd take my chances with Jake, wherever he was.

Crisp, clean air bathed my itchy skin. Praise the Lord.

"Shopping?" Jake peeled himself off the wall of the grain and feed store.

I sucked air and squealed, fully prepared to die and be done with it. "Yes."

"For bulk grains?"

"Yeah." I ran the generous material of one fancy cuff under my nose, which had begun to run. "I think I need a hospital."

Jake placed a palm against my back and guided me to a bench. "If I leave you here and go find a drugstore, will you stay or try to drive home like that?"

"Stay." My voice was off. "I think ma tong is welling." He cursed. "Do you really need a hospital?"

"I have a pill in ma caw." I handed over the keys.

"Come on. I'll drive." He hefted me onto my feet by one elbow and walked me to Stella's side door.

I fell inside and ransacked the console for my prescription.

Jake sat sideways, feet on the street, and slid my chair all the way into the backseat before pulling his boots inside. His knees framed the wheel. "This car is ridiculous."

"You aw."

He snorted. "Are you going to be okay? Do you need a doctor or can I take you home?"

"Home." I popped the pills and chased them with a bottle of water I kept on hand. "What about you twuck?"

"I rode here with Dan in the state car. I told him I'd catch up with him later."

I rolled my head against the headrest. He'd seen me. I was the opposite of stealth. I flipped the visor down and grimaced. A clear jelly-like substance filled my eyes. My chest and cheeks were splotched pink and white. No wonder those men were staring. I rolled the cool water bottle over my inflamed skin. "I'm allergic to hay, alfalfa and apparently something else that was in that store because the swollen tongue is new."

"How do you feel?" He glanced my way before taking the ramp back to the highway.

"Okay. Better. I usually take a pill before I go somewhere I know I'll have trouble. Give me ten to twenty minutes."

The ride was silent until I realized I'd fallen asleep. "Shoot." I shot upright and the seat belt yanked me back.

"Jeez. Am I drooling?" I wiped the corners of my mouth and eyes.

"Those pills really put you out."

"Yeah. Downside."

He parked outside my condo building and shut the engine down. "Do you need help getting upstairs?"

"Yes." Not at all. "Please."

Always the gentleman, Jake escorted me to my apartment and made a call for Dan to pick him up.

I changed into street clothes, which meant something entirely different to me than my sister, and returned to the living room where I'd left Jake. "Thanks for saving my life today."

"Don't mention it." He reclined on my couch, one arm over the backrest, one foot over the opposite knee.

"Can I get you some iced tea or lemonade?"

"Either." He shoved onto his feet. "Here. You sit. I'll pour."

I didn't have the energy to argue. I fell into the spot he'd vacated. "I don't think Mr. Plotz killed Dante. I think the only thing that man's guilty of is having an unfortunate name."

"Well, the evidence says you're wrong." Jake ferried two cups to the coffee table in front of my couch. "His prints were on the dagger and the piece is from his store."

I recalled the wall pegs and weapons on the ground. "There was one extra set of hangers on the wall than blades on the floor."

"Exactly. We found the last one in the lake."

"You were inventorying his collection. When I saw the plastic on the floor behind the desk, I thought he might be trying to run. I still don't think it was Plotz." I sipped my tea and sighed, thankful to breathe properly again and impressed Jake knew I preferred sweet tea over lemonade. "That guy's a marshmallow. Do you really think he has the amount of venom it takes to stab a man and drown him? What's his motive?"

Jake swigged and stared.

I waited.

Silence.

I set my glass aside. "Oh, I see. You're not talking to me about this?"

"Nope."

My mind raced with a complete inability to deal with that answer. "You have to talk to me or my head will explode."

"All you need to know is that Dan and I have this investigation covered and you don't need to worry about it."

Heat returned to my cheeks for all new reasons. "Jake. Seriously. Talk."

He set his glass down beside mine and swiveled to face me on the couch. He cocked one knee on the cushion between us. "Okay. Let's talk."

A feeling of doom settled over me, and I got the distinct impression I was in trouble.

"Do you know Angelina Weiss?" he asked.

Uh-oh. I worked the hem of my worn Mathletes jersey between my fingertips.

"Think before you answer," he warned. "Lying only makes things worse."

I pressed my lips into a tight line.

He clenched his jaw. "Tall. Scientist. The victim's ex-wife. Any of that ringing a bell?"

I wiggled my head noncommittally.

"Really? No comment? I only ask because I went to

see her and she said a weird little woman with too much hair and adorable kitten heels came to see her."

"She liked my heels?"

He closed his eyes for a long beat before reopening them. "You're killing me, Connors. I can't believe you're doing this again. You're interfering in another police investigation."

"I'm not interfering."

He pressed a finger to his temple. "I pulled the security video from her floor because I needed to see it with my own eyes."

"I didn't stay long," I hedged. "I only asked a few questions, and I never said I was a cop. She assumed that. I didn't realize her mistake until the end."

"And then you explained it to her? That you weren't there in an official capacity?"

I adjusted my glasses. "I thought her misunderstanding was a gray area."

"Do you know what she said when I got there? She told me a female detective had already asked all my questions. She became obscene when I insisted that wasn't possible and made her answer again."

A laugh bubbled out of me.

"See—" his lips twitched, but the smile failed "—you think it's funny because you weren't sworn at in Mandarin for ten minutes and called a bunch of things that weren't your name."

I covered my mouth. "I'm so sorry. I planned to tell you."

"Sure."

"I figured it would come up when we sat down to talk about the case."

His eyes widened for a fraction of a second before

narrowing to slits. "We aren't going to talk about the case, Mia. You're not a cop. When you start meddling, the department has a word for it, *obstruction.* It's against the law. You know that. Yet we keep having this conversation."

"We haven't had this conversation for a long time," I countered.

A vein in his temple pulsed out a warning tempo. "I've been gone for two months. We had this conversation before I left. Right after you found your second dead body. Any of that sound familiar?"

I bristled. "I can't help it these things keep happening. My therapist says so."

His phone buzzed and he pulled it from his pocket for a look. "Dan's downstairs." He dragged his gaze over me. "We can talk about this later. Are you okay if I go? No more trouble breathing?"

"All better. Tired but better." I walked him to the elevator.

"Good. Stay in. Sleep."

I wasn't great at reading between the lines, but I was confident the script between those read: *Stay out of my investigation or I will handcuff you in a not fun way.*

We did a weird hug and parted ways. An awkward ending to an unromantic night.

"Hey, one more thing," I called as he stepped into the elevator. "Did you check her alibi?"

"Angelina was in her office all night."

Bummer. "Okay, see you tomorrow!" I called through the closing silver doors.

Hopefully dinner at my folks' tomorrow would go better.

# EIGHT

I OVERSLEPT THE next morning, thanks to my unyielding schedule and that dose of antihistamine, so I skipped breakfast and accidentally worked all day on REIGN. My intention to add a hidden spring, accessible only to knights with sufficient valor, kept unfolding. A spring wasn't enough. If I wanted to reward the honorable, dedicated players with bonuses and health, a spring was too small scale. I needed a hidden realm. The trial-and-error process pulled me under like glorious quicksand. I emerged hours later to the sound of my phone alarm. The screen flashed: *Leave now or be late.*

Jake had left one text: running late. meet you there]]

I grabbed a pack of strawberry Pop-Tarts to quiet my roaring tummy and headed out the door. I took the longest route to the guard gate, admiring Ohio Wiring's work around the community. Wireless routers were tucked discreetly into leafy oaks throughout the neighborhood. I'd received a confirmation call that the job was done. The crew didn't run into any issues and the new community Wi-Fi was up and running.

A little thrill zipped through me. Within an hour of sending an official announcement to residents this morning, I had a dozen praising responses. People logged on to the new network easily and took full advantage as they tooled around outdoors, enjoying the weather. Wi-Fi on the golf course. Wi-Fi on the walking paths. Wi-Fi at the falls. I gave them something they didn't even know they wanted, and they loved me.

I waved to Bernie on my way out and mentally arranged a few errands in the most logical sequence to avoid zigzagging all over town and wasting time. I didn't want to be late for dinner, but I needed to stop at the bank and post office. I was low on cash and for some reason, the bill collectors wanted to be paid every month. I registered for automatic withdrawals anytime it was an option, but a few companies insisted on upholding traditions. Envelopes. Stamps. Mail carriers in navy walking shorts and knee socks. I'd tried to explain my impossible schedule to the landlord at my old building once, as the reason I was late with my payment. He was indifferent to my plight, and adamant on the late fee.

The bank and post office shared a strip mall not far from my place. I left Stella in a central spot outside the squat brick stretch of building, used the money machine, then dumped my bills into the big blue box at the curb. Goose bumps lifted the fine hairs on my skin as I rounded the hood to my driver's side door. I checked over both shoulders for a look at who was watching me.

No one. Paranoia. Just one symptom of too many run-ins with deranged individuals.

I shook it off and dropped behind the steering wheel. Next stop: Bree's favorite bakery. I waited in line twenty minutes to place a five-hundred-dollar order for a three-tier white-on-white almond-flavored cake with pairs of white fondant animals climbing from the bottom to the top in a left-to-right spiral pattern. White tigers. White penguins. White giraffes. The baker struggled to accept it as a serious order. Most shower cakes were a simple half-sheet rectangle or something shaped like a big belly.

I gave him a look at Bree's demand list, and he threw in a box of cream puffs and chocolate éclairs to get me through the next thirteen days. The joke was on him, the éclairs would be lucky to see sundown.

I jumped back into the sunshine with a sugar contact high and hustled across the short gravel lot. Instinct warned me to be careful. Pay attention. I slowed. Yes, I had a touch of PTSD, but I'd also ignored my gut on more than once occasion and ended up in a bad situation, thus my PTSD. I tuned into the strange pressure in the air and proceeded slowly to my car. A dead mouse lay several inches away from the driver's door, stiff and damp. Was it a coincidence I'd seen one outside my car at the Faire? I hadn't believed in coincidences until Jake was assigned to a second murder case involving me last fall. I started giving the Universe a little more credit after that.

I twisted for a look in every direction. The usual sights and sounds of a busy Sunday afternoon buzzed by. I beeped the door unlocked and climbed inside with a hop that cleared the mouse but made me shiver. Could I have missed seeing it when I arrived? Had a cat dropped it there and left? I reversed away from the thing and refocused on dinner. My brain rejected the mouse, and my stomach was attempting to reject the Pop-Tarts.

Dan had taken Plotz into custody for Dante's murder, but I'd looked into Plotz thoroughly before bed and found nothing. No indication he was anything other than a nice man who liked antiques. And cats. He posted images of both regularly on his Instagram. He wasn't burdened with any significant debts. No vices, ranting blog posts or peculiar fetishes.

Was his arrest a little too easy, almost orchestrated, or was I jaded? Maybe some things were simple and I was overthinking. Projecting. Nothing in my life seemed to fit the Simple category, but maybe other people had different experiences. Ohio Wiring had no problems with the Wi-Fi project. Maybe this murder case was the same way. Maybe it was only me who existed in a perpetual state of Murphy's Law.

My parents' home came into view like a mirage appearing from my mental fog. Somehow, the twenty-minute drive had vaporized as I relived yesterday's events.

The thirty-year-old ranch home never changed. The little postage-stamp yard was as well manicured as ever and lined in Mom's favorite flowers. The drive was predictably packed with family cars.

My phone rang and Nate's face appeared. "Hello?"

"Hey, are you at Sunday dinner?" he asked.

"Where else would I be?" I teased. Nate had attended more than his share of our weekly rituals. He knew the kinds of lunacy that happened in there.

"Great. Check your email. I sent you butterfly pictures." He spoke quickly and with a clear note of distress. "I've been on the phone with insect distributers all morning. There are three companies who can get you one hundred and twenty butterflies in time for the shower, but each company is having a special on a different kind of butterfly. I don't know anything about butterflies. How am I supposed to choose? What if I'm wrong and Bree blames me for ruining her big event?"

"Calm down. What are my choices?"

"Monarchs, the brown and orange ones. Painted ladies, I think those were blue, and some little white and yellow deals. I can't remember what they're called, but they're little."

"Cute."

"Have you ever seen a butterfly drink? It's disgusting."

I cut the engine and parked on the street for an easy getaway. A massive truck pulled up behind me until all I saw in my rearview was a big silver grille and headlights. "Jake's here. I'll text you back on the bugs."

I disconnected and grabbed the bakery box and file folder riding shotgun. I tucked the file into my oversized hobo bag. I'd spent the better part of my evening digging for skeletons on Marvin, and I'd come up empty. Marvin was a good guy. If Grandma didn't mind him being a lawyer, I certainly didn't. He'd helped me out of jail last summer, even before we were officially introduced. He was a lot like Dante on paper, but maybe that was what had scared her into asking for a background check. She'd thought she'd known Dante, too.

Jake's face appeared outside my window. He tapped his knuckle on the glass and mimed for me to power it down.

I obliged. "Hey."

"Everything okay?"

"Mmm-hmm." I opened the door too quickly and sent him back a big step. "Sorry." I pulled my bag onto one shoulder, gripped my keys in one hand and hoisted the bakery box over my steering wheel toward Jake. "Nate's stressed out about butterflies."

The box disappeared into Jake's grip. A strong hand cupped my elbow and tugged me to my feet. "Should I ask?"

"Thanks." I shut the door with one hip and rolled my shoulders back, hoping for a look of self-confidence. "It's better if you don't know."

"I'll take your word for it."

We made it halfway to the house before Grandma

burst through the door like the Flintstones' dog and hooked her arm under Jake's. "There you are! We're so glad you're here. We thought you weren't coming."

I checked my watch. "I'm only ten minutes late."

She leaned back to talk around Jake as we moved. "He's usually on time."

He shot me a wink. "I didn't want to arrive before the woman who invited me."

"Nonsense," Grandma chided. "You're always welcome. We could've chatted, gotten all caught up on your undercover operation until Mia got here."

Well, my bets were on Jake never arriving on time again.

Mom met us on the porch and relieved Jake of the box. She held the door with one hand and beckoned us with the other. "Thank you, Jake. You didn't have to bring anything."

"It wasn't any trouble," he told her, casting me a mischievous grin.

"Come on." She shooed us deeper inside. "The table's set. Drinks are served. I'm starved."

"Me, too." I dropped my bag under a line of coat hooks and kicked off my heels. "Oh my goodness, what did you make? It smells like I want to eat your house."

"Oh." She blushed and gave me a squeeze. "A ham and potatoes. I used your grandma's recipe. There are plenty of rolls and sides. Eat until you're stuffed and then take the rest home. Coming!" She flitted away at the sound of Dad's voice.

Jake left his boots with my heels. He toed them off with a comfort I couldn't comprehend. He seemed at ease everywhere he went. An odd feeling curled in my chest at the sight of our shoes together on the welcome rug.

I turned stiffly for the dining room. Clearly, I was losing my mind. "Ready?"

He followed silently into the room our family had outgrown several members back.

We took the last two seats at the table. Side by side, across from Bree, Tom and Gwen. Grandma and Marvin sat beside us. Grandma next to me and Marvin next to her. Mom and Dad anchored the feast at either end. Jake and the family exchanged welcomes as the bowls and dishes made their way, hand to hand in a slow, delicious circle.

Bree rubbed her belly. "I have my shower guest list."

"Really?" I'd expected more tug-of-war on that one. "You cut it down?"

"No. We need to get the invitations in the mail tomorrow. That will give guests almost two weeks' notice before the event."

"Okay." I pushed a fresh strawberry into my mouth. "I'll print them out and address them tonight. I ordered your cake on my way here. The baker said it was too much for sixty people. You knew you weren't cutting your list, didn't you?"

"Yeah." She seemed to melt into her chair. "Thanks for doing that."

I texted Nate that we needed two hundred butterflies, then opened my email and passed Bree the phone. "You need to pick your bugs."

She straightened in a snap and grabbed eagerly at the phone, but her belly stopped her. Jake intervened with his too-long arms and passed it into her hands.

"Thanks." She blushed, one arm on her bump and one hand flipping through pics on my phone. "I like the little ones. Can we get them paired by color?"

"Sure." What's one more step into crazy land? I caught Grandma's eye beside me. "I've got the paperwork together we talked about. It's in my bag. Don't forget to grab it before you leave."

She lifted her brows. "How did everything look?"

"Perfect." I made a little okay sign with my fingers.

She smiled brightly and turned to Marvin.

I was making everyone's day. What Universe had I bumbled into? And could I stay?

Jake returned my phone to the table between us. I texted Nate the bug order.

"I have some news." Mom's voice rose above the rest. She pressed her palms to the table on either side of her plate, heaped with untouched food. "You're all probably wondering why I invited you here tonight."

Half the table mumbled in confusion. "No. Not really. We come here every Sunday. What's going on? Are you ill?"

"I'm writing a book," Mom exclaimed. She stood abruptly, a human exclamation point.

We stared.

Grandma squirmed beside me. "That's wonderful." She tapped a finger on her napkin. "What's your book about?" The million-dollar question.

*Please say fiction. Any fiction. Fiction. Fiction. Fiction.*

"It's a memoir."

Uh-oh.

Bree gasped. "What? Mom, why?"

Mom took inventory of our faces. She lowered onto her seat, deflated. "Honestly, I'd expected you all to be a little more supportive. Excited even. The book is about us. All of us and our journey together from Mom and

Dad's small beginnings when I was a child to the empire she's created from that dream."

"So, this is about the company?" Bree asked in her no-nonsense researcher voice.

Mom blinked glossy eyes. "I meant this empire." She motioned around the table.

My heart thumped harder. "Mom."

Jake slid his hand over mine and squeezed.

My eyes misted. "That sounds nice."

She nodded. "I think what we have here is amazing and one of a kind. The company is a big part of it, yes, because it's just one more common ground we share. Sure, the business gives us another reason to stay close, keep talking and support one another, but it's not what makes us worth knowing. This is."

Jake released my hand. "I think it sounds great, Mrs. Connors. Good for you."

Bree made a sour face. "I agree. Can I ask another question? If the story's about us, how much do you plan to tell *about us*?" She clearly meant to say *about me*.

"Think of it as my gift to you. I'm recording our lives for posterity. With a little luck, they'll let me choose the photos."

"Photos!" Bree's mouth opened and didn't shut.

Tom rubbed her back. "Don't worry. It's not easy getting a manuscript published. We've tried a number of times with our papers and it's rough. There's a process. I'm sure you can give a little feedback along the way."

Bree closed her mouth. "Maybe you can self-publish and print one copy for each of us. A gift. Mia can help with formatting and technical stuff."

Mom gave Bree a face that said things she never would. Mostly swears.

"Mom?" I asked.

Dad looked like he was waiting for a dam to burst.

"Honey?" Grandma asked. "Are you okay?"

Mom took several long breaths. Her cheeks darkened to match the scarlet of her blouse. "I've always wanted to write a book. You know that."

The family exchanged looks. Nope. No one knew that.

"Come on!" She looked at each of us, taking her time to drink in our expressions. "I've always dreamed of becoming an author, but I've been too busy. I was an English teacher for thirty years. I raised these two." She motioned between Bree and me as if that was a more monumental accomplishment. "I help with the company. I volunteer in the community. I do everything for everyone else. I want to do this for me, and I'm going to. I don't need your blessings to do it, but you're all going to give them anyway and support me because that's what this family does."

Silence.

She turned to Tom. "I've already got a literary agent and a national publisher's attention, thank you. I met an editor while I was waiting for Mom to finish a marketing appointment around Christmastime. He was there looking at layouts for a summer cookbook and we started talking. I told him a few stories about us and he said they'd make a good book. I sent him some things by email and he loved them. His press has offered me a substantial advance to tell our story. *The Story of Us.*"

"I think that's a Bruce Willis movie," Dad said.

I snickered.

"It's a Taylor Swift song," Bree corrected.

Mom smiled, a tiny, you-people-make-me-crazy smile, and tension rolled away from the table. "I'll work on the title, and the agent is working on the deal. She says his offer was just a taste of what's to come."

Jake leaned against my shoulder and lowered his voice. "That's going to be the first book I've bought in a long time. I'll pay double for the pictures."

"Stop smiling. You wouldn't be so happy if your mother had made the same announcement."

He pushed a forkful of potatoes into his mouth and turned his gaze to Mom. "Yeah, but look at her."

Mom laughed at something I'd missed. She looked excited. Hopeful. Happy.

Grandma lifted her glass. "This night deserves a toast. I can't wait to read my daughter's book, and I'm honored to share a table with the man who got justice for my dear friend, Dante Weiss, rest his soul."

"Here. Here." Everyone raised their glass. Except Jake.

He sipped silently. When all glasses were back on the table, he cleared his throat. "As it turned out, Mr. Plotz had a solid alibi and Dan released him shortly after they arrived at the station."

Grandma looked like she'd gotten sucker-punched. "What?"

I buttered a roll and shimmied my shoulders. "Knew it."

"How?" Jake turned narrow eyes on me. "How did you know it? You're terrible at reading people, and the weapon belonged to Plotz. His prints were all over it."

I took a bite of my roll and waited to answer. "I knew because creampuffs don't kill. Unless you eat enough of them, then maybe they kill through a secondary channel like a contribution to clogged arteries or high cholesterol."

"What?" He wagged his chin. "Clogged arteries?"

"Plotz is harmless. That's all I'm saying. He probably escorts spiders outside on a tissue. He's not a murderer."

"Are you saying you can tell by looking at someone if they've killed before?"

I backpedaled. "No. Of course not. Are you certain the weapon from the lake was the one missing from Plotz's collection?"

"Yes." Jake dragged the word into multiple syllables, as if the answer was obvious. "Plotz says he gave the dagger to Dante a few days prior."

"Why?"

"As a thank-you for helping him open the store. He said he couldn't have done it without Dante's help. The dagger's worth a small fortune, so Plotz deemed it the perfect way to thank him."

I crushed an ice cube between my teeth. "The dagger is valuable? Then why did the killer toss it into the lake? That seems stupid. It could've been sold for cash or at least wiped clean."

"Maybe this isn't about money," Jake said.

My mind roamed to Horseshoe Falls. I hated the idea that a killer could live among us. "Maybe the killer didn't know the dagger was valuable."

"Maybe. Why? What are you thinking?" He scrutinized me with serious eyes.

I hated to bring her up again. He'd already griped about my visit with her once, but it seemed relevant. "His ex-wife had an insurance policy on him."

Jake pressed his lips tight. He glanced around the table before lowering his voice. "Angelina is the beneficiary of a policy purchased by Dante during their marriage, but she didn't initiate it, and there's nothing unusual about it."

"Why didn't they do something with it in the divorce?"

"Who knows? It was years ago. She doesn't need the

money now. Her financials are solid. The policy isn't significant enough to serve as motive in her situation."

"You looked at her financials."

He leaned back in his chair. "Yes, and before you go digging again, we already know she called the insurance company to notify them of Dante's death after I spoke to her. She requested the payment check be made to St. Jude's."

"She donated the policy money?" There went that theory.

Grandma sniffled. "Dante was an annual donor to St. Jude's, even when he had very little to give."

I cleaned my plate as I processed the turn of events. I needed a new main suspect.

Several minutes later, Mom swiped my plate and then Jake's, adding them to a growing pile in her arms. "Who's ready for dessert?"

Marvin followed Mom to the kitchen.

I turned to Jake, a new question on my mind. "Has Dan said anything else about the girl he's seeing?"

"No."

"Have you asked?"

"No."

I shook my head. "If you're going to keep hanging around with us, you're going to have to get nosier."

Marvin returned with a fearful look in his eyes and stopped short of taking his seat. "Um," he began, standing beside his empty chair and Grandma.

The room stilled. I pulled my cell onto the table in case he needed an ambulance. Jake scooted his chair back, ready to rescue the septuagenarian from whatever ailed him.

Marvin pulled in a deep breath, expanding his chest

to extremes. "I want to thank you all for allowing me into your lives. These past six months have been wonderful. You all know I was married once, like Mary and her husband. We shared fifty good years together. I raised a daughter, too. The experiences were monumentally fulfilling, but they were nothing like what you have here. My Priscilla, bless her soul, was a meek and humble woman. She made wallflowers seem like a Mardi Gras parade. My daughter is a grandmother now. Her entire family lives in France. We aren't close. Not like this."

I looked at Jake. What was happening?

He shrugged, still ready to assist in the old man's apparent breakdown.

"Mary." Marvin lowered his narrow, shaky frame to one knee.

A gasp went through the room.

He took her hand in his. "Mary, you are my best friend, my confidante, my compass and my guide. When I'm with you, I feel thirty years younger, like anything is possible and nothing can stand in my way. You make me laugh. You taught me what family can be. I don't know how many years are left in these old bones, but if you'll have me, I'd love to spend them all with you." He produced a telltale blue Tiffany box from thin air, in true magician style. With the flick of his fingers, he uncovered a rock the size of my head and asked the big question. "Will you marry me?"

Tears rolled over my cheeks. I swiped them away as Grandma leaped on poor Marvin, knocking him into the table.

"Wow." Dad supported the lovers with his palms, keeping them upright. "Save something for the wedding night, would ya?"

"Champagne!" Mom hustled through the room with her arms over her head. She returned seconds later with a tray of glasses and deposited one in front of everyone.

The joy on Grandma's face was worth more than anything I could imagine. In light of her friend's recent death, and what I perceived as the absolute worst timing. Ever. She was illuminated with joy. Who knew?

Tom pulled Bree closer, wrapping an arm around her shoulders and sandwiching little Gwen between Bree's belly and himself. Mom kissed Dad.

I squirmed to my feet, feeling more awkward than I had in years around the family table. "I brought cream puffs and éclairs from Johnny's."

I lined the pastries on a serving dish in the kitchen and wondered at the emotions ping-ponging in my chest.

"Need any help?" Jake sauntered to my side and rested a hip against the sink.

"Grandma asked me to look into Marvin. Do you think she knew this was coming?"

"Maybe."

I stuffed a puff in my mouth. She'd known, but she still looked utterly shocked. How was that possible?

Jake grabbed a puff. "You okay?"

"Yeah."

He bit into the flaky shell. "Allergies are all cleared up?"

"Mmm-hmm."

"Please don't keep looking into this case." All pretenses of casual were gone. His grouchy face was back in full force. "You nearly killed yourself yesterday hiding in a feed store. Imagine the danger you could be to someone else."

I fought a stupid smile. "I see. So, you're not worried about me. You're doing a public service with this request. I'm a danger to the community at large."

"Absolutely."

A laugh popped out. "I'll keep the general population in mind and try to control myself."

He grazed my arm with his hand. "I know this case is personal to you. I know how important it is to Mary that Dante get justice. I know how important Mary is to you. I understand the stakes here, and I'm asking you to let me finish this. You have enough to do without meddling in a murder investigation, and I can't do my job properly if I have to worry about what you're getting into."

Meddling. He made me sound like a member of the Scooby-Doo gang. "I take issue with your word choices."

"Wouldn't be you if you didn't."

I mulled that over. It was nice talking to Jake, but there were too many people around for me to relax. Bree and Tom always seemed to analyze every male/female interaction. "Would you like to come to my place after dinner?"

He slid his eyes closed. "I can't." He reopened them with a look of sincerity. "I promised myself to spend the rest of the night back-tracing some credit card activity on a known alias of Horton's. I can't seem to get my hands on him directly, so I've decided to start hauling in his every known associate until his supply chain is cut off. To stay this far underground, he has to rely on others for everything. I'm going to take his support system out of the equation, one by one, until he's forced to surface."

"Genius."

"Thanks. Rain check on the visit?"

"Sure." I pushed the irrational sting of rejection from my heart. He was busy. I was busy. "I have plenty to do anyway. Bree wants two hundred baby shower invitations printed, addressed and mailed immediately. Nate sent me a proposal packet to review for a REIGN contractor interview. Plus, I've got a surprise wireless network going live throughout Horseshoe Falls tomorrow. Technically, it's live now, but I'm not sure how many people read their email last night."

"Is that all?"

"That and my job-job."

"Another time, then." He checked his phone and frowned. "I've got to go."

"Where?" I scooted around the kitchen island, close on his heels. "Is everything okay?"

He darted into the dining room and dropped kisses on every woman's cheek, shook hands with the men and congratulated Marvin and Grandma.

She squeezed him to her chest. "Maybe Mia will be next."

I smacked my forehead and wobbled my glasses.

"Maybe." Jake glanced at me. "Talk about a lucky man." He zoomed back to my side and kissed my cheek.

When my lungs began to burn, I sipped in a little head-clearing oxygen. "Call me? Let me know what you find out about Horton?"

"No. I'll call, but you're off the case. Remember? Self-control?"

I followed him onto the porch. "We'll see."

He gave me a dirty look as he climbed into his truck. "I'll call."

By the time his taillights disappeared around the corner, I had a new plan and its name was Lara. Last I'd heard, she handled everything at the office, set up Dante's tee times, ordered his lunches and house-sat as needed. Lara knew everything, and it was time we got caught up.

# NINE

I woke Monday morning feeling like Garfield and left the apartment feeling like Odie. Somewhere between my wakeup shower and second cup of coffee, I remembered the excellent news I'd shared with Horseshoe Falls and the early enthusiastic response. Residents who'd tried it loved the new community Wi-Fi. I'd saved their emails. My new network was a hit. I'd intended to provide service equivalent to the speed and quality they had inside their homes, but for some, I suspected, our wireless community service was better than what they had at home.

I sprang from the elevator with a song in my step and Bree's last-minute shower invitations in hand. They looked marvelous. Printed on upscale eggshell cardstock with embossed golden edges and pastel animals marching two-by-two to a waiting ark. Somehow having two children equated to Noah in Bree's mind. She said she couldn't explain it, and I probably wouldn't have understood even if she could, but it made perfect sense to her. Regardless, the fancy invites were sealed, addressed, stamped and ready for the postman. So far, I was winning Monday.

Groundskeepers peppered the Horseshoe Falls landscape, mowing lawns and tending to flower beds. A pack of black squirrels ran along power lines overhead. Hard to believe the black squirrels were once endangered in our area. The population had thrived and boomed behind our protective walls.

I crossed the street with a smile. My dress was new. My shoes were adorable and I was ready for anything. I wasn't alone in my go-get-'em attitude. The clubhouse lot was packed. Residents had scheduled more and more services before their day jobs since I'd added the online scheduling feature to our site. Golfers slid in for private lessons. Women had their hair done before big meetings. The number of morning massages had tripled.

"Good morning, Marcella." I greeted our public relations manager with a smile. "Did I make your job easier or what? People loved my surprise." I helped myself to a disposable cup at the concierge desk and filled it with fresh coffee.

Sunlight glistened through freshly washed floor-to-ceiling windows where Horseshoe Falls architects had outdone themselves bringing the outdoors in. I raised a hand through a cloud of dust motes shimmering like fairy dust on the sunbeams. The clubhouse was stone and wood, with an expansive marble atrium. A grand tribute to nature, the space was polka-dotted with bushy greenery and the occasional pint-sized bubbling fountain. My favorite part was the concierge desk. Free gourmet coffee on demand.

"Oh, no, no." She followed me to the desk. "The people are unhappy and that is all you. You had better drink that coffee and fix this thing." Her thick Latina accent hit every syllable. Shades of pink lined her pretty olive skin.

I stirred creamer into my coffee and pondered the distinct contrast between my reality and hers at the moment. Did she say the people were unhappy? As in not happy?

No. They were thrilled. I probably had thank-you emails piling up. "They're happy." I made a big cheesy smile.

The lines gathering on Marcella's forehead deepened. She popped a hip and braced her hands in the deep curves of her waist.

I'd studied body language online, but applying the reading to reality was tough. "Is something wrong?"

"Yes, there is something wrong. The new network is down and the people are taking up pitchforks."

There. Now, I could try to fix it. Direct communication saved so much time. Except she'd made no sense.

A quick scan of the surrounding area confirmed her statement. Employees and residents clustered outside the hair salon, steakhouse and groomers, scowling and holding their phones to the sky. "My network is down?"

My network was down!

"I'm on it." I gave Marcella a weird salute and walked away at a clip, careful not to slosh hot coffee onto my hand. Why did I salute? Why did I do bizarre things? It was as if my body and mouth were sometimes disconnected from my brain. I'd never intentionally salute someone. I curtsied, on occasion, too. It was nuts.

I ducked into the mailroom on my way to IT and waved to a girl in dress pants and a white blouse. "I need these to go out with the morning mail." My gaze locked on a blue smear near her cuff. Probably ink from the packages. Hairspray would get that out. "I've already applied postage. They just need to be on their way."

She beamed. "Sure thing."

I longed to tell her about the hairspray but couldn't. Bree said strangers shouldn't give advice. Personally, I liked advice. Some of it was amazingly helpful. Some was just funny. Like the time we were leaving a luncheon and an older woman told Bree to drink more water because it helped eliminate bloat. That was useful and funny.

I shut my office door behind me and fell onto the black ergonomic desk chair I loved. "So, what's up with the interwebs?" I asked the empty room. I logged on to my laptop using the clubhouse Wi-Fi and tapped my toe. The clubhouse network was still available inside the building. I needed to shoot an email to employees about that. "Holy moly!" I lurched forward at the sight of my inbox. I'd never had so many emails at work. I scrolled through the lengthy list and clicked the arrow for the next page. "Crikey."

I scanned the top ten messages. Everyone was upset about the Wi-Fi. My bubble of happiness was officially burst. The community network hadn't lasted twenty-four hours and people were in panic mode. Emailer Number Five wanted to know if this shoddy service was what he could expect moving forward. "Oh boy." I spun my chair to clear my head. "It works." I balked at the screen. "There's just a little problem, which I will find and correct. We don't stop believing automobiles are transportation if our cars have a problem. Come on, people."

I arranged to meet the groundskeeper and wrenched out of my chair. Something had stolen my thunder and I wanted it back.

The boathouse was the central hub. I'd suggested Ohio Wiring set the access points and gateway there. Repeaters were hidden in trees, moving the Wi-Fi signal from the main access point throughout the community, thus creating a large mesh network where residents could pick up and maintain their signal anywhere in Horseshoe Falls. The fact the system had worked yesterday but not today was nonsensical. The fact it wasn't one area or another meant there was an issue at the main access. Maybe the network cable had come unplugged.

The boathouse was a gray Cape Cod–style building, trimmed in white and used for Horseshoe Falls' seasonal storage. I supposed it got its name from its location near the lake. There weren't presently and never had been any boats inside. The single-acre lake wasn't big enough for boating. Though the occasional enthusiastic kayaker would offer introductory lessons from time to time and cover the water with brightly colored vessels for an hour, but that was the most action our lake had seen before Friday night.

No sign of the groundskeeper yet. I tugged on the doors. Locked.

My cell had full signal from the tower, so I searched for our new network. Found it. No bars.

I shaded my eyes with one hand and peered into the trees. The hot summer sun stared back, forcing my gaze away. I blinked spots from my vision and circled the clubhouse.

My toe caught on something in the grass and I yelped. Memories of the stiff, gross mouse came to mind. This time, fortunately, it was a hunk of inoffensive white vinyl. I lifted it for examination, then checked the boathouse for damage.

My gaze caught on a hole in the underside of the boathouse roof.

The increasing drone of a golf cart drew my attention. A man in khaki coveralls steered the vessel to my side and climbed out. "Hey. Mia, right? I'm Clive. We spoke on the phone."

"Hi, Clive. I found this hunk of white vinyl on the

ground and a hole in the overhang. It looks like it belongs up there."

He took the vinyl from my hands. "This soffit's been down every morning since February. I say it's squirrels. They probably holed up in the attic space for the winter."

I gave the roof a long look. "Do squirrels chew wires?" If something gnawed through the cable physically linked to the network, the repeaters would be useless. No signal to repeat.

"Yep. They chew everything."

I eyeballed a line of black squirrels on a branch nearby. Jerks. "If I get the wiring repaired, can you keep them away from here?"

"Lady," he huffed. "I'm trying. Didn't you hear me? I've been fighting this battle since February."

"And you're sure it's squirrels?"

He shrugged. "Them or raccoons."

I pressed the heel of one hand to my forehead. "Can I take a look inside and see what's happened?"

Clive let me in. The space where Ohio Wiring positioned my router was stinky and hot with suspicious amounts of animal hair and acorns. The plastic coating on the cables was peeled back and the exposed wires were frayed.

"Fine." I walked outside and pulled in deep lungfuls of clean air while he locked up behind me. "I'll get the wires repaired, and I'll find out how to keep the wildlife away from my network if you can't."

"Good luck. Let me know if you come up with something I haven't thought of."

I dialed Ohio Wiring on my way back to the clubhouse and asked them to repair the main access point wiring. Next, I dialed Bernie and the head groundskeeper to let them know Ohio Wiring was coming and needed access to the community and boathouse.

Back at my desk, I shot an email to the community apologizing for the Wi-Fi problem. I advised them to go back to whatever they did before yesterday for Wi-Fi and promised an update as soon as I knew more. I also let clubhouse employees know the building network was one hundred percent. They should use it when they were inside anyway.

The thin vanilla fragrance seeping from my office outlet plug-in was supposed to soothe frazzled nerves, but it just made me hungry. The "soothing" pale gray-blue walls weren't working either. Bree had chosen everything in my office during her brief feng shui obsession. I was, apparently, immune to the laws of Chinese metaphysics.

I answered as many angry emails as I could with personalized responses before switching gears. I cracked my knuckles and adjusted my glasses. "How to get rid of squirrels." I typed the words into a search engine as I spoke. Dozens of links returned. Poisons. Sound and motion deterrents. Traps. Scarecrows. Predators. I marveled. There was an entire industry dedicated to removal of wildlife from homes and communities. Until that moment, I'd thought wildlife was an asset. Instead I discovered inconceivable dollar amounts of damage done by the little beasts.

I flipped my buzzing phone over to check the screen. Maybe Clive had already sealed the boathouse attic and my troubles were over.

It was a set of text messages from Bree. Did you mail the invitations? I made a list of florists and links to arrangement examples I like for centerpieces. Check your email.

I sent her a thumbs-up emoticon response.

Amidst the morning turmoil I'd forgotten to contact Dante's assistant about lunch. Jake had asked me to apply self-control on the matter of Dante's death, and I'd agreed, but setting up a brief chat with a mutual acquaintance was completely within the parameters of self-control. If the murder happened to come up, there was little I could do other than engage in the conversation. I opened an instant message window and typed out a request to meet.

My phone buzzed again. Jake's face appeared on the screen.

I bit my lip and kept typing. If I didn't answer, I wouldn't have to lie about what I was doing. Lying was bad, ignoring was good. I'd return his call right after lunch.

Fifi exploded into the office with enough energy to send me headfirst to the ceiling. "Good morning!"

I pressed my back to the chair and gripped the armrests. For the briefest moment, I thought she was Jake ready to bust me for meddling.

She dropped her bag and kicked off five-inch heels. "Isn't it a beautiful morning? The sun is shining. Birds are singing."

That's what I'd thought, too. She should give it a minute before she got too attached to the notion. I waited for my pulse to come down, peeled my fingers off the armrests and pressed Send on my message to Lara.

Fifi did little showgirl kicks at her seat. "I just looked at the most perfect apartment. You'll never guess where it is."

"Where?"

"In your building!" She pounded her feet into the

tight-woven carpet. "Can you believe it? The penthouse mirroring yours will be ready any day and all I need is a contractor to make it exactly what I want it to be. It's a total blank slate right now. Drywall. Subfloor. Nothing else. Not even interior walls. I can literally choose every single thing about it."

"That sounds exhausting."

"You mean amazing?"

Not even a little. "Yes."

She went back to imitating a kick line.

At least she hadn't brought a party horn.

My laptop dinged. Lara accepted my invitation for coffee, but her workload was insane, so she had to eat at her desk.

No problem.

I picked up gyros and Greek fries from a place downtown and headed her way. I had to roll my window down to circulate the meat-scented air away from my face. Lemon juice, feta and oregano-doused fries called to me, tempting me to eat and drive. The odds of eating my meal en route without crashing or ruining my dress were zilch. So, I suffered.

I salivated all the way to the tenth floor.

"Mia!" Lara met me in the hallway with a stack of files. Her royal-blue wrap dress matched the carpeting. Her hair was sleek and gray, bobbed at her chin and wedged in the back. Her eyes were puffy and the makeup was nearly gone. "I was on my way to the copier, but that can wait. Come in. Oh no! Did you get gyros? You shouldn't have!"

I followed her into a conference room where she dumped the files into a heap on a massive black table and unloaded the food bags with gusto. "I was going to offer to share my salad from home or order in. I didn't accept your invitation as a way of bilking lunch." She slid my food across the table with a methodical flick of her wrist.

"Don't worry about it. I wanted to do this. Besides, I nearly ate both on the way."

"Well, I wouldn't have blamed you." She spread a napkin on her leg. "How are you? I'm so glad you called. Can you believe he's gone?" She peeled the foil back on her sandwich and bit into the folded pita, eyes closed.

I was already there. Tzatziki sauce clung to the corner of my mouth. "I'm as shocked as anyone. I found him. Did you know that?"

Lara ran the pad of her thumb under each eye and sighed. "No."

"Yeah." I wiped my lips and distracted my heart from the weighing emotion.

Framed pictures of people in suits covered the conference room walls. The people stood shoulder to shoulder with a smiling Dante. Some of the photos had plaques at the bottom. Some had hospitals and museums in the background.

Her bottom lip quivered. "I'm so thoughtless. I should be asking if you're okay."

"Grandma's a mess. The community's afraid there's a killer living among them. It's been a rough few days."

Lara blinked glossy eyes. "Absolutely horrendous."

"You've been his right hand for a decade. How are you holding up?"

"Oh, you know, staying busy. Keeping my mind off the details. There's so much to do without him. I'm contacting all his appointments to cancel and letting everyone who's waiting on money know it's not coming. I've got to get in touch with his bank contacts so they don't push loans through with his co-signature. I'm not sure if I'll be paid for this or if I should go home and look at the want ads or what."

I forked a French fry and nodded, hoping she'd continue. Pressure seemed to build in the room. "I'm sorry. I wish I knew what to say but everything that comes to mind feels inadequate and stupid."

A tear slid over her cheek. "Thanks."

"You know what bugs me?" A recurring thought slithered into mind. "I wish I knew what made him call Grandma that night." I set my fork aside. It seemed most likely that he'd needed money for an escape, but if he was in the laundering business, he probably had access to cash. "Why drag her into his mess? They didn't keep in touch outside birthday and Christmas cards." As far as I knew. Maybe Grandma wasn't telling me something? Why call a friend who thought you were an angel if you were on the run from someone like Terrance Horton?

"Maybe he wanted your help?"

"Mine?" I wrinkled my nose. "No. He called Grandma, not me. I hadn't seen Dante since high school. I barely recognized him." I bit my tongue.

"It's okay to be frank with me, Mia. Everyone knows you're involved with the police somehow. You're in the papers every few months. You solved two murders. Maybe Dante hoped Mary would ask you to help him."

"With what?"

She lifted and dropped one hand, mystified. "We'll never know."

Lunch expanded in my stomach and turned to lead. Had Dante wanted my help? What could I do for him? "The local papers made me out to be more instrumental than I was. I'm not involved with the police. I've had a run of bad luck. Nothing more."

She dipped her head. "Are you undercover?" Her whisper cut through the quiet space.

"No. I'm a hindrance. Ask anyone in Homicide." Or at the marshals' office…maybe at FBI Cyber Crimes, too. "I'm a mess. I couldn't have helped him. I don't think that's it."

Her expression turned angry. "Then why are you here?"

"I don't know." Memories of my every misstep in previous cases stampeded through my mind, reminding me of how I'd nearly gotten myself killed by butting in. What could I do besides muck up Jake's investigation?

Lara pushed away from the table and walked out of the conference room.

I hurriedly cleaned up lunch, puzzling through what had happened and how I could fix it.

Lara returned with a kick of her foot, arms full. The door swung open and banged the wall. She marched inside and set a massive laptop on the table where my gyro had been. "I don't know what you're up to, but I believe you helped solve those cases like the papers said. You're scary smart. Even if you didn't help the police those times, I want you to help Dante now. This is his private laptop. The detectives haven't come for it yet, but they will. They took the desktop from his office Saturday morning."

My fingers twitched with the urge to log in and uncover Dante's every secret. I did my best to look unaffected, but ideas mounted in my brain and spilled over. My mind sectioned off. Deciding the possible passwords. Wondering if I should call Jake and walk away. Longing to hug Lara for this gift. Hugs weren't my thing, so I gave her a thumbs-up and started typing. I'd tell Jake about this the next time we spoke. "Why didn't you give this to the police when they took the desktop computer?"

Lara fell onto the chair beside mine. "Dante didn't always associate with the nicest people, and to be honest, I wasn't sure if the men who came were really the police. I searched their names online when they left, but when they came, I froze. I was still processing the fact Dante had been murdered and hoping the men in front of me weren't the ones who'd done it."

Understandable. "I'm going to sweep his history and files, save anything that looks promising to an external memory device, and ask you to call the detective who came for the desktop. Did he give you his card?"

"Yeah. Detective Dan Archer. Handsome. No ring. You should be here when he comes back."

That was a big no. "You know what? Maybe don't mention we've talked."

She frowned. "Okay."

My fingers flew over the keyboard, willing the accounts into submission. Demanding all they knew. "Let him know you found this laptop. Tell him he can have it if he wants it. I don't want you to get in trouble for withholding evidence. I'll see what I can make of his files."

"Anything you say."

I dug a thumb drive from my purse and shoved it into the laptop port. The little silver US Marshal star stared at me in disappointment. Jake had given me the drive as a gift last fall. Now, I was using it to snoop where he'd asked me not to. "Shut up," I mumbled as I transferred another line of files. I'd come clean to Jake. He could have any information I had. As soon as I had a quick peek.

I left the office an hour later with a smoking thumb drive. I'd saved his heated emails, personal calendar and sites he'd frequented. Also a few pictures. I kept anything I wanted to take my time with.

I dashed along the sidewalk to my car, one hand on the pocket with the USB drive, until I saw them. Two dead wet mice lay on my windshield.

# TEN

I FOLLOWED THE Ohio Wiring van from the highway to Horseshoe Falls. Perfect timing. I waved to Bernie as I stopped behind them at the gate. She smiled and chatted with the driver a minute before raising the lever for us to pass. I rolled in on their exhaust and zipped into the clubhouse parking lot. The van kept going.

I dialed Jake as I hurried down the hall to my office. The call went straight to voice mail. Probably for the best, I didn't have time to talk anyway. I copied the thumb drive contents onto the cloud via my laptop and hurried outside to greet the wiring guys.

Nervous energy coiled and burned beneath my skin as I bustled along the cobblestone path from clubhouse to boathouse. I needed to talk to Jake. Not just about the files I'd found on Dante's laptop. There was also the mice. My chest tightened at the memory. One mouse in the grass and gravel was a possible coincidence. Two on my windshield was a message. Instinct said I'd caught the killer's attention, but I'd barely talked to anyone about anything. Dante was a family friend. For all an outsider knew, I'd visited Angelina to give my condolences. Lara and I were online friends. So what if we'd had lunch? It wasn't logical that I'd be followed already. I was innocent. Maybe the mice were unrelated. Maybe I'd upset someone else without knowing and they called in a dead mouse deliveryman. Like sending flowers, but when you're mad. I shook my hands out hard at the wrists, hoping to toss away some anxiety with each flick. I especially didn't like the fact that the mice were wet, as if the person who drowned Dante enjoyed that sort of thing.

Maybe Jake was right. I'd barely gotten started and already I was in the crosshairs. Or maybe Jake was wrong. Maybe the killer saw me pull Dante from the water and talk to the cops. Maybe I'd sealed my fate the moment I jumped into that lake.

I stepped off the path onto emerald-green grass and pulled in settling lungfuls of heady summer air. Wildflowers and backyard gardens perfumed the world inside our walls. Walls I chose to believe kept me safe, despite what had happened at the lake.

Residents milled around the white logoed van near the boathouse. Knots and clusters of onlookers sprinkled the lawn, some craning their necks to see up a silver ladder leaning against the boathouse.

Clive climbed down and hung a hammer into a loop on his tool belt.

"How's it going?" I gripped the rattling aluminum to steady him as he reached the ground.

"It's a losing battle." He turned his khaki ball cap backward and huffed. "The wildlife's running this joint. I'm thinking napalm could help."

A collective gasp rolled through the crowd.

I waved hands. "He's kidding."

The look on his face suggested I was wrong. "Something's torn up the whole attic. Soffit's secure now, but it'll be down again tomorrow. All winter I replaced the soffit. Over and over. It's a nightmare in that attic. Poop and hair everywhere. The insulation is destroyed. We need to call our insurance guy and get that taken care of."

Thank goodness for insurance. "What about the squir-rels?"

"A-bomb?"

"Be serious."

He shook his head. "They aren't up there now. It's not like they're sitting around waiting for something."

I stepped away from the ladder. "Have you spoken to the wiring guys?"

The boathouse door swung open and a pair of men in matching white polo shirts and black slacks crossed the wide wooden porch in our direction. Labels over their pockets identified them as Ohio Wiring Technicians.

The taller one with black wavy hair stopped in my personal space. "Mia Connors? I'm Trey. I think we spoke on the phone."

"Yes. How'd you know it was me?"

He shot Clive a look. "Someone described you to me." His smile was charming. His cologne was enticing and his vibe was straight womanizer.

I looked past him to the smaller, less cocky man standing at a normal distance. "Everything okay up there?"

"Not really," the second guy said. "It's pretty filthy. We needed masks and coveralls to install the cables this weekend. We're going to need them again to replace the distressed wires."

"Were you up there today?" Their crisp white shirts said otherwise.

"Didn't need to be," Trey said. "Got a good view from the ladder. Something gnawed through your network cable at the main access point. Without a physical connection to the internet, the main access can't send the signal to the repeaters we placed around the community."

I held a palm between us. "I know how the mesh network works. I sent your company the plan. If I had time, I would've done it myself."

He laughed.

I stared. "Something funny about that?"

"What about the squirrels?" a voice called from the crowd.

Clive turned on the mob. "There are too many of them. We need to thin the population."

A murmur spread through the onlookers and morphed into an ugly growl.

I lifted my hand. "Can we put a pin in this? No one will touch the squirrels in the next ten minutes. Hold your pitchforks." I turned to Trey. "Can you fix the wiring or not?"

"Yeah. We have to come back with the right equipment."

"Why didn't you come with the right equipment? I told you what I thought had happened when I called."

He smirked. "Most times we follow up on a call like this, the system's unplugged or in need of a reboot."

Of course he'd assumed I didn't know what I was talking about. I was a woman. I couldn't turn it off and back on again without his help. I ground my teeth and locked my attention on his partner. "When can you be back with a replacement cable? And can you get the job done while the attic's in that condition or do we need to clean up the space first? We'll contact the insurance company, but that's going to take time and these people want wireless now."

"We can get it done." Trey moved toward the van. "We'll get our gear and come back."

"Thank you."

He popped the door open and hesitated. "Won't be

the last time we replace the cable if you're keeping animals up there."

I turned my back on him.

Clive lifted a cell phone to his ear. "Marcella? This is Clive. I'm on my way over. You got time to talk about the squirrels?" He moseyed to his golf cart and drove away.

Smart. She'd take care of the insurance claim and settle the people.

I faced the crowd. "Something chewed through the network wire. That's why it went down right away. Apparently some local wildlife made the boathouse attic their home last winter and they chewed through my network cable last night. Clive thinks it was squirrels. We're going to try to get rid of them, but the network will probably continue to have problems until we do."

A bearded man raised his hand. "I can help trap and release them."

"Great. I'll put you in touch with the gamekeeper."

"Oh, no, you don't." A woman in yoga pants and a tank top crossed her arms. "Trapping is inhumane. Animals can be injured in the process. They can cut themselves on the hinges or break their teeth trying to get out."

"Okay. We have other options," I told them. Hot afternoon sun beat down on me, a relentless interrogator. How had I become in charge of saving the squirrels? I tugged the neckline of my dress away from my skin to circulate the stifling air. "A number of things might keep wildlife away from the wiring. We can try scarecrows or audio deterrents with motion sensors. Maintenance can seal the building once we're certain the space is empty."

"Seal them out?" someone cried in a strangled voice. "It's their home!"

"The attic is not a squirrel house," I countered. "It's community storage. Animals can't live there."

A woman in walking shorts and a T-shirt with GRANDMA embroidered on the chest shoved her way to the front of my audience. "You said they lived there all winter. To them, that's home. And they'd be fine right now if you hadn't installed cables up there and caused all this trouble."

My mouth fell open. I had to force it shut.

The bearded man spun on her. "I don't care what they think is home. I want the Wi-Fi." He turned back to me. "I say move the squirrels."

The crowd erupted in argument. Half demanded preservation of the quarter-million-dollar squirrel house and the other half were sane.

A sharp bark drew everyone's attention. Sam, the goose-chasing, body-finding dog, wheezed and gagged under the strain of his collar as he dragged Polly to my side.

I dropped to rub his ears and regroup my thoughts. The residents were divided on the state of the squirrels, but like it or not, squirrels couldn't live in the boathouse.

I left Sam for a better look at his person. Polly was a shambles. A few women stroked her back in comfort. She didn't seem to notice. Her clothes were askew, and her hair was a mess. "Are you well?"

She shook her head. A fat tear rolled over her cheek. "I can't get that man's face out of my mind."

Silence befell the smattering of residents still lingering nearby.

"It gets easier," I whispered. Not a lot, but still. "It takes time."

She rubbed a sleeve under her nose and sniffled.

"Who do you think killed him? They only found one car. Bernie only let one in. I asked."

A number of expectant faces turned my way.

"Do you think a killer lives among us?" she asked. Her limbs trembled. "I can't sleep or eat. I think the killer lives here and knows I found the body. I think the killer suspects I saw something I didn't and I might be next. I might be a loose end."

I'd had the same thoughts about myself, and I ached for her. I feared very few things more than I feared the unknown. The truth was that no one knew who the killer was or what he saw or what he might have planned.

Sam rolled round brown eyes skyward and tipped his muzzle back. He moaned long and low. He felt her pain, too.

I slid one arm around her back and gave her a weird side hug. "No." I shook my head in the absence of better words. Just *no.*

"How can we be sure of anything right now?" another woman asked. She clung to her husband's chest, fingers clenched in the material of his shirt. "We were owling that night. What if the killer thinks we saw something and comes for us next?"

"No." I rubbed my lips. This group needed reassurance. Polly needed professional intervention. Maybe something to help her sleep and manage the anxiety short term. Emotional trauma was inexplicably awful, worming its way into a mind's forefront life long after it should've been forgotten. Like an autoimmune disease of the emotions, attacking you for no reason, sometimes without prompting.

"It doesn't work like that," I said. "This isn't a scary movie. There's no boogeyman plotting to wipe out our community. We have to stay calm and be sensible to get through this."

Polly vibrated in my grasp. "Are you suggesting there's something sensible about murder? About fear? About the fact someone died right there!" Her voice burst into maniacal shrieks. She shot her arm up, finger extended toward the lake several yards away.

I let her go. My heart hammered painfully and I swallowed gulps of air. "Everyone is safe here. Don't be afraid. Fear is contagious." And so was panic.

"If we're safe," Polly warbled, "then why's the detective back? If he doesn't have a suspect inside these walls, then why return? Why ask all these questions if the killer's out there and hasn't returned?"

I straightened. "Who's here?"

"The detective from that night."

"Which one?" I scanned the area for one of the Archers' giant trucks.

"Handsome. Brown hair. Blue eyes."

She'd just described every Archer ever born. "Was he wearing a dress shirt and tie or a T-shirt and jeans Friday night?"

"Tie."

Excellent. Dan was here. "Where is he now?"

Several people turned and pointed at the stables.

It never failed. I got in a hurry and I missed things. Bernie probably would've mentioned Dan on my way in, if I hadn't blown past her in a rush to meet the wiring guys. What else had I missed? "I'll be back," I told Polly. I faced the people. "Don't be afraid, and don't riot about the squirrels. Give me a little time and I'll figure things out."

I speed-walked around the crowd and headed for the stables.

My mind raced as I hustled to catch Dan before he left. What had I missed? A photograph of the moon had revealed a clue in my first case. Something someone had said resonated in the second case. So far no one had said anything useful, so I nixed the latter idea. What about pictures? If residents were owling that night, could someone have taken a picture and captured a clue? Probably not. They were the in-the-moment types, not the sort out to document their sightings. Still, I'd ask around.

The stables brought something else to mind. Security cameras. Every major building in the community had them and many houses, too. Maybe someone had caught something on video. I stopped and turned in a slow arc. Lush, leafy trees separated nearby homes from the lake and surrounding trails.

Dang it. I needed something to work with.

Dan stuffed a little notebook in his jacket pocket when he noticed me headed his way.

I did a bendy-finger wave.

"Mia. Nice to see you." He checked the area over my shoulders. "I see you've formed an army."

I twisted at the waist in search of his meaning. Across the field behind me, Polly and the handful of residents had formed a motionless line, gaping in our direction. I'd promised they were safe, and I needed to come through on that.

I smoothed my skirt and turned back to Dan. "They're scared. They want to know they're safe and that potential witnesses aren't being stalked or worse."

"That's highly unlikely."

"I agreed, but why do you?"

"Well." He widened his stance and rubbed his chin. "I've checked the victim's records and reviewed the GPS in his car. He hadn't been to Horseshoe Falls before that night as far as I can tell. There are no records of a relationship with a resident here either. We checked all available electronic and paper documentation. If he knew someone here, other than your grandmother, they met outside these walls and maintained a distance from the community. Horseshoe Falls residents can relax."

Relief and disappointment washed through me. "I didn't think to check those things."

"You aren't a detective."

"I'm not *not* a detective either." I was great at puzzles and a gold medalist at leading killers to my door.

"No." His congenial expression turned clinical. "You aren't a detective. You're curious, and curious makes you dangerous. Mostly to yourself." He continued to appraise me with steely blue eyes. "You're obviously attractive, but contrary to the evidence before you—" he used his hands as air frames around his face "—attractive doesn't make you a detective either. In your case, it probably makes you more dangerous. I submit my brother as evidence."

"Funny."

"Thanks." He gazed across the field. "What was with the panel van? Planning a stakeout?"

"No. I'm planning community Wi-Fi. The van was from a wiring company."

"Huh."

I dug the toe of my best Mary Jane into lush green grass. "What are you doing here?"

His sudden smile disarmed me. "Same thing you're doing, but I get paid, and I get to carry a gun."

"I'm licensed to carry a gun," I bragged. I'd completed my concealed carry courses in college and kept the license renewed since. I had no intention of carrying a gun, but I liked knowing I could.

He tented his eyebrows. "Yeah? Do you go to a range and practice?"

"Sometimes." When Nate and I were bored with our usual methods of passing time or when one of us needed to let off some steam, we'd spend an hour or two ruining paper targets. Loser bought dinner.

"Are you any good?"

"Yep." Dad was a retired cop and serviceman. He supported my interest and occasionally joined us at the range. Aside from his influence, I had a lifelong addiction to learning. Any subject was fair game. Except knitting. Knitting made me swear.

He didn't seem surprised. "I don't suppose you know of any hidden cameras around here that might've recorded the events of Friday night?"

"No. Horseshoe Falls policy forbids cameras in community areas, and home surveillance wouldn't have picked up anything as far as the lake."

"I didn't think so. I walked the perimeter that night, talked to everyone. I thought you might have an inside scoop. Secret security cameras for insurance purposes? Perverts with camera drones?"

"No. I've already thought of all that." I turned my shoulder to his and surveyed the community at his side.

Polly and the line of residents had mostly dispersed.

I spun a silver band around my first finger with my thumb. "This couldn't have been a planned murder. The killer would've had to know there would be a lake and that Dante would run in that direction. The stabbing feels violent and angry, not calculated. If the killer didn't plan the location and timing, he didn't plan his escape either."

He crossed his arms. "So, we're missing something."

"Yeah." I just needed to figure out what that was.

"Door to door?" he asked.

"I'm right behind you."

We visited everyone who was home and reviewed personal security feeds from every house with a camera between the lake and the gate, hoping one had caught a glimpse at the killer making his escape.

Fifteen camera feeds later, the sun had set and we'd found nothing. Not even footage from the street where Dante's car was found.

I dragged back to my office at dinnertime with Dan on my heels. He followed me into my office and greeted Fifi on her way out the door. He stole her empty chair and wheeled it to my desk. "What do you know that you haven't told me?"

"What?" One traitorous hand dropped to cover my pocket.

He homed in on the action and sucked his teeth. "What's in your pocket?"

"What are you? A detective or something?" I liberated the thumb drive and held it out for inspection. "You can have this if you answer one of my questions first."

He made a sour face but didn't object.

"Did Dante die from the drowning or the stab wound? The ME said it was the stabbing, but that was preliminary. What's the final verdict?"

Dan leaned forward, resting elbows on knees. "Officially, he drowned, but the blood loss would've killed him anyway." He opened his hand, palm up.

I pulled the drive to my chest. "More, please."

"A few small round bruises turned up on his chest and shoulders after we got him to the morgue. My best guess is someone held him underwater, probably with a branch or stick, whatever was available."

Confirming my theory. This was unplanned. A crime of passion. "So the killer was strong. Otherwise, Dante could've easily pulled him into the water with whatever was being shoved at him."

"If both parties were healthy, yes, but Dante was weak and hurting."

"Adrenaline?" I handed him the drive.

"Doubtful. Anything else?"

"How's your girlfriend?"

He pulled in a long audible breath. "I meant do you have anything else to give or tell me? What's on this drive?"

Dead mice came to mind, but I choked on the words. If I had to say them aloud, I'd wait to tell Nate. Nate would let me know if I was overreacting courtesy of PTSD and a rough year of lunatic run-ins, or if I needed to tell Jake. My gut said *tell Jake*. "You'll get a call soon from Lara at Dante's office. She has his personal laptop."

"She did. I sent a uniform to pick it up after lunch." He turned the drive over in his fingertips. "You plundered and pilfered it first?"

"I took a quick peek. Those were the files I thought deserved a closer look."

"Do you realize tampering with evidence in a murder investigation is against the law?" He shook the drive in the air. "Don't answer that."

"I realize that, but I didn't tamper-tamper. His assistant brought the computer to me and asked me to take a look. I did and I'm handing my findings over to you."

He grunted.

"She thinks I work with the police."

He narrowed his eyes. "You do not."

"I told her that."

"Have you told yourself?"

I made a swipe for the drive, but he pushed it into his pocket. "Thank you for the files. It would've taken me forever to break the password protection, and our tech lab is jammed up. Their turnaround is at least a week."

"You're welcome."

He stretched to his feet and arched his back. "I'm going home. You should do the same and leave this alone." He patted his pocket.

"Fine."

"Fine. Tell your grandmother and Marvin congratulations for me. Jake told me the news."

"I will." I walked him to the glass clubhouse entry doors and waved goodbye.

He stopped at a nondescript sedan with government plates. "Mia?"

I lifted my chin. How had I not noticed the government plates on my way in after lunch? I needed to slow down, or he needed to go back to driving his giant truck. Give a girl a little warning.

"Call me if you find anything else." He reversed out of the clubhouse parking lot and vanished through the guard gate exit.

The image triggered something in my gut. A gush of oxygen rushed from my lungs.

The killer hadn't left in a car. He'd jogged right out the front gate!

# ELEVEN

I FILLED TWO to-go cups with coffee from my pot and went to meet Bernie at the start of her shift. She'd been off duty when I'd visited the guard booth before going to bed. Not that I'd slept. Images of Friday night's pack of joggers plagued my mind. One piece of the group had broken off and headed for the gate. It happened sometimes. Plenty of runners sought a more ambitious track than the winding roads of our little community. Still, what if I'd literally crossed paths with the killer and watched him jog away? How was I supposed to sleep until I knew for certain, either way?

I visualized the pack of joggers. Had anything been different about the one who broke away? Had the overzealous jogger killed Dante? Was I looking for the killer in the right places? Had I seen something that night, or any day since, that held the answers? Something fluttered in my chest as I whirled mentally through five long days of crazy.

Shards of amber and gold pierced the pale gray sky. I tilted my chin to embrace the arrival of a new day. Sunrises were my favorite, but I hadn't seen one in years. Somewhere along the way, my life had taken a turn for the nocturnal. Instead of early mornings that preceded days of leisure, I'd moved into days of ongoing chaos that led to late nights and mornings where I pried my eyelids open with caffeine after hitting snooze twelve times.

"Mia?" Bernie's smiling face popped into view. Her kind eyes settled my rampaging heart. "Are you okay? What are you doing out here before dawn?"

"Thinking."

She hung her jacket on a peg inside the small booth and pulled up a stool at my side. "You shouldn't drink so much coffee. It'll give you wrinkles."

I sank into her warm Hawaiian accent. If Bernie was a peaceful harbor, I was a dinghy in a storm. "I brought one for you."

"Aw." She accepted the offering but set it aside to give me a hug.

The coconut scents of her lotion got my empty stomach in a tizzy. I pressed a palm against my shirt to quiet the ruckus.

"Tell me what I can do to erase that frown."

"I passed a group of joggers on my way to Grandma's Friday night." I adjusted my glasses, allowing her to catch up.

"Oh. Friday." Her smiled turned sad. "Of course."

"Do you remember them? They were coming from the direction of the lake. Not exactly, but generally, and I passed them between the lot outside my condo and the gate."

She kneaded her dimpled hands. "I remember. They jog every night at sundown. I interviewed them once for my blog. I'd thought night jogging was a new thing. Turns out it's a scheduling issue. Those residents work long hours and commute quite a distance. By the time they get home, change clothes and eat, it's late. They'd run into one another willy-nilly during irregular morning jogs and decided they should jog together at night instead. A nice story of community support, but I'd been hoping for a secret society of night joggers, or breaking news on the next new health trend. It's harder than you'd think to uncover a story around here."

"Tell me about it."

"Do you want the names of the joggers?"

She wasn't the eyewitness I'd hoped for, but this was good too. "That'd be great. I also wondered if you noticed one jogger break away and leave Horseshoe Falls that night."

"Sure. We have several marathon runners here."

"Only one left on Friday. Did you see who it was?"

She pressed her lips together. "No. I guess I didn't notice which one it was."

"It's okay. I'll take the list and go from there."

"All righty." She grabbed a notepad and pen from the booth.

My phone erupted into the theme song from my favorite television show. I tapped the screen and gave Bernie a thank-you smile. "I'm meeting Nate for breakfast before work. That's my reminder. I'll stop here on my way back and pick up the list."

Bernie set the notepad and pen aside. "That's all right. I'll text it to you. You'd probably like that better anyway. Thank you for the coffee."

"Anytime." I hastened to my car and gunned her little engine to life. Joggers were common. Joggers leaving the grounds were common. Maybe my theory was junk. If so, I was back to having no leads. Which wouldn't be as bad if someone wasn't following me around, putting drowned mice on my car.

I checked the rearview mirror a hundred times on the way downtown. No one seemed to be following me. Then again, I hadn't noticed anyone before either. I shook the

fog from my brain and climbed onto the sidewalk behind Nate's truck.

Nate leaned against his big white Navigator outside
the PC Consulting Company. Steam swirled in the air
around his Daredevil travel mug.

"Hey, Wannabe," I said. "Nice cup. It's as if you're
only carrying it because Netflix told you to."

He twisted the mug, examining it at eye level. "Excuse
me? Do you have a problem with my cup?"

"Not at all. I'm a huge Matt Murdock fan. Always
have been. You never liked him before he became available for instant streaming, but that's okay. You and soc-
cer moms everywhere are finally cool."

He snorted and pushed away from his truck. "Oh, I'm
sorry." The words dripped with sarcasm. "What about
you and Jessica Jones? Are you the pot or kettle here?"

I stepped onto the sidewalk in front of Nate. "I am
Jessica Jones."

"Uh-huh."

We boarded the elevator with a bunch of people in suits.

I folded my fingers together and stared at the ceiling,
hoping none of them were sick or perverted. Crowds
weren't my favorite. Crowds in little metal closets were
worse. The overstuffed vessel stopped on every floor,
delivering and retrieving strangers. I imagined a killer
cloaked in black depositing dead mice on my unattended
car. At least the city had security and traffic cameras. I'd
get a look at who was following me if they tried anything
while I was in the meeting. And if the culprit was brave
enough to wait for my return, I'd have a giant ginger at
my side. A ginger with a killer left hook.

"Are you ready for this?" Nate asked.

"I guess. Did you check the site today? I added a link

where users can volunteer as part of a test group. We'll be alerted after every twenty-five registers. Then, we can sort the volunteers according to their answers on the registration form about their experience. I'm working on questionnaires for each experience level, so we can meet players where they are. I started roughing out a few question sets geared toward specific aspects of our game, but I fell asleep."

He gave me a sad face. "Mia, you don't have to do that stuff. That's why we're here, so you don't become the youngest person in Ohio to die of some stress-related illness."

*You're welcome.* I mashed my lips shut and focused on the crush of strangers packed around us.

By the eighth floor, I was edging internally toward insanity. The stairs felt like a better option every time we stopped. "How's things with Fifi?" I blurted, desperate to escape my prison.

Nate turned his face to mine in slow motion. He squinted bright green eyes. "Fine. Thank you for asking. I'm definitely in love. I think she's the one. What do you really want?"

I widened my eyes in faux innocence. "Nothing. I'm doing small talk."

He waited.

"Fine. I hate this elevator, and I don't want to hire a project manager."

"Mia. I don't know the first thing about marketing or half the stuff we need accomplished."

"I do." I pointed to my face. "I'm an amazing and experienced project manager. I'm not a bad programmer or web designer either, and no one loves REIGN like I do."

"All true, but you don't have time to take on something this important right now. You said it yourself."

I looked away. "Fine. I have something else to run past you." I ignored his smug face and kept going. My heart pounded frantically as I said the dreaded truth aloud. "I've found drowned mice on or near my car on three separate occasions since Dante's death."

The elevator dinged.

I pressed one palm to my chest and made the sign of the cross with the other. The machine was out to kill me, by claustrophobia, panic attack or stroke, it was anyone's guess.

One traveler got out. Four new suits pressed their way inside.

Nate nudged me to go on. "What did Jake say?"

I rolled my head against the cool metal wall behind me.

"You haven't told him?"

The doors closed and we lurched upward once more.

"Jake's hard to reach."

Nate angled to face me. "Well, reach him anyway. You need to tell him. Those mice are threats. You know this. Twice is a coincidence. Three is a pattern."

A few strangers turned their ears our way.

I pinched the fabric of his jacket between my fingers. Either Nate had a sudden influx of fashion sense, or Fifi bought the outfit. Silver slacks, white shirt, sky-blue tie. The cut was premium. He looked like a *GQ* model. "Where'd you get this?"

"Nordstrom. Why are you changing the subject?"

I gave my outfit a long appraisal. Maybe I should've worn a suit. Something structured instead of a flowy dress and flats. I looked too young. I was dressed too casually for a proper barter. Nate looked like the stronger

player here, and I hated what that did to gender stereotypes everywhere. I dug into my purse for some bobby
pins and an elastic band.

"What are you doing?"

I twisted my heavy locks into submission and se-
cured them in a librarian bun on my head. "I can't represent REIGN looking like a twenty-something. We'll get
crappy rates on consulting fees, and it'll be my fault for
wearing this dress." I pulled the long strap of my handbag over my head, freeing it from my body. I hung the
bag, in the crook of one elbow, by its smaller handles,
and tucked the longer strap inside. "I'm aging myself."

"The Powerpuff Girls nail decals might work against
you."

"Shut up. I couldn't sleep last night. The manicure
lifted my mood and distracted me. I wasn't thinking
about this meeting at the time." I scraped away the tiny
decals on my pinky nails. "You have no idea how complicated it is to be a woman."

His patronizing face proved my point. "It must be really hard to be so smart, rich and adorable. I'll bet people
mistreat you all the time."

"I'm going to mistreat you in a minute."

The man in front of us coughed to cover a laugh.

I folded my arms and my boobs instantly looked bigger. Jeez. I relaxed my stance and shook my head.

The elevator whooshed to another stop and dinged.
I didn't jump.

Nate inched forward. "This is us."

The riders parted as I followed Nate off the car.

I gave the cougher an angry face as I passed. He was
cute.

The PC Consulting offices were immaculate and obsessively modern in design. Glass walls and endless windows. Metal-framed white couches and chairs. Spotless glass tabletops and counters. White carpets and upholstery. A chandelier of glass balls hung in strands from the soaring ceiling like bubbles headed into the ether.

Nate stopped at the welcome desk to announce our arrival.

I slunk off to the waiting area, picking tiny superheroes from my nail polish.

The receptionist greeted Nate with a wide smile. Her blouse was stunning, and the gray designer pencil skirt paired amazingly. Her stilettos made my toes hurt just looking at them. I'd never seen an outfit so on point. Why hadn't I worn something more professional?

Nate crossed the narrow room in two long strides and took the seat beside me. "She's letting them know we're here. Is anything else going on with your private investigation? Besides the mice, which you need to tell Jake about ASAP. Leave him a voice mail or text him if you have to."

I fiddled with the purse on my lap. "I went to Dante's office and had a look at his computer. I found several appointments this month with someone named Keith Orson."

"Did you tell Jake about the files?"

"No, but I gave them to Dan yesterday."

Nate stretched long legs before us and crossed them at the ankles. "Given the mice situation, is it safe to assume you have no idea who the killer is, but it's highly likely the killer is on to you?"

That didn't deserve a response.

"I mean, unless you've peeved off someone else or become the modern Pied Piper."

The Pied Piper led rats out of Hamelin. That had nothing to do with this. "We shouldn't assume anything."

The receptionist rounded her desk and smiled at Nate. "The team's ready for you now."

We followed her down a brightly lit hallway to an oversized, ultra-modern conference room complete with full wall of flat-screen monitors demonstrating various games and a massive oval table covered in action figures and puzzles. "The team" wore jeans and dress shirts with wacky vintage ties.

A guy my dad's age opened his arms and encouraged us to take a seat. His tie had Space Invaders. "I'm Bartholomew Sanders and this is my team." He introduced everyone before joining us at the table and beginning an enthusiastic presentation of all the things he could do for our company.

Nate smiled from start to finish.

I did my best not to be too impressed by their obvious skills. I could've done the same thing with a little time.

After our meeting, we were given company-logoed thumb drives with the team's presentation for quick reference.

Nate walked me to my car, still smiling. "I liked them."

"You like everyone."

He shrugged and checked the area for mice. "All clear."

"See," I said, thankful to change the subject to anything else. "Maybe three is sometimes a coincidence."

"Talk to Jake or I will."

I CLIMBED OUT of my car at Horseshoe Falls, thankful not to have seen another mouse, and hoping I'd somehow blown the whole thing out of proportion. Denial was my favorite coping mechanism.

The Ohio Wiring van rolled to a stop near the clubhouse and beeped. Trey climbed out of the passenger seat. "We replaced the shredded cable, but you need to get rid of whatever caused the damage or we'll be back replacing this cable every week. I can call it job security, but I'm not sure your boss will approve."

"Thank you. I'll keep that in mind." I waved him off and headed for my office. Apparently, winding my hair into a bun didn't stop some people from thinking I was an idiot.

I made it through the double glass doors before Marcella flagged me down in the lobby.

I forced a small smile and met her at the concierge desk. "Yes?"

"The people are in an uproar. They want the community Wi-Fi you promised."

"Great. It should be working now."

She nodded too quickly, like a gorgeous Latina bobblehead. "Yes. For now. What about tomorrow?"

"Did you talk to Trey?"

"Yes. He says keep the animals away from the wires, but the people are divided. Mr. Lionel owns a national chain of Outdoor Sportsman stores, and he says he'll get rid of the squirrels one way or another if we won't." She drew one finger across her neck in demonstration.

"Yikes."

"Yes, yikes," she echoed. "Mr. Peters has the pro-wildlifers all worked up. He's obsessed with tracking their little squirrel behaviors and making a case for animal rights."

She'd lost me. "Who's Mr. Peters?"

"He was the one who brought the first pair of black squirrels into the community. He feels like they're his responsibility. Like their human grandfather or something nutty." She pressed a hand to her mouth, trying not to laugh at the unintentional joke. "He has a squirrel family tree." She paused again. "A lineage chart."

"Gotcha." Peters was a wackadoodle, and leading the charge against my Wi-Fi. Peters equaled Enemy.

She squinted down the hallway. "Maybe we can hire trappers to haul them out of here under cover of night."

That wouldn't work. "They'd just come back."

She did some quiet swearing in Spanish and walked away.

I hurried down the employee hallway to IT. Squirrels were the least of my problems at the moment, and I'd met my quota on crazed researchers. I had Bree. Marcella could deal with Peters.

Fifi bustled around our office, comparing two flyers in-hand with new ones from the chugging printer. "There you are." She shoved the flyers at my hands. "I think the answer to all this community drama is a party."

The printer ground to a stop and beeped.

She huffed. "How old is that dinosaur? It sounds like it's going to die."

"It's out of paper." I flipped between the flyers she'd handed me.

Fifi stuffed the printer with blank white paper and stroked her blond hair. "What do you think of the flyers? I have more variations on the desk."

I glanced around the room. Yes, there were flyers on the desk. Counter. Floor. "Wow. How long have you been at this?" I checked my watch. Ten after nine.

"I came in at eight. I thought about the party all night, but I wasn't sure if I was allowed to work on that during work hours since it's technically a PR issue, not IT. I'd planned to stop by nine, but then I couldn't pick a font. What do you think?"

"I think these are great. The Wi-Fi issue makes this IT related, and Marcella will be thrilled for the PR help." I perused the flyers papering our room. A clip art oak tree anchored one side of the announcement. Cartoon squirrels lined the branches. Some chewed acorns. One gnawed a wire that swung from his jaws and disappeared off the page below. Stick figures with frowns and cell phones stared at the sky; others smiled and pointed binoculars at the furry rats. "I think you've depicted the problem fairly."

"Thanks." She bounced on her toes. "I think getting all the angry people in one place is the answer."

I blinked. "It sounds disastrous."

"Yes, but this group of grouches has a solid sense of community in common. Whatever their stance on the wildlife, they care more about this place and each other. I think some refreshments and a properly moderated heart-to-heart is the answer."

"Uh-huh." Wherever the moderator-sign-up sheet was located, I'd be headed in the opposite direction.

I dropped into my desk chair and waded through email. Thanks to the week's incessant hoopla, my day flew by. At six, I called Grandma to let her know I was running late for the Ren Faire. I had a quick stop to make on my way.

I parked in the lot outside Keith Orson's pet store and checked the area for lurkers, lookie-lous and animal killers, then dashed into the store.

Fins, Feathers and Fur was a boutique pet shop with high-end custom items, personalized accessories and enough live animals to keep pet lovers cooing.

Keith stood over a chinchilla play yard, filling food bowls. A name tag hung from his shirt pocket, but I recognized him from a few online searches. According to his Match profile, he was an entrepreneur with a penchant for fine wines and gourmet cuisine. From where I stood, he looked more like a cheeseburger-and-beer guy. His profile pictures were all taken from the chin up. Some lucky ladies were going to get a big surprise.

"Mr. Orson?" I pressed the girth of my velvet gown against my legs and side-stepped between displays.

He straightened and froze, chinchilla food in hand. "Can I help you?"

"I hope so. I'm Mia Connors. My grandmother was a friend of Dante Weiss. I believe you knew him."

Keith moved closer. "How can I help you?"

A wall of glass habitats lined the far wall. White mice scurried through tubes and tunnels, burrowing under piles of bedding and sucking madly on water bottles stuck to the glass. My empty stomach flattened against my spine. Heat rolled up my neck and across my cheeks.

"Uh." I pried my gaze off the mice and fixed it on the large man before me. "You had a lot of meetings with Dante before he died."

"Yes." He stepped closer. "And?"

"And I wondered if you might want to tell me why you were getting together so often."

He moved into my personal space and stared down at me. "May I?" He motioned to the desk at my side.

I craned my head back for a better look at him and stumbled out of the way. "Sorry."

He pressed through an opening in the counter space and halted on the business side of his register. "I don't think my meetings with Mr. Weiss are relevant or any of your business, frankly."

I forced the sound of a dozen mice on running wheels from my head. "I'm not sure if your meetings are relevant. That's why I'm asking. My grandmother is bereft over his death and she's my business. I promised her I'd ask a few questions." I moved closer to the front door and kept my eyes on his hands, in case he kept a weapon behind the counter.

"Did she ask you to wear that getup too?"

"Yes." Wearing the Queen Guinevere costume to question Orson wasn't my first choice, but it was a scheduling necessity, and Bree would be at the Faire tonight, which meant I was on a clock.

He moved like ooze behind the counter, slinking with every step. He dropped his hands to his sides.

My heart kicked into overdrive. My mind hurled images of hidden weapons at me. Guns. Baseball bats. Throwing knives. Daggers. I gulped. "Do you keep dead mice here?"

His eyes flicked up to meet my gaze.

"Like for snake food or something?"

His greasy smile speared my gut. "Predators generally prefer to chase their pray."

The door swung open and a couple with children strode inside. They headed for the turtles, oblivious to my intense relief. He wouldn't shoot me with witnesses.

I refocused my thoughts on the reason I'd come to the shop. "Mr. Orson, why did you see Dante seven times in the three weeks before he died?"

He took his time deciding to answer. "We were working on a new venture for invisible indoor pet fencing. A way to keep cats off the counters and dogs off furniture. We had to hash out the details and financing."

"Can anyone substantiate that?"

"Yes."

"Who?"

He trailed the family of shoppers through the store with his gaze. "We met with Project Management Central last Thursday. Someone there can confirm the venture and our plans to move forward." He pushed the words through gritted teeth. Rage burned in his eyes. "I had no reason to kill him and you have no reason to be here anymore."

Amen to that. I rushed back to my car and pushed the power lock button ten times once I was inside.

Keith Orson might not have had a reason to kill Dante, but he sure looked like he might have wanted to.

# TWELVE

THE REN FAIRE was in full swing when I arrived. Surprisingly, I wasn't late. The fast getaway I'd made from Fins, Feathers and Fur, coupled with some hasty driving, had made up the time lost during my brief inquisition. Even in the car, I couldn't seem to put enough distance between Keith Orson and myself. He'd raised all my internal flags. Beady eyes, smarmy face, entitled disposition. I couldn't manage any of those things on my best day, definitely not with a ketchup stain on my belly. A shudder rocked across my shoulders. Hopefully it was only a ketchup stain. *Poor animals.* Surely he wouldn't harvest his pets for harassment when they were meant for profit? Was he the kind of man who would hurt something so tiny for sport? What about a grown man in anger?

Grandma met me with a toothy grin and an open palm. "Good day."

"Good day." I turned my cell phone over to her and curtsied.

I hefted a basket of samples and moseyed magnanimously around the interior of our booth, nodding and delivering the goods to onlookers.

Women dressed as woodland faeries sashayed whimsically through the crowd. Children splashed in water basins, lovingly painted with signs like *Cool down ye hot mess!* and *Wash thy stinkers!* A minstrel band entered the nearby meadow, followed by ladies in brightly colored skirts, swaying to the merry tune. All in all, the Enchanted Forest was earning its name.

Unfortunately, Orson's glass wall of mice habitats haunted me. I started at the sound of jousters colliding in the field beyond the market and nearly dropped my basket. A round of exuberant applause rose into the air. I shook off the panic and located my Zen. I pushed Orson from my thoughts again. He couldn't reach me here. Here, I was Queen Guinevere of Camelot.

I really wished I hadn't gone to see him in costume.

Nevertheless, I inhaled the moment and let the yeasty scents of a vendor's soft pretzels take my worries away.

Grandma eyeballed my wailing abdomen. "Good grief, was that your stomach?"

"No."

She opened her giant handbag and ladled out a mess of fruit leather and granola pouches. "Here. Eat before you fall over."

"I'm fine." I ripped a chunk of fruit leather between my fingertips and shoved it in my face.

"Stop that," Grandma complained. "All that groaning and sighing will scare the customers."

I popped my eyes open. When had I closed them? "Sorry." I shoved another bite in carefully. "Was it scary to accept Marvin's proposal?"

She pursed her lips. "Yes."

"But you agreed anyway."

"It's shameful to say, but losing Dante changed my ideas about a lot of things. I'm not promised another day of life or health. I'm going to enjoy both while I've got them." She lifted her fist and bumped it to mine. "Right on."

I laughed. "I guess."

She perked suddenly and headed to the opposite side of our booth. "Get ready. Here comes the money maker."

I followed her gaze into the distance. Bree.

"When she's here, I can't take shoppers' money fast enough." She dashed along the booth's interior, adjusted displays and hoisted fresh supplies onto the counter. Her long gray braid swung wildly against her backside.

I bit into the fruit leather and watched a body that looked a little like mine, but more and more like a parade float, wobble through the parting crowd. A white satin gown adhered to Bree's burgeoning belly like a second skin, revealing every secret she'd ever had. The slits on the skirt's sides stretched to her hips. Delicate golden roping underlined her breasts and hung suggestively under her bump. A thin golden cape floated in the breeze behind her.

"Oh, boy," I told the fruit leather. "She's got a new costume."

"Good day," Bree said upon arrival. A heartbeat later, her cape flitted to a stop against her back. Her skin was flushed, and her bosom heaved. "May I trouble ye for some water, milady?"

The crowd closed in.

I uncorked a bottle from the hidden cooler and poured it into a glass. "What are you supposed to be dressed as?"

She gulped the water like we were in the Sahara. "I'm fertility."

"You don't say."

She rubbed the back of one wrist across her forehead. "The walk from the gate is awful. Tom dropped me off, but my goodness."

I looked over her shoulder. "It's like fifty yards."

"Try doing it when you're forty pounds heavier and growing a human being inside you."

A hush crossed the crowd.

I forced a smile. "Of course. May I get you a seat?"

"No, thank you." She stretched a hand in my direction. "Would you boost me onto the counter? I'd like to sit up there so I can get a better look at all these glorious faces."

I placed a stepstool outside the booth and rolled her onto the counter.

She toyed with her skirt and cradled her bump in her hands. "How do I look?"

Like Buddha.

The adoring crowd gazed up at her in anticipation.

Her belly button resembled a popped turkey timer, but she'd threatened me the last time I mentioned that. I arranged her cape over one shoulder and tried to cover her cleavage.

She tossed the material off her. "I think my life is actually enchanted. I've never been so happy, you know?"

I didn't answer.

"I look okay?" She fished again for a compliment.

I smiled brightly. "Exactly like Humpty Dumpty."

Her lips twitched. "And you, milady, are the oldest of all the maidens."

I curtsied deeply, enjoying the moment of silliness before the dark cloud I stumbled underneath began to rain again. "Yet I am still younger than you."

"Ha."

I blew her a kiss and stepped away.

Grandma climbed onto the vacated stool and raised a large basket of Bree's product overhead. "The Pampered Womb Collection is a complete system for worshipping your blessed maternal skin."

That was my cue to go anywhere else. I swapped the samples in my basket for ones from Bree's new line and headed into the crowd. Shoppers dove for me like vultures on a fresh kill. My basket was picked clean in minutes. I wrestled flyaway hairs back into position and straightened my gown. "Good grief."

Grandma dumped a fresh load into my basket. "Told you."

Bree finished her portion of the spiel and answered consumer questions while Grandma and I raked in the money. I fought the smile working over my face. Bree drove me completely bananas, but she was pretty great. Even in her weird maternity slave Leia outfit.

My parents arrived at the height of chaos. They fell into position, picking up slack and smoothing the wrinkles in our assembly line until all the shoppers were satiated and Bree was back on her swollen feet.

Mom folded shopping bags and marveled. "That was amazing, Bree. Great job, sweetie." She kissed her cheek. "I keep expecting the response to mellow out, but it never does."

"It will when I have the baby," Bree said, looking slightly disappointed at the notion.

Whether she'd be sorry to see sales drop or her pregnancy end, I couldn't say. Maybe a little of both.

"I'm hoping Mia can take the torch after that."

"What torch?" I wiped Bree's butt print from the counter and stacked our scented soaps in a pyramid.

"Creating the next addition to our family, duh."

What would I do with a baby human? I killed plants regularly. Goldfish died before I finished paying the clerk. I'd considered a cat once, but there wasn't room for any more sass and judgment in my life. Stupidly, Jake's face popped into mind. He was great with kids, and during a rare heart-to-heart before his undercover assignment, he'd admitted to wanting a brood of his own one day. I gave Bree's burgeoning belly another look and imagined she was a mirror instead of my sister.

"Never mind that." Grandma flopped a three-ring binder onto the counter and opened it. "Now that you're all here, we can begin sorting out details for my wedding."

I peeked around Grandma's arm. She'd only been engaged for five minutes. Where was this coming from? Her binder was at max capacity. Brochures and printouts poked free from the pockets on both sides, and the little metal rings threatening to pop at any moment. "This must have taken weeks. Did you know Marvin would propose?"

Grandma turned wide eyes on me. "No. Of course not. It was a complete surprise."

I leaned in at her ear. "Then why'd you ask me to check up on him?"

She blushed. "I was going to ask him to move in with me."

The flush of her cheeks seemed to seep from one face to the next around our circle, first to Mom, her daughter, and then to me. Grandma had planned to shack up. There would have been premarital sex. Grandma sex.

I lifted my gaze to Bree, who beamed.

I'd rather think about the mice.

Grandma turned to the book's center. "This section is for the wedding reception. I'd like to make it a black tie event with a black-and-white color scheme. Some punches of red for flavor. Top hat centerpieces filled with red roses, and decks of playing cards on the tables. Magic wands at each setting."

This was my kind of party. "Where did you find the time to do all this?"

Mom and Bree shot me a warning look.

Grandma turned the page. "I'm not sleeping well. There's a lot on my mind."

"Oh." I mentally kicked myself. She covered her stress

so well, I'd forgotten how much she was hurting. "Right. I'm working on it. I promise."

"I know you are," Grandma said. "I just wish I knew what he'd wanted from me. Why would he call me out of nowhere like that? He was in huge trouble. Why call me? What could I have done for him? What did he want to say to me?"

I wrapped my arms around her on instinct. I wanted to cover her pain and mend her heart by osmosis until I had the answers she needed to truly heal. "Maybe Dante wanted you to stitch him up?"

She disentangled herself from me. "What?"

"You were a nurse when you met him. Maybe he needed medical help."

Dad poked his way into the estrogen circle. "You think he was already injured when he called?"

"Maybe." I was running on pure theory and speculation, but it made sense.

Dad nodded his retired-cop head. "I'd assumed he needed money, but your way makes sense. If he was into some shady business and packed for a fast escape, he wouldn't have wanted to go to a hospital. Hospitals are required to report violent injuries. Stabbings qualify. It would've been hard for Dante to get away once the hospital staff had him in their care, and it would've been easy for whoever hurt him to find him. Hospitals are the first place an attacker would have looked."

A tear dropped from Grandma's cheek.

My family stopped breathing.

I reached for the big binder and pointed to the magic-themed reception photos. "I love what you've put together so far. Marvin is an incredible illusionist and you are a gorgeous assistant, but what about the Faire? Have you considered adding a dash of the Faire here? Some of your personal pizazz?"

She caught a tear on the pad of one thumb and accepted my abrupt subject change. "The Faire was your grandfather's thing. His and mine. We were married under the willows in full Renaissance regalia. It was who we were then and what I needed raising Gwendolyn."

"And now?"

Wrinkles gathered around her eyes and lips as her smile grew. "Vegas, baby."

I laughed.

"What?" Mom yelped. "I thought you'd get married in the church where Bree and I were married."

"Nope. My work here is done. My family beats the pants off any other family I know. I've won at motherhood, grandmotherhood and business ownership." She opened her arms in evidence.

Mom pulled Bree and I against her sides. "I can't argue with that."

Grandma smiled impossibly wider. "Marvin and I have decided we're making our golden years everything they can be. When we were young and responsible for so much, we had to behave ourselves. Little eyes were watching. We had to lead by example. Now we don't. We're going to have fun!"

"Huzzah!" A round of applause went up.

Her speech had gathered a crowd.

I blinked emotion-filled eyes. "Well, good for you. You deserve it. You deserve everything and anything you can dream up."

Mom released Bree and I. She hugged Grandma's neck. "That was absolutely wonderful. That's going in my book."

Dad groaned. "Not the book."

I'd forgotten about the book. How insane was my life

that I'd forgotten my mother wanted to air the details to anyone with some cash or a search engine?

I loved my life, but I was smart enough to know it was crazy.

NATE AND FIFI picked me up for drinks and pizza after the Faire. Part of me wanted to feel like a third wheel, but I couldn't quite manage. I knew them too well. Fifi was fast becoming my best friend, and Nate was like a brother. The three of us were painfully alike in all the best ways. That fact earned us some strange looks after Nate took off his hoodie and we realized we'd accidentally coordinated outfits. Nate had on a T-shirt and cargo shorts. I had a blouse and capris. Fifi wore a halter top and skirt. All light blue tops. All khaki bottoms. We looked like a bizarre prom trio, but less casual and without the leafy corsages. Mostly, people laughed. One guy in a BEER T-shirt asked if Fifi and I were sister-wives. Nate directed him elsewhere before I could answer.

Five hours, four stops, three mega slices of pizza and two drinks later, I was headed home in Nate's big SUV, music blaring. I'd have felt ten years younger, except ten years ago, I would've been at the library, not out with friends. Until Nate, my only friends were classmates with competitive grade point averages who grouped weekly to study and pound espressos.

I stroked the tinted window with my fingertips. "This was fun. I'm so glad you guys came and got me."

Someone turned down the stereo.

Nate caught my eye in the rearview mirror. "I checked out the changes you made to REIGN."

My tummy tightened. "And?"

His face split in a wild smile. "They're fantastic! Are you kidding? I happen to have plenty of valor, so I headed straight for the spring and entered the hidden realm. Players are going to flip when they see the spring, happy to heal their wounds, then boom, they get a whole other level to explore."

"Did you see the volunteer links?"

"I signed up." He stopped at a red light and turned to look at my face. "They're really good, Mia. You did all that in a couple of sleepless nights? Imagine the changes we could make with a full-time project manager."

I wanted that sentiment to end differently, like, *what if you were the full-time project manager?* I deflated. "Yeah. I know." He was right, but the reminder killed my happy buzz. I needed a new subject. "Did I tell you my mom's writing a book about our family?"

Fifi twisted in her seat. "How's it going?"

"I don't know. I forgot until today, then I started watching her. She spent half the evening stage-winking and scribbling in a little notebook."

Nate caught my eye in the rearview mirror. "Maybe the book is a guise. Maybe it's actually a social experiment designed to test you guys and see if you turn on one another, divulging secrets and retaliating."

"You go dark when you drink."

"I'm not drinking, nerd."

"Dork."

Fifi held her hand up. "I bet you can decide the content of your mom's book by working with your family outside her knowledge. You can get a group consensus on which stories to tell and which are off-limits. When she interviews you individually, she'll get the same info from everyone. Ultimately, you'll have determined what was published."

I collapsed against the soft leather seat. "You're an evil genius."

"Thanks." She gave Nate a high-five.

He hooked an elbow over his armrest and glanced my way. "You should talk about the time you and I solved a crime the FBI couldn't handle."

"Sure." I rolled my eyes. "Jake would love it if I exposed that story."

"Then tell her about how we met the Archers. No, tell her about the time we rolled down our street, right past Dan on stakeout." He roared in laughter. "That was awesome. I was stalking him. He was stalking me. He had no idea I was there all the time."

I jerked upright. "Nate! You're bloody brilliant."

"And you're British?"

I pushed his head. "I know how the killer got into Horseshoe Falls. He doesn't live in my community. He rode there in Dante's car. Hidden in the backseat, just like you hiding from Dan last year." I pulled my phone from my pocket and scrolled through Contacts. "After the deed was done, he jogged right out the front gate. Bernie texted me a list of joggers." I found Jake's face and made the call. "Jake's going to flip out. They probably weren't even processing the backseat for evidence. I just opened up a whole new land of potential clues."

"It's just a backseat," Nate deadpanned. "Maybe five square feet. Hardly a whole new land."

"Shut up. I win."

# THIRTEEN

I STEPPED OUT of my morning shower with purpose. I'd gotten Jake's voice mail last night, but I left a message, so that was done. I drank a pot of coffee and obsessed over what I knew and what I needed to find out. The next mouse I found was going in a shoebox until I discovered its origins. A quick internet search revealed that mice like the ones I'd found were often bred for shops to sell as pets or as food for predatory pets like snakes. They were shipped in bulk, warehoused and distributed in mass quantities. I'd never given much thought to how mice were produced before. Part of me had assumed it worked, at least loosely, like cats or dogs. Not even close. Orson was a business owner. He bought mice from somewhere, which meant there were records of the transactions, and if the next furry threat to turn up on my windshield was one of his, he was going down.

I toweled off my hair and started the blow dryer. Time to concoct a plan to make myself easy to follow. First, I'd be more predictable. Use the same routes to the Faire and back. Keep a schedule. Maybe revisit the scenes of previous mouse deliveries.

My phone lit with a voice mail. I stopped the dryer and checked the message.

Jake's voice crackled across the line. Wind buried a few of his words, but I got the gist. He wanted me to know he got my message last night, and he'd have Dante's backseat thoroughly processed for evidence of someone hiding back there.

Trading calls had become our thing. Basically, I got more face time with stray community cats than my boyfriend, if that's what he was to me. Semantics were a pain in the ass. I would've toiled over the right word longer, if it wasn't dead last on my list of unsolved puzzles.

I swept my hair into a messy pony and dialed Jake's cell. While it rang, I planned my message for him and gathered my laptop bag, purse and keys. I lost the call in the elevator and redialed in the lobby. I grimaced at my reflection in the glass as I headed into the day. I needed stronger coffee than I kept in my apartment. As was evidenced by my outfit. Blue sleeveless swing dress with yellow polka dots and matching skinny belt. My patent-leather peep-toes were cute, but that was where it ended. No accessories. Not even a headscarf or earrings. It was probably a minor miracle I'd remembered shoes.

"Archer." Jake's deep tenor pulsed through the line.

"Hey." I stopped to collect myself. What was I supposed to say when he actually answered the phone?

"I just left you a voice mail."

I headed for Dream Bean. "I was in the shower."

"You had a good idea last night." His voice gave my heart a much-needed pick-me-up. "If we find a single thread, it could break the case, and if there's anything to find, we'll find it. Unless he wrapped himself in plastic wrap and shaved his body, we'll get him."

"*If* he was really in the backseat." It was only a theory, and I was known to be wrong.

"We'll get him. I promise."

I looked both ways and crossed at the double white lines. A pair of women on Segways slowed for a gaggle of geese. I steered clear of both. Not every Segway owner knew how to keep them upright, and the geese liked to chase me.

Jake's truck's engine roared through the phone. "I'm out for the morning. Following a lead. Are you available for lunch?"

A woman in a Kent State Black Squirrel Festival shirt darted into Dream Bean.

I cringed. "No. I've got to help Marcella and Fifi with a community meeting about squirrels."

He blew out a sigh. "Are you blowing me off, or are our schedules really this incompatible?"

I tugged the door open at Dream Bean and nearly collapsed. If Heaven had a smell, it was this. Soft scents of spun sugar and fresh-baked treats mixed with French vanilla and caramel coffees. The shop was wall-to-wall with resident-protesters. Fifi's flyers had done the trick. Everyone was geared up to make their stand. A few carried stuffed squirrels. Most wore variations of Save Our Wildlife apparel. Others were dressed in full hunting camo. Not good. I took a seat near the door and calculated the distance for an escape. If a brouhaha erupted, I'd get out first and call for help second. I still had phantom pains in one elbow from the summer's butter battle.

"Mia?"

"Sorry." What did he ask? Oh, right, the squirrels. "I put in community Wi-Fi and it tanked."

"Did you do a mesh network?"

I lowered my voice to a whisper. "Yeah, but the squirrels ate it."

Darlene hustled between customers, delivering coffee cups and white pastry bags, a look of panic on her brow. Luckily, the residents weren't arguing. In fact, the utter silence was worse. It was like anything could happen at any moment. Despite the soft shuffle of clothing and shoes, I could hear myself breathing.

"Are you okay? Why are you whispering?"

I shook my head. What could I say? "The community's in upheaval. The usual."

"So no lunch."

"Right." I shifted in my seat, hyper-aware of prying eyes and listening ears. "How about dinner? I'm visiting a shower venue with Bree before the Faire, but if you can stop by the orchard, maybe I'll treat you to a pint of ale and a proper dumpling."

"Can't. I've got a family thing."

"Okay." I tugged my bottom lip between my thumb and first finger. A flurry of little white mice ran through my mind.

He cleared his throat. "Is there something on your mind? Anything you want to talk about?"

I'd hoped to tell him in person, but apparently, that wasn't in the cards. Stupid Universe. "Someone put drowned mice on my car. Twice. Well, three times, if I count the first one, but that was in a field where mice belong."

"Start over."

"The first dead mouse was beside my car in the field outside the Faire. The second time was at the bakery. One mouse in the gravel. The third time, there were a couple mice on my windshield."

"Drowned mice?"

"Yeah. I think they're supposed to represent Dante. He drowned."

"I recall. Any idea who left the mice?"

Yes. The only man I knew with a big wall full of them

and reasonable reason to have them. "Maybe. Dante met with a man named Keith Orson several times before he died."

"I'm aware."

"I went to see him. He owns a pet store. Not a friendly guy."

Jake groaned. "You promised to stop looking into this."

"I promised to try. Besides, the pet store is a public place. I might be a regular shopper there. Maybe my visit was completely ordinary."

"Had you ever been to Fins, Feathers and Fur before?"

"No." I drew a circle on the shiny white tabletop with my fingertip.

"Okay, first of all, I need you to stay out of this investigation before you get yourself attacked. Again. I will put you under house arrest if necessary."

My finger froze on the table. "You wouldn't."

"Would."

"For what cause?"

"Assurance of personal safety."

I gasped. "That's not a thing."

"Arrest me." He snorted at his unfunny joke. "Seriously, though. I think the drowning angle sounds more and more like Terrance Horton. I wasn't convinced at first, but the mice are his speed. He's a white-collar criminal with a flair for the dramatic. Drowning mice is dramatic. It won't be long before we wrap this case, so can you please leave it alone?"

"After I check on the mice. I can trace them to the warehouse where they were purchased and check the invoices to see if Orson bought them. I don't have to see him again for that. No one will know I'm looking." Of course, I needed to wait for another mouse to be delivered since I'd consistently left the evidence behind.

Silence stretched for several long beats. I checked the phone to see if I'd dropped the call.

"Fine," he finally grouched, "but look into it from home. No more inquisitions."

"Fine. Did you say you know where Terrance Horton is now?"

"My team's closing in on him. We scooped up a known accomplice last night. I'll ask if he knows anything about Horton and mice."

It sounded like a long shot to me. "Orson owns a pet store with tons of mice."

"Orson's on my list too. I saw the same files you did, Connors." His engine quieted and a car door slammed. He'd arrived at his destination. "I'm glad you told me about the mice."

"Okay."

We disconnected with an awkward goodbye. Phone calls were the worst.

I waded through protesters toward the coffee counter, doubly in need of a boost after our draining discussion. "Hi, Darlene."

Her brown eyes widened at the sound of my voice. She scanned the area and dropped her gaze on me with relief. "Mia." She wrung her hands into a dish towel and headed my way. "I almost didn't see you."

Whispering began behind me at the sound of my name.

"Short girl problems." I shrugged. If anyone understood it was her.

"Preaching to the choir. What can I get you?" She

leaned across the counter and grabbed my hand, slowly mouthing the words *you have to fix this* before letting go.

I swallowed hard. "Iced raspberry mocha latte, triple shot of espresso, please."

The whispers grew into a murmur. I swiveled in the confined space and pressed my back to the counter to examine the faces around me. No one smiled.

She worked quickly behind the counter, jostling containers and mixing her potions. She claimed there was no magic, just quality ingredients and love. I didn't see how that was possible. I'd tried to recreate my favorite Dream Bean drinks multiple times. I'd failed magnificently.

"Iced raspberry mocha latte." Darlene's voice cut through the rumble of disgruntled voices. "Heavy on the caffeine."

I angled toward her and dropped money on the counter. "Thanks. See you at the meeting?"

"I'm bringing the coffee."

I gripped the large plastic cup with both hands and gave the crowd a parting glance. "Bring decaf."

Tension rolled away as I put distance between myself and the coffee shop. Fifi might have overestimated the level of community around here.

I swept through the clubhouse double doors with a jaunt in my step. The most delicious coffee on earth was kicking in.

Marcella paced the lobby with a scary clown smile. "There you are."

I checked my watch. "I'm early."

She crossed the distance to my side. The click clack of heels reverberated off wide marble floors.

"Are you okay?" Close up, the smile bordered on lunacy.

"I didn't sleep. I baked all night in preparation for this

meeting. My phone buzzed incessantly with resident con-firmations. We had to move everything to the big room."

Wow. The big room was saved for conferences and an occasional guest speaker. Sometimes penny-pinching residents held office holiday parties there, but it was mostly used for storage and novice employee hanky-panky. No one went in there. "How many people are coming?"

"Two hundred."

"How many?" I'd misunderstood. Obviously. "I thought you said two hundred."

"Ay." She grabbed my arm and hauled me down the employee hall toward the big room. "Two hundred, *gorda*." Her grip tightened. Her stage whisper bit into the air.

We stopped outside a set of double doors, and she re-leased me. The doors were propped open and adorned with huge Welcome signs. Helium balloons floated at half-mast on both sides in shades of brown and green. Paper squirrels were taped to the walls inside.

Fifi circled through the rows of seating, dropping leaf-lets on each chair. "Come in!"

Marcella entered first. "I made comfort foods. Brown-ies. Pound cakes. Flan."

I followed her to the nearest row of seats.

Lunch tables lined the far wall, covered in cloth and weighted with sweets.

Fifi fanned her face with the pamphlets. "I ordered finger sandwiches from the clubhouse restaurant. They're being delivered about twenty minutes before the meet-ing. What do you think?" She opened her arms like a game show hostess.

"I think you've both worked very hard." I wasn't great

at lying, and though she motioned to the room, she meant *how do you think the meeting will go*? It would probably go poorly. Ask any member of the silent mob buying coffee.

"Guess what?" Fifi moved to my side and rocked on her heels. "I loved the empty apartment beside yours. I think it's fantastic, and I'm going to buy it. There's an unbelievable amount of square footage for the price. And those windows." She hung her mouth open.

"When did they finish it?" I hadn't heard any construction work since I'd moved in last summer and the condo mirroring mine was a big empty rectangle then. I'd liked the view from there better, but my penthouse had been move-in ready and the other was all drop cloths and drywall dust.

"It's still unfinished, but I'm having a ton of fun making design decisions. I've got an appointment to look at cabinets and faucets after work."

"Faucets."

"Mmm-hmm. There are at least a hundred decent choices. I'm putting off the floorplans. It's hard to know how big my closet should be. I don't want to cut into the space for my shower, but I don't want to part with any shoes either. You know what I mean?"

I slid one eye closed and rubbed the corresponding temple with my fingertips. "Absolutely. Well, it looks like you two have this under control, so I'm going to let you finish while I prepare some speaking points for the meeting."

I navigated the corridors back to my office, sucking the dregs of my latte as I went. Thirty minutes later, I pressed the order button for some recommended motion sensor toys. Multiple wildlife-loving websites said the toys would keep animals at bay. The toys worked like robotic scarecrows. If anything came in view of the sensor, the toy would light up and move around or make a sound. Animals would flee. My network would live.

I had a sneaking feeling residents who treasured the peaceful ambience of Horseshoe Falls would hate the idea, but I ordered a boatload of rechargeable batteries anyway. I planned to position the toys as sentinels inside the boathouse attic and use them sparingly outside the insulated confines. Keeping the peace was worth a little robotic intervention.

Next, I hit up a baby couture website and ordered two hundred white onesies and a bunch of gender-neutral sleepers and itty-bitty socks. I planned a shower craft for the onesies and a clothesline of rainbow-colored clothing as a decoration over the gift table. All items would hang in twos of course, and each with a different featured animal, two green froggy sleepers, two white bunny hats, two yellow bunny sunsuits, etc. I paid for the express delivery and said my daily prayer of gratitude for technology. If this was the nineteen hundreds, I would have had to drive all over Ohio looking for all this junk, and I'd have had to quit my jobs to do it.

I turned an ear toward the office window. Voices carried through the glass. One at first, then more.

I used my feet like Wilma Flintstone to propel my office chair across the room. I tugged the blinds up. A mob spread through the clubhouse lot. Save the Squirrels signs bobbed over their heads as they marched toward the building, amped up on coffee and ready to be heard.

Marcella appeared in the lot several moments later, smiling that demented smile and handing out cookies.

Behind them all, a taxi cab filed into the community and headed toward the stables.

Taxi cabs. A hazy idea percolated. I dialed Bernie at the gate.

"Horseshoe Falls, where nature is nurtured and so are you," she sang into the receiver.

"Bernie. It's Mia. Where was that cab headed?"

"Let me see." Papers rustled on her end. "Do you need an address or a name?"

"No. Neither. I mean, why is it here?"

The rustling ceased. "Oh, cabs take people to the airports."

I pressed my palm hard against my temple. "I always see limos or car services doing that."

"Most residents use those. Some just call Yellow Cab."

I bounced in my seat a little. "Will I see you at the meeting?"

"Of course. I'm covering it for my blog."

"Be careful." I disconnected and hurried back to my desk, considering taxis with each pull of my feet. I could count the number of times on one hand that I'd taken a cab, excluding vacations. Cabs weren't part of exurban Ohio life.

Assuming the killer didn't live within jogging distance, which I'd already dismissed as a probability, he could've drowned Dante, exited the gate, called a cab and been home in half an hour. I just needed to know which cab had picked him up and where he went. Thanks to technology and business records, that should be a cinch.

I grabbed my trusty keyboard and opened a search engine. There were only a few cab companies in my county. If one of them had picked up a jogger dressed in black, near Horseshoe Falls, on Friday night between eight and nine, I was going to find him.

# FOURTEEN

THE BIG ROOM was packed by eleven with standing room only inside the doors and a handful of residents positioned in the hallway.

I wiggled around the crush of bodies at the sweets table, silently rehearsing the main points of my presentation and trying not to knock anyone over with my laptop. "Excuse me. Hello. Pardon me." I took the empty seat beside the podium and opened my laptop's lid.

Marcella lifted the microphone. "Welcome. This meeting has two rules." She lifted a finger into the air. "Only one person is permitted to speak at a time—" another finger went up "—and *everyone* is treated with respect. I know the squirrels are a sudden point of contention among you, but we're here to find a path of peace, not start a war." She turned to face me. "Mia."

"Thanks." Feedback from the mic screeched through the room. I adjusted my stance and plugged my laptop into the podium ports. The PowerPoint presentation I'd created while researching local cab companies appeared on the screen behind me.

I peered into the sea of unhappy faces. "Hello."

They stared and grunted, as if to say, "Why is she standing there? Why isn't she making me happy?"

"Hi." I started again. This time, I pressed the button on my laptop and moved on to the slideshow. "I'm Mia Connors. I know many of you. For those I haven't met,

I'm the IT manager here. I'm the one who set up the community Wi-Fi."

A deep rumble swept through the crowd.

I powered on. "As you're aware, my attempt to improve life at Horseshoe Falls through technology failed briefly." I dragged hair off my burning neck.

Marcella passed me a bottle of water. Condensation ran down the sides and over her fingers, as if she'd pulled it directly from an ice bucket.

"Thanks." I cleared my throat repeatedly before cracking the lid and taking a few easy sips. I set the drink aside and rubbed wet palms on my skirt. "I recently installed a new Wi-Fi network throughout the community. It's called a mesh network, and it sends signals from place to place until the whole area is covered in Wi-Fi. It worked beautifully until—"

"Squirrels." A man in fatigues raised one fist in the air. Outdoor Sportsman was embroidered on his ball cap.

"I was going to say 'the main network cable was damaged,' but 'squirrels' might also be correct. The technicians at Ohio Wiring believe local wildlife had a hand in bringing down the network. They suggested that squirrels chewed through the cable, ending the signal and disabling the network before many of you had a chance to enjoy it."

A woman in the front row stood with a jolt. She smoothed her skirt against the backs of her thighs. "What are you going to do about it?"

The crowd grew restless. It was the question of the week. The reason we'd come together carrying bad attitudes and picket signs.

I took another sip of water. It was harder to swallow this time.

Fifi stepped onto the stage. "It's your community. What do you want?"

I recoiled. Wrong question. I stepped back, positioning Fifi in front of me in case a food fight broke out. "Bad idea," I whispered. "You're going to cause a riot."

As expected, dozens of arguments broke out and rose to a crescendo.

"Hey!" I beat the mic against my palm until half the room covered their ears. "Hey!" I hollered into the device. "One at a time. Remember? Respect one another." I lifted my hand. "Show of hands. Who wants the community Wi-Fi?"

They turned red faces on me.

"I should've polled you before I installed the new network. There are a number of things I would do differently if a TARDIS was available, but I have to move forward since I can't time travel, yet." The last word slipped out, but no one took notice. "Wi-Fi is important to me. I installed it as a surprise, expecting you to feel like me about it, and that was, in hindsight, an error, but like I said. I'm late on this exercise, but better now than never." I stretched my arm higher. "Who wants the Wi-Fi?"

Fifi stepped forward, hand raised. "I want community Wi-Fi."

Hands went up around the room. Almost everyone.

"Okay." I inched my shoulders away from my ears. "Good. That's great. I can give you that."

A man near the refreshment table jumped to his feet. "I won't allow it at the expense of my squirrels."

I adjusted my glasses and gave him a hard look. *His* squirrels. "Mr. Peters?"

He lifted a bushy white eyebrow over round wire-rimmed glasses. "Yes. Have we met?"

"No, but your reputation for dedication to the local squirrel population precedes you."

His neatly pressed black slacks and cream Mr. Rogers sweater were telling of his age and poor circulation. The fact he'd made a living at studying animal behavior said he'd likely been well respected in his field at one time or another. Surely, he would see reason, or at least be useful in ending the residential standoff.

I left-clicked the pad on my laptop for a new slide. "I've done some research, not as much as you, I'm certain, but I've taken the issue seriously and found a number of noninvasive measures for removing and/or discouraging squirrels."

I pointed to the screen at my back and pushed play with my clicker. A little video came to life. A monkey like the one from Stephen King's book cover banged its cymbals. "This is a child's toy. There's a sensor to make it move. I've ordered a box of these for the boathouse attic, where we believe the animals are nesting. According to my research, toys like these make good deterrents."

A long pause followed the video.

"No!" Everyone was on their feet, outraged but united in agreement. "Those are terrifying! My grandchildren will never come to see me! Those toys will ruin our peace and quiet! You'll scare the squirrels to death! No! No! No!"

A new idea sprang to mind. "What if we aren't dealing with squirrels? A gamekeeper mentioned the possibility of raccoons. What if I install night vision cameras for a week to confirm it's a squirrel problem before we go any further?"

Angry expressions turned to stink faces.

The woman from the coffee shop twisted on her seat.

Her Black Squirrel Festival shirt looked like a target for haters. "Raccoons got into my attic once and it cost me nearly ten thousand dollars to repair the damage."

I nodded. "Can we agree on positioning a few motion sensor cameras for a week?" I asked. "Strictly for the purpose of clarifying the problem. I'll remove them immediately afterward."

Mr. Peters lifted pale wrinkled fingers overhead.

"Yes?" I asked.

He shifted his gaze around the room and rolled his shoulders back. "You might not need to set up new cameras."

My heart thudded. "What? Why not?" Better question: Why had he said *new* cameras? There weren't any old ones.

He made a pinched face. "As you've heard, I've been tracking the squirrel population here for years. I know how the squirrels are related, who sired who and which family lines are longest."

I left the mic on the podium and headed into the room. "You have cameras out there?"

A gasp rocked the big room.

He backpedaled as I drew closer. "I don't always record. Mostly, I view live feed during the day or when I'm up at night."

I stopped in the aisle at his side. That story was all bull. I knew scientists. Scientists didn't do anything casually, especially not research. They obsessed. Peters had recorded footage. With any luck, he had footage from Friday night.

The crowd turned in Peters's direction, and the questions began anew. "You have cameras out there? You've been taping us?"

He confirmed with one stiff jerk of his chin. "One camera in the willow."

*By the lake.* I patted his shoulder and adjourned the meeting until further notice.

I'd put a hold on the discussion until we could find a way to remove the raccoons or incite a spontaneous relocation of the squirrels. I had my hopes set on raccoons, which no one seemed motivated to defend.

Most important, Peters assured me access to his recordings.

Back at my desk, I started making phone calls.

By five o'clock, I'd spoken with three local taxi companies and a half dozen cabbies. Shift managers provided the contact information of on-duty cabbies from the night Dante died. It took some coaxing and one moderate bribe to get what I needed. My life would've been a lot easier with a badge. Without call transcripts or service logs, I had to call every cabbie and leave messages. Now all I could do was wait and hope they returned my calls. In hindsight, I probably should've pretended to need a ride, then questioned them in person.

Next I contacted the joggers from Bernie's email. All five answered their phones. None recalled anyone joining along last week. Three admitted to blasting music through earbuds and fantasizing they were somewhere else entirely. One recalled the meal she'd planned in great detail for three point one miles, knowing all the time she'd have her usual grilled salmon and greens. The final jogger was a new mom and local CEO. She confessed to crying for at least a third of her run.

I tossed my pen onto the desk and dropped my head back.

My phone's alarm went off. Time to grab a Guinevere gown and meet Bree at Congress Lake before the Faire.

I fielded return cabbie calls all the way to the shower venue. No one had picked up a man fitting my description within six blocks of Horseshoe Falls that night. I pulled into the parking lot ten minutes late and crossed the callers off my list. There were only three cabbies left. I considered expanding my perimeter to ten blocks, but unless the killer was also an actual jogger, no one walked ten blocks on purpose. There weren't even sidewalks.

Bree rapped on my driver's side window and I screamed. She jumped back and grabbed her bump.

I flung open the door. "I'm so sorry. I didn't see you walk up."

The bodice of her pink dress heaved in time with her rapid breathing. "Holy shit, Mia!" She smacked my arm. "Are you trying to start my labor?"

Yes. This was all about her. "Sorry," I repeated. "You surprised me."

"What were you doing? Why are you late?"

I gave my future niece or nephew a look before dragging my gaze to meet Bree's. "We're having trouble with the community Wi-Fi."

She relaxed. "Oh, Grandma mentioned that. I'm sorry about the squirrels."

"It's okay." I beeped Stella locked and followed Bree down a beautiful flagstone path through lush flora and around tiny ponds and stone benches. She cooed at every fountain and fish.

Grandma swung the door wide as we approached the regal-looking hall. "This place is fantastic. Maybe I don't want to go to Vegas for my wedding."

I grabbed the door. "What are you doing here?"

"Hello to you, too." She raised a quilted bag between us. "I'm wedding planning. Do you know how many magazines and websites are dedicated to this nowadays? I thought the staff here might have some advice. Your parents agreed to man the booth."

Bree breezed through the incredible space. Polished wide-planked floors were outlined by a wall of windows and capped in soaring wooden beams. A balcony at the rear of the room led to a wide staircase, perfect for a bride's entrance, not so perfect for Bree's new balance issues. "This is gorgeous."

Grandma spread her binder on the nearest table and made notes. "I'm going to need a wedding planner." She looked pointedly at me.

I did my best to look honored but unworthy. "Bree's been through it. She's got experience."

Grandma wrenched upright and cocked a hip. "Weren't you her planner?"

Dang it. "Maybe."

"Besides, Bree will have a new baby soon, and she already has a toddler, grant and husband to contend with. What are you doing?"

I splayed my fingers on my face. Was that a serious question?

A man in a white chef's coat appeared, pushing a wheeled silver cart. "Menu sampling and cake testing." A woman and two men followed, each with their own cart.

Dinner!

I cleaned my tiny white plate several times before we finished the tasting. I'd need a muscleman to tighten my corset before fitting into my Guinevere gown. I walked the space, praying for speedy digestion and giving Bree room to interview the chef and manager.

My phone beeped with an incoming text from Nate.

A diamond solitaire ring filled the screen. A line of text came next. What do you think?

I skittered back across the room for privacy and typed a stupid response. About what?

The phone dinged. About the ring.

What's it for? I tapped the phone to my forehead. He and Fifi had only been dating six months. He couldn't be serious. He couldn't propose. It was too soon. Wasn't it?

I checked his response with one eye closed.

I'm going to ask her to marry me. This is important. Will she like the ring?

Holy crap. Nate was ready for marriage, and I was lucky to see Jake without a crime scene between us. I blew out a slow breath and responded. Yep.

Nate and Fifi were getting married? *If* she said yes, but of course she would say yes. And Grandma. Two weddings.

Bree's reflection drew nearer in the windows as I processed Nate's intent. "Why are you pacing?"

I froze. "I'm not."

"Yes, you are. Something's wrong. I can feel it. I *know* it. We're twins, remember." Bree thought we had a mystical connection. I thought she was nosy.

Grandma arrived next. "Is this about Dante? Do the Archers have any leads?"

"It's not about Dante. I was texting with Nate."

"What's happening with Dante's case?"

"I'm not sure. Jake asked me to keep my distance."

Bree shot me a droll look. Grandma raised an eyebrow.

"I'm working on it from a distance."

Grandma tipped her head over one shoulder. "Safely,

I hope. I don't want you getting into harm's way for me. I shouldn't have asked. I got carried away in the shock of things. I'm sorry."

"It's okay. I'm safe, and I don't mind asking questions."

Her apologetic expression turned curious. "Do you have any new leads?"

"Not really, though I could contact some of the people who'd sent angry emails." None of them had seemed mad enough to kill, but who was I to judge?

"Have you made a list of people who stood to gain from his death?" Grandma asked.

"Not yet."

Bree shifted foot to foot, stroking her belly. "Or a list of who would be hurt by his life?"

They exchanged looks.

I resolved to look into both. First, I had obligations to family.

I turned the phone over and sent a more enthusiastic and supportive text to Nate. Congratulations! She'll love it.

I gave Bree an awkward side hug. "This place is perfect. Your shower will be legendary."

"Do you really think so?"

"Absolutely."

She laid her head against my shoulder, happiness radiating from her.

"Come here. Grandma." I pulled her into our group hug and ignored my belly protesting all the sample foods.

This was my life. Encompassed by wedding plans and baby showers and a killer on my six. I needed a massive antacid.

# FIFTEEN

I TAPPED MY fingernails on the kitchen counter, regretting another hasty decision. Propelled by instinct, as usual, instead of caution, I'd made a risky move and emailed Josh Chan, Dante's angriest client. I'd linked his office phone number to the texts from That Guy in Dante's phone. After rereading every correspondence file I'd copied from Dante's laptop, I'd decided Josh was the only one who seemed truly upset with Dante. The other senders were run-of-the-mill impatient, self-important CEO types. Their snippety and demanding dispositions came with the titles. Their hostility wasn't directed at Dante.

Josh Chan, on the other hand, was a headhunter turned entrepreneur who'd recently signed a contract with the Shop At Home Network for over three million dollars, and he was ticked. It didn't make sense. I wanted to know why, so I asked if we could meet.

I refreshed the screen again.

All I needed was a time and place, preferably somewhere with lots of people under the bright summer sun. Once I had Josh on the hook for a face-to-face, I'd share my intent with Jake. He could come along or listen in, if he wanted. Maybe he or Dan had already spoken with Josh. Either way, I wanted to meet the man who created Luminatti, the fastest-growing paper lantern company on the East Coast. Not bad for a headhunter.

*Who gets mad about landing a three-million-dollar contract?*

The pot of water on my stove roiled to a boil, and I dumped a box of twisty noodles into the bubbles. Steam filled the air. I inched my laptop back a few inches from where I'd positioned it on a stack of never-opened cookbooks. The noodles zoomed and flipped through the pan, both supported and assaulted by the water.

Who needed recipes when instructions were printed on the box?

I shoved a silicon spoon into the mix and stirred. I couldn't get past Josh's anger over a six-figure contract. He'd had a reason to celebrate, but based on the number of times he'd texted and emailed Dante with descriptive ideas about where he thought Dante should go and what he should do when he got there, Josh was definitely mad.

I adjusted the heat under my pot and stared at Josh's face in an online photo taken earlier this year. I needed a new thread to pull on my floundering investigation, and he was the best I had. *Maybe he wanted more money and had blamed Dante for a lowball deal?* If receiving three million had him swearing like a sailor, he was clearly unreasonable. It wasn't a stretch to imagine him lashing out at Dante if he wound up in striking distance.

I'd decided, during a walk around the lake at lunchtime, that the stabbing was probably a crime of passion and improvisation. The drowning, I guessed, was meant to cover the stabbing, or at least get rid of the only witness. The reason behind the stabbing was still unknown. I didn't even have a guess. It had been six days since Dante was killed, and I was right where I'd started, wondering who would want to hurt him and why. Never mind the fact I practically lived at the crime scene.

Ten minutes later, I carried a heaping bowl of macaroni and cheese to my couch. I set my laptop up beside me and propped my fuzzy-socked feet on the coffee table. I opened a new window and searched for images of Terrance Horton. I hadn't given the fugitive Jake was looking for much serious thought before. Bad guys had strategies and silencers on guns. Dante's killer had chased a bleeding man into a lake and held him down. His killer wasn't calculated, he was cuckoo. Terrance didn't look cuckoo. He'd been on the run for a while, so he probably didn't look anything like the images on my screen anymore, either, but I was desperate. The cabbies I'd spoken with had freely described the riders in my time and location window, but none had sounded like what I saw before me. The man online was pushing fifty with the physique of Ichabod Crane. Hard to forget. The cabbies had picked up portly middle-aged businessmen with bifocals and briefcases, couples headed for the airport, and a few miscellaneous women. I doubted Terrance had found a fountain of youth, gotten shorter or changed genders before Friday night, so he seemed like another dead end.

For good measure, I texted his picture to the cabbies who'd had a hard time recalling what their passengers looked like. Unsurprisingly, they'd had no trouble remembering the score of the ballgame on the radio that night.

I scooped starchy noodles and simulated cheese sauce into my mouth. Memories of previous botched investigations came to mind. I'd found the killer before the cops, but nearly paid for the revelation with my life. I needed to involve Jake, tell him what I'd been up to with Josh and the cabbies. We could hash out the details and set a plan. I stabbed my fork into the noodles and sent Jake a text. Dinner tomorrow at my place?

Someone knocked on my door as I hit Send. I recognized the little shave and a haircut number. The building's FedEx guy. I shuffled into the foyer with enthusiasm and used the peephole just in case. Yep. Delivery. I swung the door open with a smile. "Hello."

He tipped his logoed ball cap. "Ms. Connors." He scanned the label on my package before handing it over. "Hope you enjoy your new box. Have a nice night."

"Thanks." I ducked into my apartment and locked the door. A Taboo Toys logo was printed on every side. "Just the reminder I needed." I peeled back the tape and opened the box to confirm. A dozen motion-sensored, cymbal-banging monkeys. The residents weren't very responsive to the monkeys as deterrents, but these were desperate times and I'd already ordered the creepy musicians.

I flopped back into place on the couch and refreshed my email. Nothing from Josh.

No matter. I still had Mr. Peters's secret tree footage to review. I sent him an email asking when I could come over. He'd ignored my last request, but I knew where to find him if he dodged me again. Worst case scenario, I'd give up my preview option and take Jake to his door to demand the video files.

My phone dinged. Jake said yes to dinner.

I danced my feet along the coffee table's edge. Now, I needed juicy information to share with him. Maybe one of the cabbies would recognize Horton's picture or Josh would accept my invite by tomorrow. Either of those options would make great dinner conversation.

My phone lit again and I swooped it off the couch.

This time the message was from Nate. Good meeting this morning. We're halfway through the consultant interviews. Do you have a favorite so far?

I hated interviewing consultants. Even if I could figure out how to live without sleep, I still needed time to eat, shower and blink. Sometimes life was unfair. I liked the first guy.

The baby?

I shook my head at the phone. He was twenty-two with a related degree and four years of documented professional experience. Not to mention a lifetime of gaming. Plus, I discovered afterward, a decade of amateur hacking. I traced his screen name for three days after we met. He's good.

Someone knocked on my door. Not the fun delivery knock. A neighborly are-you-home knock. Hopefully I'd find people, not drowned mice, outside my door. I split my droopy ponytail down the middle and pulled both sides, shooting it to the top of my head. No one got into my building without a fob or an invitation. I was safe.

Nate responded to my text with a cradle emoticon. Everyone has a lifetime of gaming experience. Good at playing the game isn't the same as qualified to improve it.

I headed for the door. Being young doesn't make him inexperienced. It makes him our target audience.

Fine.

Fine. I checked my peephole.
Fifi stood outside with a tall, dark and handsome man

at least twice her age. She was yammering full-speed, though the words were muffled by my door.

I flipped the deadbolt and gripped the knob. My phone buzzed. Have you spoken with Fifi?

Not since work.

How was she?

She was Fifi.

I hesitated. She wasn't wearing an engagement ring. Why? Did she say no?

Fifi knocked again.

I opened with a too-broad smile. "Hey!"

Her expression fell as she took me in. "Are you in your pajamas? I thought you'd be on your way to the Faire."

"Oh." I'd forgotten how I must look. I checked my shirt for fallen noodles or cheese marks. "Tom went. They didn't need me, so I got a night off."

She wrinkled her nose. "Well, I came over to give you this." She extended her hand to me. A keyring covered in wispy hot pink feathers dangled from her finger. A key swung beneath.

My phone dinged. I bobbed my head and tried not to stare at the stranger beside her. "Cool."

Fifi looked at my phone. "Aren't you going to see who's texting you?"

Right. I turned the phone over.

Nate: She didn't say, no. I haven't asked.

Nate: Why?

Nate: Do you know something? Doesn't she want to marry me?

I shoved the phone into the pocket of my baggy cotton bottoms and jerked my gaze back to the pair on my doorstep. The man looked too disinterested to be her friend. They stood two feet apart. She wasn't making a point of our introduction. Who was this guy? Middle-aged security detail?

He turned his eyes to me.

I started, jerking my attention to Fifi. "What's the key for?"

She pointed across the hall. "For my new penthouse apartment! I bought it and I'm moving in!"

My phone vibrated against my thigh. "That's great."

Fifi craned her neck to see around me. "Are you sure you're okay? You seem distracted."

"No, no. I'm good. Really great. Peachy." I stepped aside. "I'm sorry. Do you want to come in? I made macaroni."

"No," the man at her side answered swiftly.

I caught my breath. He reeked of authority. I had a finishing-school flashback and straightened my posture.

"Oh, Mia, this is my father, Pembroke Wise the third."

His sharp blue eyes looked bored and out of place in the building's hallway. His tailored suit and Italian leather shoes belonged in a window at Harrods. "Nice to meet you." His tone and expression said he was lying, and he made no move to shake my hand, a gesture that had been drilled into me since childhood.

I crossed my arms and regretted answering the door. "I don't normally look like a slob when I'm meeting new people," I explained. "It's just that I've already put in nearly sixty-five hours this week, and I haven't had nearly enough sleep. Someone died here on Friday."

Fifi gritted her teeth and closed her eyes.

Oops. Her dad probably wouldn't want her to live where people were murdered.

I waved off the news. "Don't listen to me. It's the sleep deprivation talking. My mind's everywhere. Clubhouse responsibilities, squirrels, my RPG and the Renaissance Faire."

He raised his brows and turned to his daughter. "Squirrels. Renaissance Faires. Rocket-propelled grenades? Is this to be your neighbor?"

I laughed loudly. The forced noise was frightening, even to my ears. "No grenades."

Fifi jumped. "No, Daddy. Role Playing Game. Mia co-owns REIGN with Nate, remember? I've told you this before."

I covered my mouth and tried not to make another sound as my phone continued to buzz conspicuously in my pocket. Somewhere in Ohio, Nate was having a series of strokes about the state of his relationship.

"Mia's my boss," Fifi continued. "She's the CIO of Guinevere's Golden Beauty. Tell me you've heard something I've said to you tonight."

Recollection lit in his eyes. "Ah, yes. The holistic beauty mogul." He frowned, probably trying to unite his idea of a mogul with the woman in front of him wearing a Space Invaders T-shirt and vibrating pajama pants.

He stepped away with a nod of acknowledgement and headed for the elevator, i.e. escape hatch. "I'll give you two ladies a minute. It's a lovely apartment, darling." The elevator doors parted, and he stepped aboard. "Think about my invitation. Maybe bring a friend." The words were there, but his heart wasn't in it. "Don't dawdle."

"I'd never dress like this in public," I told the closing doors.

Fifi laughed.

I covered my face.

"Sorry," she said. "I never would've stopped if I thought you were relaxing. I assumed you were on your way out and we'd share the elevator or just exchange hellos. Plus, I wanted to give you the key." She wiggled it.

"Oh!" I took it. "I'm so sorry. My brain." I pressed a palm to my head. "This is great. We're neighbors." I rewound the words. It was great, right? I'd enjoyed having the whole top floor to myself, but I loved Fifi, so sharing was okay. Right?

"I think I'm going to ask Nate to move in," she said. "What do you think? Am I crazy? Is it too soon? It's too soon, isn't it?"

"No." Neighbors with Fifi and Nate. Mixed emotions collided with my over-processed dinner.

"No?" Her doe-eyes widened impossibly further. "You think he'll say yes?"

"I think he'll say yes."

She squealed and hugged me, successfully pinning my arms to my sides and my lungs to my back. "I'm so glad you said that. I really want him to live with me. I hate when he has to go home, you know?"

"Yep." I wiggled her off me and took a whole breath. "You're very strong."

"I guess I should go." She didn't look like she wanted to. "I'll call you and tell you if you're right."

"I'm right."

She pushed the button to call the elevator. Wise not

to keep her father waiting. He didn't seem like an overly patient man.

A burst of curiosity hit. "What did your dad say about an invitation?"

"Oh. He wants me to attend a fundraiser for a guy I've never heard of, a mayoral hopeful. Dad's big into local politics. All the rich old geezers are. It makes them feel powerful, pulling the strings. The wealthy decide who runs, and who wins, with their fat pocketbooks. Essentially all politicians are puppets."

"Wow. Tell me how you really feel," I deadpanned.

She puffed air into her platinum bangs. "I hate politics."

"You have a law degree."

"For Daddy. I've always wanted to be an interior designer."

"Of course. So who's the party for?"

"Someone named Crispin Keyes. He's hosting the fundraiser as a guise. He wants to get a bead on his support. I told Daddy that Nate and I have plans." She dug into her clutch and placed a red, white and blue button in my hand. "But, hey, Vote for Keyes."

"Right on." I laughed. "Thanks again for the key, neighbor."

Fifi grabbed her phone and beamed. "It's Nate."

"See you tomorrow." I waved and went back to the couch.

I set the key and button on the coffee table. Was Fifi right about rich old men and politics? I pulled the laptop onto my legs and typed Dante's name into a search engine, along with the titles of various locally elected positions.

Bingo. I hit the motherlode with "Dante Weiss State

Senate." I opened a slew of tabs and scanned articles. Dante had publicly and enthusiastically supported Vince Adams for state senate. This was the lead I needed. I couldn't think of a single politician who'd be glad to have his or her name associated so tightly with Dante's, a man people would soon know as a criminal informant and associate of fugitives.

Next time I saw Fifi, I might kiss her.

# SIXTEEN

I'D OFFERED TO COOK, but Jake insisted on picking up take-out. I wasn't sure if that was exceptionally considerate or a comment on my cooking. Either way, I was glad not to have to clean the kitchen again. I'd spent the evening cleaning house in preparation for his arrival. Now, instead of a giant mess, there was only one small one on my kitchen counter. Bree's request for rainbow fruit skewers was proving to be an issue with the Congress Lake caterers. Guess who got to figure it out?

I piled disposable plates, cups and napkins on the island and mentally tallied the information I'd gathered on Dante's murder since I'd last talked with Jake. I hadn't gotten anything new or useful from the cabbies, but I had some following up to do. Two still hadn't returned my initial call and another hadn't responded to the photo of Terrance I'd texted last night. Josh refused to acknowledge my email, so I was forced to cyber-stalk his social media accounts all night. From what I could tell, he wasn't dead or a killer who'd fled the country. In fact, based on his hardcore Instagram dedication and frequent Twitter updates, there was no doubt he'd gotten my email and chosen to ignore it. No one was online as much as Josh Chan without checking email.

Mr. Peters was another man playing hard to get. He'd dodged my calls from the office today, and I couldn't understand why. He'd told me about the camera and agreed to share the footage. Why the sudden urge to hide? He was either bluffing about the camera or erasing parts he didn't want me to see. The latter plucked my curiosity. What could he have caught on camera? Owling? Night fishing? Skinny-dipping? I shuddered. The average Horseshoe Falls resident was between forty-eight and sixty-nine. I didn't want to think about what moonlight did to age spots.

My doorbell rang.

"Open up, ma'am. US Marshal Service."

I rubbed sweat-slicked palms against soft denim shorts and hurried to the door.

Jake looked at me around a stack of brown paper bags stapled shut, receipts blowing in the blast of wind from my opening door.

"What seems to be the trouble, officer?" I took half of his load to the kitchen. "Marshal?" I was terrible at improv. "Thanks for bringing dinner. You didn't have to."

"I wanted to. I was glad to get your invitation last night." He unpacked an impressive mix of lidded containers and small paper pails. "I have no idea what you like."

"So, you bought everything?"

He made a grouchy face. "Yep."

He'd told me once the angry look was his "thinking" face. Now, I never knew if he was thinking or pissed off.

He scooped fried rice from a pail with a plastic spoon. "I can't believe how hard it is to make time to eat dinner together. Our schedules are total crap."

"Accurate." Spicy scents of red peppers soaked in Szechuan cleared my head and enticed my tummy. I bit into the crispy shell of a fried wonton with reckless abandon and savored the cream cheese center. "This Szechuan is so much better than the macaroni and cheese I made last night." Lines of small talk circled my head. How was traffic? Work? The weather? "Any new information on Terrance Horton? Did his former associate cave to your interrogation prowess as expected?"

"Nope."

I smiled. "Nope?"

"This case is a nightmare."

I dragged the corner of my wonton through a puddle of duck sauce. "If it makes you feel any better, I'm not doing great either."

He laughed. "Yeah?"

"Yeah. I see your dead-end former associate and raise you a squirrel-watching scientist with secret footage of the lake at the time of Dante's death."

Jake stopped chewing. His eyebrows stretched into his hairline. "What?"

"His name's Mr. Peters, and he's dodging me, but I'm going after him tomorrow. I've already set time aside in my schedule to show up on his doorstep."

"I'm going to need to come with you for that." He wiped his mouth and looked expectant. "Anything else?"

"Did you know Dante was an avid and vocal supporter of a state senator?"

"I did not."

I poked a hunk of orange chicken with my plastic fork. "Senator Vince Adams. There's a ton of online material about Dante's financial support of Adams's campaign. I think you should talk to him."

"So do I."

"He had a lot to lose if news of Dante's involvement with money laundering or his ties to Terrance Horton got out. Adams could lose the next election. His life would be put under a microscope. His reputation would be ruined."

Jake filled his mouth with pepper steak and chewed slowly.

"It seems reasonable to assume he'd take measures to protect himself."

He struggled to swallow the food in his mouth. "You think Adams hired a hit man? Do me a favor and keep that to yourself. Those are the kinds of things we don't say out loud unless we've got rock-solid evidence to back them up. Accuse him wrongly and *your* life will be ruined."

I went to the refrigerator for bottles of water. I set two on the island. "That's why you should talk to him."

Jake cracked open a bottle and sucked greedily until his red face returned to a more normal hue. "I'll contact his people and schedule a time to talk with Adams."

I made a hopeful face. "Or."

"No."

I dropped my fork. "You haven't heard what I'm going to say."

"I know what you're going to say. It's something cockamamy and likely to get you arrested."

"By who?" I scoffed.

He chomped a hunk of steak on his fork hard enough to break the tines.

We ate in silence for several minutes while he settled down.

I tried again when he stopped eating. "Fifi's dad invited us to a fundraiser tomorrow night. Would you like to go?"

The frown returned. "What are you up to? Start with why Fifi's dad would invite me anywhere?"

I lifted a finger. "Technically, he invited her and she

declined, but I'm sure if I ask, she can still go and bring three guests."

"Me, you and Nate."

"Yes. She said the fundraiser is really some kind of cover for a guy who wants to be the mayor, and he's trying to figure out who's going to support him."

Jake nodded. "You think Adams might be there."

"I know he will. I called his office from work today, pretending to be a reporter attending the event tomorrow night. His admin told me to save my questions for the fundraiser."

He dropped his empty plate in the trash. "Anything else?"

I pursed my lips. "She might have asked me not to call back."

The makings of a smile played across Jake's mouth, never finding purchase. "I meant, do you have any other information you need to share?"

"You didn't answer me about the fundraiser."

He unearthed his phone from a pair of very fortunate jeans and tapped the screen to life. "I'll go. You have to promise not to talk to Adams. You can listen and observe, but no direct interaction."

"Can I ask the other partygoers about him?"

"No."

"Can I ask them about Dante?"

"No."

I pushed my plate away. "What am I supposed to do if I can't talk to anyone?"

"Enjoy the party. The evening. Time with friends. Time with me."

I ignored the twinkle in his eye and blew a quiet raspberry. I dialed Fifi to see if she'd reconsider going to the fundraiser and add Jake and me to the list.

"Flight of the Bumblebee" burst through my phone speaker and I winced. It was the ringtone I'd assigned to Bree long ago. An accurate depiction, I'd thought.

"Take it," Jake said. "If you don't, she'll probably come over here."

Good point. "Hello?"

"You answered." She sounded stunned and took a minute to recover. "Are you okay?"

"I'm fine." I edged away from Jake for privacy. "Don't seem so shocked that I answered. You're the one who called."

"Exactly."

"And you want…?" I prompted.

"Oh. I want to know if you think hiring a band for the shower is too much. Is it too showy? Will the guests think I'm being a princess?"

"Depends on the band."

"Do you think Maroon 5 is available?"

I laughed. "Yes, I think they only do weddings."

"Maybe Adam will make an exception. A woman only gets two baby showers in a lifetime."

"Sure."

"See if he'll play something upbeat but family friendly. I want to keep it a G-rated affair."

Jake was watching me from the kitchen island while he scrolled and tapped his phone screen.

I headed for my laptop and searched for local bands. "Got it. Anything else?"

"Yes. Thank you for this. I know you're busy, and I can sometimes be a little demanding. If I get on your nerves, imagine how annoying it is to *be* me. Anyway,

I don't say it enough, but I really appreciate all the hard work you're doing to make this special for me."

"You're welcome."

"One more thing. Can you get a swing band as backup? You know, just in case Adam runs into traffic."

"Already on it." I disconnected and refreshed my email.

My phone buzzed with a text from Fifi. "Yes! Fifi says we're in. Nate's going, too."

Jake drained the bottle of water and tossed it into my recycle bin. "Guess I'd better pick up a nice suit tomorrow."

"I'm sure you own a nice suit."

"Aside from my birthday one? No. I've got a bunch of cheap blazers and dress stuff for work, but that's it."

I couldn't stop the cheesy smile spreading on my face at the idea of Jake in his birthday suit. "Need any help looking for a suit?" *Or finding that one?*

He rubbed the stubble on his jaw. "I'm shopping at Dan's closet and borrow-mart. Your money's no good there."

"Maybe I should shop in Bree's closet. Give one of her gowns a night to remember."

Jake caught me in one arm and kissed my head. "I'd love to help with that."

I tilted my face for a look in his strong blue eyes. "I'll allow it."

He kissed my lips gently, chastely, before releasing me with a broad smile.

I leaned against the counter for support and swept my tongue across my bottom lip on instinct. "Who were you texting? Was it about the case?"

"No. It was Nate."

"My Nate? When did the two of you start texting?"

"He's helping me out with something."

"What?"

"Guy stuff." Jake circled the island to a white pastry bag but stopped short of opening it. "What did you do to this banana?"

*The banana.* I let my head hit the counter, sexist comment forgotten.

"It's blue."

I raised my head with a sigh. "Bree wants rainbow fruit skewers at the shower. The fruits need to go in proper rainbow color formation. Red, orange, yellow, green, blue, indigo and violet. So, I placed the request with the caterers for two hundred each, strawberries, orange slices, pineapple chunks, kiwi cubes, blueberries, raspberries and blackberries. They can't get the blueberries. There's some issue with their wholesaler. I don't know. It sounds like excuses instead of ingenuity. So, I pulled a banana from the fridge and shot it with food coloring, thinking they could just slice and color bananas. It didn't work, plus it got squishy and brown after sitting out. Bananas are not a hearty fruit once they've been disrobed."

Jake threw the banana in my trash and capped the tiny food coloring bottle. "I'll get the blueberries."

"Really?"

His expression of disbelief was almost comical. "You colored a banana."

I laughed. "Yeah." The laughter kept coming.

He shook his head. "You're a good sister. I'll get the blueberries. Nana's bushes are heavy with them." He opened the white paper bag. "I'm not sure it goes with Chinese food, but I remember you commented on the baklava at Eric and Parker's reception." He lifted two gooey pieces from the bag.

I'd almost single-handedly wiped out the dessert tray to avoid dancing that night. It was practically our first date and I'd thought more than once what it would be like to be with Jake in front of the priest or spinning into his arms in a white strapless Vera Wang original. That thought series inevitably led to the honeymoon and a bevy of things I'd like to try.

I focused on my dinner in case the sudden bout of dirty thoughts was written on my face. "Thanks."

"So, you've got an old guy with a hidden camera and a politician in crisis. I hate to ask, but anything else?"

I cleared my throat and sucked down half a bottle of cold water. "Not really. I've been in touch with about a million cabbies, hoping to find one who picked up the killer and drove him home that night. So far, nothing."

"I'm going to need a list of those cabbies and their contact information."

"I'll email it. I also went back through the files I took from Dante's laptop. One guy was really mad, so I tried to get him to meet with me, but he won't respond."

Jake dropped his head back. "There it is. You promised."

"Hey. I planned to ask you——" or Nate "——to come along, if he said yes."

He lifted his head. "You can't write to Chan again, and if he responds to the letter you sent, let me know immediately. Don't go anywhere near him alone."

I squinted. "I didn't say his name was Chan."

Jake patted his pockets, pretending to look for it. "Have you seen my badge, lately? Has a big star on it. Says this isn't my first rodeo."

Yeah, yeah. He had the same files I had. "Why are you looking at Chan?"

"Did you pull up his priors?"

No. I'd flipped through dozens of social media pictures of his dogs, jogging routes and healthy meals. "What kind of priors?"

"Restraining orders from two past girlfriends. They were issued a decade apart, but that only means the women in between were too afraid to file or they didn't stick around until he got attached. He's also got a black belt in tae kwon do. He's got a history of emotional instability and he's trained to fight. Please avoid this man."

I mulled that over. "So Josh's a stalker?" That was exactly what his emails to Dante had made him sound like. "I always think of stalkers as men stalking women."

"Stalkers do all kinds of weird shit. Do yourself a favor and don't research the topic unless you hate sleep."

"I love sleep."

He smiled. "Me, too. I'd indulge more often, but something's always going haywire in the world."

My phone's Skype app began to ring. I shot Jake a look. "Someone's calling from my mom's account." I'd created it years before but she'd never used it.

"Answer it."

"What does she want?"

He pressed the accept button without answering me. "Hi, Mrs. C."

"Oh, dear." She looked left and right. "I'm so sorry. I was trying to get Mia, but I don't know what I've done wrong." She slid glasses on her nose and peered into the camera until I could see her pores. "I don't know what happened. The screen says this is Mia."

I pulled my phone in front of me. "Hi, Mom."

She jumped back. "Mia? I thought I'd called Jake."

"Why were you calling Jake?"

Her cheeks turned pink. "I don't know." Her degree of frazzle increased with every rise and fall of her chest. "My publicist told me to get on the social medias and meet people."

"Skype isn't what you're looking for, Mom."

"I think it is."

"Nope."

Jake extended the phone away from my chest until we were both in the shot. "I can help you sometime, Mrs. C. I miss working online."

She stared. Mouth open. Confusion evident.

I sighed. "Jake's at my place, Mom. We were having dinner."

"Oh!" She slapped her table and did a big belly laugh. "I thought I'd really done something advanced! No problem. We can talk later. I need to know which trip was your favorite family vacation, but it can wait. Enjoy your macaroni." She walked away from her desk.

Jake and I stood shoulder to shoulder, arms extended to support the phone, as Mom hummed her way around the living room, patting pillows and flipping channels.

"Oh my goodness." I hung up. "She didn't disconnect. She's a train wreck."

"How's her book coming?"

"I'm not sure. She eavesdrops and stage-winks a lot more." I set the phone aside and refreshed the email on my laptop. It would be great if Josh agreed to meet while Jake was here so we could coordinate our schedules. *New message!*

I opened the mail. It wasn't Josh, but it would do. "Mr. Peters says he's home now." I hit the highlights. "He didn't appreciate all the messages I left for him while I was at work. I can come over and look at his video files now if I want, otherwise, he'll be gone until Monday."

Jake stuffed half-empty takeout containers into my fridge. "Let's go. I'm in."

I hadn't doubted that for a second.

# SEVENTEEN

I DROPPED THE box of mechanical monkeys in my backseat and led Jake toward Mr. Peters's home on Lake Drive. The moon hung bright and low in the sky. Millions of stars twinkled overhead. Every one of them knew exactly what had happened here last Friday night, just like Dante, the killer and the squirrels, but no one was talking. Maybe no one had to. I visually trailed a family of black squirrels along powerlines overhead and wondered if Mr. Peters's obsession with the destructive creatures would be the unlikely key in solving a murder. Maybe he'd unwittingly caught the awful events on camera and his footage would serve as judge and jury. Case closed. Criminal punished.

Starlight glistened on still lake waters. Jake's arm brushed mine as we moved. Bree would've insisted the moment was fiercely romantic, walking with my beau across a quiet field, a stolen moment of peace in the midst of two busy lives and we'd chosen to share it. She'd have clutched folded hands to her chest and made Disney eyes at me until I agreed. Thank goodness she wasn't here.

I scanned the area and crossed an arm over my tummy. Ours wasn't a romantic walk, it was a moment with no witnesses, beside a lake that had taken the life of someone dear to Grandma, someone who might jump out from the trees and eliminate two people looking for answers.

No, Jake wasn't my boyfriend tonight, he was a Deputy US Marshal and my trusty sidekick.

The boathouse came into view. I paused. "Did the police find any other clues near the lake? Anything else at the bottom?"

"No." He tilted his head back for a better look at the building's roofline. "What are you going to do about the squirrels?"

"I bought a bunch of motion sensor monkeys."

He lowered his eyes to mine. "What?" His expression was strained. "Why?"

I scanned the area for armed killers, lying in wait. "To use as scarecrows."

"That's nuts."

"Do you have a better idea? Don't say kill them. I'm not allowed to kill them, and I don't want to."

He turned in a circle, surveying. "You could plant corn. Choose the locations strategically, near plenty of trees with squirrel boxes. Lure them into more suitable sections of the community."

"I already bought the monkeys."

He blew out a long breath. "Let me know if you want me to shoot them."

I opened my mouth to protest, but the twinkle of mischief in his eye stopped me short.

My phone buzzed with Bree's theme song. "Hang on. I've got to take this again in case she's in labor."

"Mia?" She asked before I'd had time to say hello.

"Hi, Bree."

"Oh! Good. I thought I might get voice mail. Are you busy?"

I glanced at Jake. Was I busy since her last call, twenty minutes ago? "Depends on what you need."

He turned his head away with a smile.

"Can you give me the number of that pretty photographer of yours?"

I puzzled. I didn't have a photographer. I hadn't had professional pictures taken in ages. "Who?"

"You know," Bree pressed, "the sassy one with the tall dark and yummy husband. She took those fantastic photos of you and Jake last fall. I want to get some pregnancy photos taken before this baby's born."

I closed my eyes. "Tennille." Tennille King was a resident photog who'd helped me solve a murder with her photos last summer. In the fall she took some ornery pictures of Jake and me, which turned out to be pretty great. We didn't realize what she was up to until we received our copies. I'd framed mine. "I'll text you her number."

"Great. Hey, can you come over tomorrow to help Mom and Grandma make a mold of my stomach?"

"Uh, that's a big no."

"Why not?" Her voice hitched. "This will probably be my last pregnancy. Is it wrong that I want to commemorate this? You know I'd do it for you."

"I'm supposed to work at the Faire tomorrow, and also yuck."

"My stomach isn't gross, Mia."

"Of course not." I puffed my cheeks out. I hadn't actually seen her stomach since she was in labor with Gwen a couple years ago, but I remembered it clearly. Pale with blue veins and a dark line dividing the hemispheres. I pressed a palm to my abdomen in memory. Her stomach was mine, genetically speaking, and the whole thing was unnerving. I didn't want to touch it.

There was a long pause on the other end. "Text me Tennille's number."

"Yep." I disconnected and rolled my head over both shoulders. "She wants me to make a mold of her stomach."

Jake had walked several feet away while I spoke with Bree. He squinted at the water. "Eric and Parker did that before Eli was born."

"Did you help?"

He turned those blue eyes on me. "Did I touch my brother's wife's bare belly?"

I smiled. I hadn't thought that through. "Right. Gross."

"I don't think it's gross." He made his way back to me at a slow saunter. "What she's doing, what Parker did, I think it's a miracle."

I turned back toward the road and sidestepped the minefield of goose poop. "I think you've never seen a woman give birth. Speaking of—" I segued poorly "—how would you like to come to Sunday night dinner again? This week we're meeting at Bree's house and Tom is throwing a gender reveal party, so it should be..." I struggled to finish the impossible sentence. *Bizarre* came to mind, but felt wrong. "Interesting?"

Jake thumbed his cell phone screen. "Well." He spun the phone to face me. "I just got a text from Dan, who is apparently with the mystery girl again tonight and making plans for tomorrow."

"Why's he telling you?"

Jake turned the screen back to him. "He wants to know if you and I will meet them for dinner tomorrow."

"Oh." Was I supposed to answer now? He hadn't answered me about Sunday night yet, and I asked first.

We stood in the dark, facing off as if we might bow, step into warrior poses and begin kung fu fighting.

Jake curled long fingers around the phone. "I'll go to the baby thing if you come with me tomorrow."

"Deal, but we can't miss the fundraiser thing. That's tomorrow, too."

He stuffed his phone into his pocket and took my hand in his, instantly warming me and scattering my thoughts. "You're wrong about what you said earlier. I've seen a woman give birth."

I gaped. "When?"

"During my first tour in Kuwait. A roadside bomb sent her into early labor." There was wonder and regret in his voice. "It was terrifying as hell, but she was strong, and they both made it, no thanks to me or my team of bumbling grunts. None of us had more medical experience than some basic triage we were taught on base. She did it all. It was enough to make me consider medical school. I never wanted to feel that helpless again."

I squeezed his hand in mine. "Medical school, huh?" I imagined his bedside manner would be something like "Suck it up" or "Rub some dirt on it." I loved hearing about the things I'd missed in his life, and discovering who he was when he wasn't saving the day. "I know you want a big family, but how big? In a perfect scenario?"

"In a perfect scenario? Where money's no object and I have time to be the dad they deserve?"

"Yeah. Then?"

He took his time before answering. Another thing I loved about him. He didn't talk to talk. He meant everything he said. "I don't know. I think that's something you just know instinctively once you get started. The same way we know the person we're in love with is the only one we ever want to be with."

I gave him a side glance. "I think you're right."

We made our way in companionable silence toward Mr. Peters's home. I mulled over all he'd said about his future family. He seemed so sure. Why did everything he say seem so possible and reasonable and lovely?

"I can't believe Dan's seeing this woman two nights in a row," he said. "This must be getting serious."

"It's only two dates. Do you realize we also have plans for tomorrow and dinner on Sunday?"

He smiled. "I'd see you more if you weren't so busy."

"I'm a woman in demand, sir."

By the time we reached Mr. Peters's door, my heart was tap dancing and my mind was in full overdrive with questions about what the future held for Jake and me. The rational part of me insisted this wasn't the right time to think about that. We had a murder to solve. I needed to focus. Concentrate. Act my age. But what should I wear on a double date with the Archers?

We stopped at a mailbox shaped like a mallard. Acrid scents of a smoldering campfire peppered the air.

Peters's house was a lot like the other homes in Horseshoe Falls, expansive, expensive and custom. This one definitely suited its owner. I'd called it "The Treehouse" for years, never knowing who owned it, assuming, correctly it seemed, that it belonged to one of the more serious nature enthusiasts in residence. The enormous two-story home was covered in cedar shake and giant windows. The Treehouse was nestled among a cluster of evergreens planted at the time of the build and a well-manicured garden established shortly afterward. Bird and squirrel feeders hung abundantly from strong sap-covered limbs. Solar lights and a flagstone path led to the front porch stairs before forking east and west around the sides of the home. A series of small koi ponds scrolled down the gentle slope near his porch, each rock-lined structure spilling into the next, where frogs and various fishes cohabited with duckweed and lily pads.

Jake marched up the front steps and rapped on the door with authority.

The massive door was outlined with stained-glass sidelights and a matching transom. Colorful pictures of hummingbirds and wildflowers struck a delightful contrast with the home's earthy shake and natural stone. The door swung open with a whoosh.

Mr. Peters stepped into view and adjusted his glasses. "Yes?"

"Mr. Peters?" Jake asked.

"Yes." He glanced at me, confused. "I'm Mr. Peters."

"I'm Deputy US Marshall Jake Archer. I believe you may have some evidence in my murder investigation? I'd like to come inside."

"Uh…certainly." He hopped aside and shoved the door away so we could pass.

I followed Jake into the foyer. "He's with me."

Mr. Peters rubbed his eyes beneath his glasses. "It's cost me some sleep, but I've reviewed all the tapes, and I have one you should see. Come this way." He headed through the foyer and down an arching hallway with shiny wooden floors and a series of small chandeliers overhead. "The motion sensor on my camera is easily engaged, and most of my footage is useless, even to me. I've accumulated hours of nothing but wind in the trees, but this is something." He frowned over his shoulder.

The hall spilled us into an atrium filled with plants and domed in glass. The wooden floor gave way to intricately patterned stones nestled in grout and glazed to a perfect shine. A set of French doors opened to a cozy study with more floor-to-ceiling windows and massive built-in shelves behind a cluttered desk. The shelves overflowed with figurines and books on nature. Statues and small paintings of indigenous Ohio animals sat atop little pedestals and rested on miniscule easels. A big globe in a wooden apparatus sat beside a telescope near the windows.

I walked my fingers over the globe, turning it until Ohio faced up. The telescope pointed at nothing but trees. Surely he didn't stand at the window watching squirrels.

"Birding," Peters said.

I spun in his direction.

He stood behind his desk with Jake, watching me. I recognized the curiosity in Jake's eyes. Peters's expression held something I couldn't name.

"The telescope," he explained. "I use it for birding."

Jake helped himself to the leather desk chair and grabbed the computer mouse. He brought the machine to life with the flick of his wrist. "What sort of birds?"

Peters turned his wary expression on Jake. "All of them. Finches, blue jays and cardinals, orioles, hummingbirds. They're quite fascinating."

"Here." Jake jerked his head up and motioned me over to him. "Got him."

I hustled to his side and leaned forward, determined not to miss a thing. "Go."

Jake clicked the computer mouse. A grainy black-and-white image snapped to life. The lake view was partially obstructed by the veiny limbs of a willow dangling and blowing across the lens.

Peters leaned over one of Jake's shoulders. "This is where they come in."

Two shadows crossed the top of the screen, one bleeding into the next under the light from a full moon. The shadows changed direction suddenly and two figures emerged, running straight for the lake. They gained momentum on the downhill slope toward the water, their inky counterparts thinning in the field behind them.

"The camera's too far away," I complained. "Can you zoom in?"

Mr. Peters gave me a disbelieving look. "I bought the camera from Amazon, not MI6."

"Shh," Jake warned. "Look."

The first figure stopped abruptly near the water's edge. It raised its hands.

"Is there any sound?" I asked. "Is that the dagger in his hand?"

Jake tapped the screen. "Look at the way the second one is hunched slightly. I think that's Dante. He's hurt, but chasing his attacker."

His *armed* attacker. I peered closer, willing the grainy forms to clear. "No way." Who does that? "I don't think…"

The hunched figure dove at the other one, tackling it onto the grass and stopping me mid-sentence. They rolled toward the water like one massive log. Something flung free and bounced on the ground.

"What was that?" I asked.

"Shh," the men warned.

I gave them the stink eye but they didn't pull their gazes from the silent flat-screen monitor. "It's not like there's anything to hear," I mumbled.

The human log barreled headlong toward the water, barely missing at first, then splashing into the smooth surface's edge. They peeled themselves apart, scrambling away on their hands and backsides like crabs. They pushed to their feet and stood motionless. *What were they saying? Was Dante pleading for his life? Threatening to put the attacker in jail? Reasoning with him?* They circled methodically like wrestlers. I presumed the slower one to be Dante, injured, bleeding and out of breath from a run and a tumble. He lunged forward on wobbly legs, then stumbled sideways and backward, unable to stay upright any longer. He splashed into the lake, sending ripples in every direction.

The first figure ran to the water's edge and froze.

Adrenaline pumped in my veins, desperate to help the hurting man on-screen and capture the monster who hurt him. "What's happening?" Frustration shook my voice. The irrational part of me wanted to tear through Peters's home and out the front door. I longed to run into the lake and try again to save Dante, but he wasn't there. The figures were memories, images from another time and long gone. I'd had my chance to save Dante and failed. All I had now was an opportunity to find the killer.

The remaining figure dropped to the ground, crawling, moving up hill in a zigzag until he raised something into the air and chucked it into the water. *The dagger.*

Dante splashed wildly, raising his hands overhead.

The second figure lifted a fallen branch and extended it to him. When he drew near, the figure pressed it to his shoulders and pushed him under. Dante's flailing hands couldn't capture the stick, they bounced off and slid along the bark until they stopped reaching.

"Here come the joggers." Jake tracked them across the screen with his finger. "And there he goes."

The figure tossed the stick into the lake and ran along

the shadowed tree line as the pack of runners passed by. He tagged on to the back of the group and kept pace.

Jake clicked through screens. "Do you have any other cameras hidden around Horseshoe Falls? Any chance you caught more of the crime, maybe their run from the car to the lake or the killer's escape route?"

"No," Peters promised with gusto. "I've only hidden one camera, and I've felt awful about it since the day I set it up." He looked at me with pleading eyes. "I knew it was wrong. I needed consent or community approval. I should've posted a sign, but then someone would've taken the camera. I just wanted to watch the squirrels."

I stared, unsure what to say.

"Retirement is hard," he continued. "The squirrel research was my greatest on-the-job success. I didn't want it to end."

From where I was sitting, roughly forty years away from anything remotely like a vacation, retirement didn't seem so bad. More like a unicorn. I bit my tongue and weighed conflicting emotions. Boredom seemed a flimsy and selfish excuse for taping an entire community without consent, but if he had evidence of Dante's killer, I wanted it.

Jake turned to face Mr. Peters. "I'm going to need this footage and anything you have in the days immediately before and after."

"Of course." Peters opened a drawer and produced an external hard drive. "I copied the entire week before this footage and everything I've recorded since onto this. You're welcome to copy more if you'd like, as much as you want, but please don't take it from me. I review the tapes from time to time, looking for patterns in squirrel behavior."

Jake didn't take the hard drive. "We need access to all the footage."

Peters nodded. "I'll make a complete backup."

Jake replayed the footage. "We're going to need an official backup. I'd like to contact our tech team."

Mr. Peters flushed. "Yes, of course. Whatever you need."

I stared at the grainy screen. Dante's killer might've escaped the crime scene, but he wouldn't get away with murder on my watch.

# EIGHTEEN

JAKE PARKED HIS beast of a truck outside Buffalo Bill's, a popular local steakhouse. The blue behemoth was the largest in our row, but there were several identical models elsewhere in the lot. Women in sundresses and cowgirl boots chatted up men in dark jeans and big belt buckles. I'd stopped in once for lunch. The food was good but the atmosphere was weird. I couldn't understand an adult's motivation to throw peanut shells on the floor, so I hadn't been back.

I released my seat belt and sighed. "We're late and overdressed. On a scale of one to ten how mad will Dan be?"

Jake shut down the engine and pocketed the key. "He won't care. He knows we're coming."

Well, that was different. "Maybe he could talk to Bree. She has no tolerance for tardiness. She actually said that once." I stared at the building, hoping for the best. "What do we know about Dan's date?"

"She's out with Dan again, so she must be crazy."

"Excellent. She'll fit right in." I gathered my clutch and reached for the door handle.

"Wait." He raked his gaze over my black beaded dress again.

I'd chosen an off-the-shoulder number with a heart-shaped neckline and waist-trimming liner. The hem was three inches above my knee and I felt closer to sexy than

I had in my life, especially when he looked at me like that. I reached for the pins in my chignon and let my hair fall in thick loose waves for coverage.

He released a low wolf whistle. "Scandalous."

"You're making me nervous," I confessed.

He tipped his mouth into a smirk, leaned across the small distance and kissed me. His lips lingered over mine when he pulled away, as if he might be torn over going in for seconds. "I'm going to stop."

"Kissing me or making me nervous?" I whispered against his waiting mouth.

His lips curved as they returned to mine, catching only my bottom lip, and leaving me half loopy. "Okay, I lied. I have big plans for both."

Oh boy!

He straightened and checked his phone. "We've got one hour here. Are you ready?"

"Ready." One hour to double date, then we had to fly across town and meet Fifi and Nate at her dad's friend's faux fundraiser, where I'd hopefully have the opportunity to question the senator.

Dan appeared outside Jake's window and rapped on the glass. He looked a little miffed.

Jake opened the door. "What's up?"

"You're late."

"Couldn't be helped." Jake climbed down beside his brother and looked at me.

Dan followed his gaze. His jaw dropped. "I see."

I lifted my palm. "Hi."

Jake rounded the truck to open my door and help me down. The women in sundresses gave him an appreciative look as we passed. Country music wafted through hidden speakers in the restaurant's roofline. Dan and

Jake tugged the large wooden double doors apart and the yeasty scent of fresh-baked rolls and salty butter rushed against my face.

Patrons in boots and flip-flops packed the waiting area. I bumped a vintage Chanel pump into Jake's Italian leather dress shoe. Everyone stared.

Dan slid past the hostess stand. "We're in a booth in the back."

I edged through the crowd with Jake's hand against the small of my back. Tension rolled off him in waves, etching into my fading calm.

"Are you okay?"

He lowered his head to my ear. "Notice anything about the way these cowboys are looking at you?"

I caught the leer of several twenty-somethings with glossy eyes and a shared pitcher of beer. I tipped my head back for a look into Jake's eyes. What I got was a view of the underside of his chin. "Jealously is a very unattractive quality."

He stared down an approaching man in a John Deere hat. "I bet it looks better than a black eye."

"Probably," I admitted.

We stopped at a large wooden booth with red padded benches.

A tiny woman with frail-looking hands and birdlike features smiled up at me. Her golden blond hair was pulled back in barrettes on both sides, and bangs hung like thick curtains above large blue eyes.

Dan slid onto the seat beside her. "This is my brother, Jake, and his girlfriend, Mia. Jake and Mia, this is Reese."

I looked at Jake for input on the name-calling. He motioned me to slide in ahead of him.

"Hello." Jake extended a hand across the table to her.

"Nice to meet you." I shook her cold little hand next.

"Thanks. You, too." She circled a finger in front of her eyes. "I like your glasses."

"Thanks." I'd chosen dramatic black frames to accent the dress.

"How long have you two been dating?"

I looked at Jake. He smiled at me.

Dan cleared his throat. "They've been like that since they met. You'll get used to it."

I smiled. We had been like this since we met, though he used to make me a lot madder.

"We already ordered drinks and appetizers." Dan paused to ogle his brother. "I'm sorry. Why are the two of you dressed like that?" He gave Jake a crazy face.

Jake looked like a *GQ* model in his sleek black suit. "We're going to a party from here."

"What kind of party?"

I tugged my tennis bracelet with two fingers. "Fifi invited us to a fundraiser tonight."

Reese smiled sweetly. "That's a pretty bracelet."

"Thanks." I stopped fidgeting. "It was a graduation gift."

"Oh." She perked up. "Where did you go to school? Kent State? Ohio State?"

"Yale, then Brown."

"Wow." She looked at Dan.

I looked at Jake. Was I supposed to respond to that? How?

Jake nudged my knee with his. "So, Reese, what do you do for a living?"

"I'm a ballet teacher."

I pressed my lips together. Suspicions confirmed. I

had nothing in common with this person. I helped myself to a cheese fry.

Dan hadn't taken his eyes off his brother. "The last time you dressed like that you were undercover."

Jake shook his head. "No. I wore a suit for Eric's wedding. This one look familiar?"

He gave the jacket another look and laughed. "Tell me about this fundraiser. Is this part of your investigation? Did you find a new lead?"

I took another fry.

"Howdy, y'all!" The waitress arrived with big hair and a smile. "I see your party's all here. Are you ready to order?"

Absolutely.

Reese asked for a house salad, light dressing on the side. Dan went with ribs and a baked potato. Jake ordered a filet, medium rare, side salad and steamed veggies. I got a bronco burger with bacon and potato skins.

My phone dinged with a new email. I flipped my clutch open and scanned the notifications. Energy zipped up my spine. "It's Josh Chan." I angled the phone to Jake and opened the email. He read silently over my shoulder.

Who are you? Stop emailing me. Dante Weiss is a crook. I'm suing him, and if you continue to harass me, I'll file charges against you, too.

"Rude." I lowered my phone onto the table.

Jake settled back in his seat and rubbed both palms down his thighs. "He said Dante's a crook. *Is,* not was. Sounds like he doesn't yet know he's dead."

Dan shifted forward, leaning his forearms on the wide

wooden table. "Sounds like a dead end. Was that your lead?"

"One of them," I said.

"Any other suspects you want to tell me about?"

Reese shifted her gaze around the table, seemingly unsure what was going on.

I leaned forward, matching Dan's position. "There's also a pet shop owner who had a beef with Dante. He has access to white mice. He's angry and kind of a jerk."

Jake swung an arm across the booth behind me. "That guy's another dead end. I checked him out. Keith Orson didn't kill Dante."

I flopped open palms onto the table. "What? Why didn't you say anything to me?"

He shrugged. "I made a trip to the pet shop as soon as you mentioned him. I also tailed him to a church and followed him into the basement where he was attending an AA meeting. The group leader said Keith attends faithfully. He was there at the time of the murder. I confirmed it with the group and local business security cameras."

I considered how much I didn't know. "What about the mice?"

He scowled. "I'm working on that."

"Do you know why Josh Chan is so angry about his mega deal?"

Jake shook his head. "I've got a call in to his lawyers."

Reese's bright eyes were wide with understanding. She smiled at me. "You're a detective, too? Is that how you all met?"

"No," the Archers answered in unison.

I rolled my eyes. "Not exactly."

Jake pointed a finger in my direction. "We met Mia during an investigation last year. I was looking into a series of identity thefts and cyber fraud. Dan was dealing with a murder."

I wrinkled my nose at Reese. "And they both suspected me."

Her smile grew heavy on her face. "Oh."

The waitress delivered our dinners, and the table went silent as we filled our tummies. Dan and Reese stole glances at one another and looked at their plates a lot.

Jake was first to break the silence. "How did the two of you meet?"

Reese set her fork aside. Her fingers were probably exhausted from pushing the lettuce around for so long. "Daniel registered for dance lessons at the studio where I work. He came twice a week for a few months before your brother's wedding."

"Interesting," I muttered around a giant bite of tender smokehouse burger, rich cheddar cheese and bacon. She called him Daniel? I squashed a brewing smile.

She made doe eyes at Daniel. "He's a natural. Lithe. Agile."

He caught her looking and she turned red.

I barely swallowed the food in my mouth without choking. "How old are you, Reese?"

"I'll be twenty-four in three months."

"I see." She was twenty-three. I pushed the burger back to my lips before I made a joke about cradle robbing, babysitting or adoption.

Dan cleared his throat. "Where did you say you're going? A fundraiser?"

A swift redirection. Nicely played.

Jake fought a smile, presumably over the age of Dan's date. "It's for a mayoral hopeful. Fifi and Nate are meeting us there in twenty-five minutes."

"Is this another lead?"

"More of a hunch," I said. "Dante was a major supporter of Vince Adams. We want to see if he knew Dante had ties to some shady businessmen."

"Vince Adams? The senator?" Dan asked.

"Yeah."

He swigged his drink. "Call me afterward. I want to know how it goes."

THE FUNDRAISER WAS at a house that made Horseshoe Falls homes look like fishing shacks. A line of limos and town cars outlined the block, awaiting their turn at the gate. Eventually, it was our turn, and one man shined a flashlight inside the truck cab while another walked the perimeter of the vehicle with a mirror on a stick, checking underneath. The flashlight guy checked our photo IDs against a list of names before waving us through.

Inside, the property was adorned in white twinkle lights and guests wearing couture. A valet took the key to Jake's truck and left us on foot at the back of another line. Jake scanned the area on a continuous loop, holding his gaze from time to time on something or someone of interest before beginning the circuit anew. A second set of security personnel guarded the gaping front doors. Their standard black suits, blank faces and curly wires running from collars to ears were overly cliché.

I leaned against Jake's arm and tipped my head up, cuing him to lower his ear. "How are we going to get near the senator with this much security?"

"You aren't. This is an observation mission."

I resisted the urge to step on his shiny black shoe. That was his plan, not mine, and I wouldn't miss an opportunity or change my objective.

Soft jazz music drifted from the home's interior as we shuffled closer.

Nate was inside and easy to spot. His ginger head rose above the others. He was sipping from a glass flute and smiling at someone too short to see from my position. Fifi, I presumed.

I stared hard, using the Force to will his eyes in my direction.

Bingo.

He turned. Nate caught my gaze and headed in our direction. Fifi appeared at his side. Her red satin gown clung to her perfect figure. Her hair was carefully twisted into a knot at the nape of her neck.

I touched my waist-length curls with regret. This was definitely an up-do kind of gig.

The couple stopped shy of the doors and waited.

We announced our names once more and were finally allowed inside. It was hard not to feel like we were in danger or doing something wrong.

Jake gripped Nate's hand. "White tuxedo. Bold move."

Nate dusted invisible lint from one shoulder. "Bond. James Bond."

"Hey." I interrupted Nate's posturing. "What are you helping Jake with?"

Fifi gave Nate a weird look.

Nate smiled over my head, presumably at my date. "Guy stuff. We get together sometimes and volunteer."

I knew he was baiting me, but the curiosity was too much to bear. "Doing what?"

"Helping dainty lady folk. We go to the mall and lift heavy shopping bags for them. Sometimes we visit home improvement stores and local garages to explain complicated man things."

Fifi laughed.

I did not. "Would you like a little blood on your pretty jacket, Mr. Bond?"

Nate smiled. "You can tell your sister I'm her new hero. Thanks to this guy, there will be two hundred live Monarch butterflies delivered on the morning of the shower. I gave the venue address to the company. I'll email you care instructions."

I relaxed my expression and didn't fight the subject change. Curious as I was about what he and Jake were up to, this was better. "You're going to be the *opposite* of her hero." I grinned. "Maybe even on her hit list. Orange-and-brown bugs will ruin her strict white-on-white plus rainbows color scheme."

"Monarchs aren't ugly," he said. "They're hearty and native to Ohio. I doubt Bree wants to be responsible for the deaths of two hundred helpless, foreign white butterflies."

"Just admit you couldn't get the white ones."

"Never."

Jake leaned against my back. "What's the deal with all the security? They're everywhere. Don't look, but the couple canoodling against the doorway at three o'clock is clearly carrying, his holster shows whenever they change position and her stance suggests a piece worn on a thigh belt. The man pretending to admire the hall paintings has an earpiece. Several men dressed as waitstaff do as well."

Nate, Fifi and I turned to check out each of these alleged undercover operatives. Jake was right.

Fifi snagged a drink from a passing waiter's tray. "It's always like this."

"Why?" And where could I get one of what she was having?

She sipped her new drink. "The host has a personal security detail but also hires a few guns for the event. Half the guests also have a trusted security team that they don't leave home without. It's worse when the fundraiser is an auction. High-end items require added security for insurance purposes. By midnight, it's usually a sixty-forty split with security outweighing guests."

Good grief. I made a face.

Nate rubbed his palms together. "Where should we start?"

"Depends," Jake answered. "What's the fundraiser tonight?"

"Gambling." Nate straightened his bow tie. "Casino Royale." He pointed down the hallway behind him.

We were in the midst of a grand foyer. Italian marble stretched out in every direction, morphing into a massive double staircase with balusters and handrails the size of my waist. A chandelier large enough to hold four grown men illuminated the cavernous room. Arching mahogany doorways to the left and right stood open, filled with guests and lively chatter. A string quartet played in one room. A buffet of finger foods and desserts drew guests into the other. Beyond the split staircase, a wide hallway led to a room with wild cheering.

Well, that explained the hooting and applause. "Let's go."

We followed Fifi into a makeshift casino in the heart of the home. Felt-covered game tables were sprinkled throughout the room's center. Slot machines were positioned against one wall, floor-to-ceiling windows covered another. An open bar and cashier finished the room.

I pointed toward the cashier. "I'm going to buy some chips." I slid into the mass of bodies before Jake could stop me. The cashier line consisted of people in clusters talking politics and investments. I popped through a tightly knit group and out the other side.

Free from my team, I sidled up to a man of interest at the bar.

Senator Adams bobbed an olive in his drink with a long plastic toothpick. His gray suit and powder-blue tie were pretty but at odds with the grandiose Casino Royale theme. He looked more like management than the whale he was.

I smiled at the bartender. "Pinot grigio."

"Coming up."

The senator turned for a look in my direction and promptly abandoned his olive. "Hello."

I smiled wider and batted dramatic false lashes. "Hello."

"I'm Vince Adams."

"Mia Connors." I lifted my fresh glass of wine in a silent toast.

He inched closer. "I don't think I've seen you at one of these events before. What's your line of work, Miss Connors?" His voice hitched on the *Miss*, as if to confirm my single status.

It was a smart play. Aside from confirming my availability, he'd devised a way to find out if I was a reporter, while setting me up to return his question. If I went along, he'd have an organic reason to announce his position as state senator without sounding pretentious.

I played along. "I'm the CIO of Guinevere's Golden Beauty. This is a first for me. My friend Fiona invited me."

"Guinevere's Golden Beauty," he repeated the words slowly. "Why does that sound so familiar to me?"

"Depends. Are you a fan of organic bath and beauty products?"

He chuckled. "I'm fairly certain I'd love them on you."

I bit the inside of my cheeks. Who said that to a woman he'd just met? Why were politicians such notorious womanizing morons? "I believe you knew a friend of my grandmother's."

He furrowed his graying brows and dragged his gaze over my body once more. "Your grandmother?"

"Yes. Dante Weiss helped her launch the company several decades back. He's probably the reason it grew to be what it is today."

Senator Adams downed his drink. "I think we're done here." He turned away, punctuating the statement with a view of his back.

I opened my clutch and dug for a business card.

Jake manifested on Senator Adams's other side and extended his hand. "Senator Adams. I'm Jake Archer, Deputy US Marshal investigating the death of Dante Weiss. Do you have a minute to talk?"

Senator Adams spun in my direction. "You set me up?"

"No. I ordered a glass of wine."

He scoffed and redirected his attention on Jake. "This isn't the time or place. You should know better, Mr. Archer."

"Deputy US Marshal Archer," Jake corrected.

"Mr. Archer. If you want a quote from me, you'll need to go through the proper channels. Contact my people. Leave your request. Someone will get back with you." He tossed back the remains of his drink. "Don't approach me again or you'll be escorted off the premises."

Jake bent slightly at the waist, a strange half bow. "Of

course. Thank you for your time." He shot a pointed look at me. "Mia?"

I pretended to struggle, juggling my purse, wineglass and napkin. I bumped into Senator Adams as I passed. "Oops. Sorry. It was lovely to meet you, Senator Adams." I slid my card into his jacket pocket as I regained my balance. I'd written *off the record* on the back of the card before I left my apartment in case of an opportunity like this one.

I held the senator's gaze and hoped the Force would work on him as well as it did on Nate.

"I knew you weren't really going to buy chips," Jake whispered. "I'll call his office on Monday and see if I can arrange an interview or confirm an alibi. Meanwhile, we watch him tonight and see if he behaves strangely. I'll make a list of anyone he spends more than a few minutes with while we're here. We can split up if needed and follow anyone leaving suddenly after a chat with Senator Adams."

"Right." There could be any number of accomplices or crime scene cleaners, especially for a man with wealth and power. I drifted along at Jake's side, fingers curled in the crook of his arm. Something in Adams's voice said he wouldn't do more than prepare a generic statement for the Marshals. Whether he was involved with Dante's death or not, it was in his interest to uncouple their names, and he was already working on that.

But, if the Force was strong in me, I'd be hearing from him soon.

# NINETEEN

I PARKED STELLA on the street outside Bree's house and jumped out, brushing the goose bumps from my arms. I couldn't shake the feeling I was being followed, but I wasn't. I'd spent as much time watching my rearview mirror on my drive over as I had watching the road. After meeting Keith Orson, I half expected to find dead mice anytime I approached my car. Dan said Keith had an alibi, but couldn't he also have an accomplice? Or be one? It seemed careless to so quickly discount a man with infinite mouse supplies. Who else would have dead mice to spare?

"Mia!" Mom raised her hands overhead in excitement.

Bree's toddler, Gwen, mimicked Mom's move. "Meeee!" She abandoned the fairy garden where she'd been playing and ran full speed in my direction, kicking ceramic toadstools and tiny gnomes out of her way. She collided softly with my legs. "Up!"

I hoisted her onto my hip and kissed her nose. "Hello, Little Miss." I straightened her bright red T-shirt. "What's this?" The white circle on her tummy was straight out of a Dr. Seuss book. "Thing One." I snuggled her to my cheek and tickled her ribs. "Whatever happened to shirts that said Big Sister?"

Mom swayed, peering around me in both directions. "Nate dropped it off earlier. He said he and Fifi are meeting a contractor and can't make it for dinner. Where's Jake?"

Nate. "Well, that explains a ton." I tickled Gwen until she wailed in desperation.

"Is Jake coming?" Mom rephrased her question.

"He had a work thing." He'd sent a last-minute text.

Running late. Be there when I can.

What did that mean? Was he really running late? Or was the text Jake's version of a polite cancellation?

Mom pulled her lips to the side. "I've never met a couple with such busy schedules."

"It's complicated." Though I liked the thought of being a couple with Jake very much. He hadn't argued when Dan introduced us that way. Semantically, we were a couple. We dated only each another. We clearly cared for one another, even if those precise words hadn't been exchanged. He certainly kissed me like he meant it.

Mom moved to my side and wrapped a warm arm around my shoulders. "Well, it doesn't have to be complicated. I'm sure the two of you will figure it out."

Bree appeared at the front door of her adorable cottage and swung it open. Hers was the smallest on the block when she bought it on the cheap and got the steal of the century. Five years of love and elbow grease later, there was a swing in the oak out front, a picket fence around the yard and flower-filled boxes under every window. Her little one-and-a-half story clearance-priced home had become the stunning centerpiece on a street of mini-mansions. She looked at me like my hair was on fire. "Where's Jake?"

"Working." Scents of garlic and herbs on melted butter soaked the air inside her home. I floated inside on a whiff of ecstasy.

"Why are you early?"

Mom peeled her body away from mine and shooed Bree along so we could pass.

I slid into her narrow front hall. "I was in a hurry to get here. I'm super excited for your big gender reveal."

She gave me a skeptical face before turning her gaze onto Mom. "What were you two just talking about?"

"Birds and bees."

I patted Bree's tummy. "Maybe she should talk to you next."

"Seriously, Mia." She scooped Gwen off my hip. "Why are you early? Are you okay? Dinner won't be ready for a few minutes. We can talk if you need to." She pierced me with her weird *twins are cosmically connected* face. "I know something's wrong. Talk to me."

I blinked to break her spell. "I'm fine."

I wasn't. Bree knew it, but this wasn't the time to lay it out there. And she wasn't the one I needed to talk to. I checked on my car through the window. Waning sunlight reflected through the windshield. No sign of a stalker. Maybe the mice were a fluke. Maybe I was wrong to worry.

I'd pulled Dante from the Horseshoe Falls lake nine days ago, and after more than a week, I had no viable suspects and too many questions. Marshals were hunting the fugitive Dante had planned to rat out. Dan believed Keith Orson was innocent. I couldn't get Josh Chan to talk to me. The antique shop guy and Dante's ex-wife were dead ends. I had a feeling I couldn't get a straight answer from Senator Adams if I asked him about the color of the sky.

My efforts had tanked. All I had left were the two cabbies I hadn't been able to reach by phone. I'd try them again in the morning. Maybe pay for a ride so we could talk privately.

"Whoa." I gasped at the crepe-paper-covered kitchen and tried to absorb the madness. "What happened in here?"

Tom poured pale pink liquid into a line of plastic martini cups positioned alongside matching blue drinks with minuscule sailboats floating in their centers. "Hey, Mia." He set the drinks aside and opened his arms for a hug. "You're early."

"Yep."

"What do you think? Are you going with It's a Boy Blueberry punch or It's a Girl Strawberry Fizz?"

"What?"

Mom shoved her way between us. Excitement blazed in her crazy eyes. "We each pick a drink before the big reveal. Pink if we think Bree's having a girl. Blue if we think she's having a boy. If we guess right, we get a prize." She pointed to a baby carriage filled with presents wrapped in white paper.

"Uh-huh." I drifted toward the dining room. The table was set with Grandma's china. A massive bouquet of wildflowers was centered on the sideboard. Boy and girl paper dolls were stretched across the china cabinet. A six-foot teddy bear slumped in the corner. Two giant pacifiers hung around his neck on strings. Pastel balloons flooded the floor. Little signs clung to the walls. It's a boy! It's a girl! Some were simple white squares with thick black question marks in the center. "It's like a party store blew up in here."

The doorbell rang. *Thank goodness*. I turned on my toes and went to welcome Jake.

Mom beat me to the door and squealed. She pulled a rail-thin woman into her arms and rocked side to side. They patted one another on the back and giggled without breaking the embrace.

Gwen hit me with a spit-covered balloon. "Boom!"

I lowered my face to hers. "Do you know who Grandma is hugging?"

"Yeah." She pushed the balloon against her mouth and tried to bite it.

"Who?" I whispered.

"Her!" She swung a dimpled hand toward the women.

"Thanks." I went looking for Dad. "Mom's hugging a woman in the front hallway. I've never seen her before. She's not a friend or neighbor of Bree and Tom's." Unless they'd just met her. Would they invite a new person to the gender reveal? Maybe. Bree was off her nut lately. Would Mom hug a new person with such enthusiasm? Maybe. Same reason.

Dad shook the wrinkles from his newspaper. "It's probably her publicist or whatever you call it. Marvin and your grandmother went to get her from the airport."

I snapped upright. "Her publicist?" She'd invited her publicist to this kooky event? People would think we were fruit loops. "Is Mom planning to put this in her book?"

Dad rolled tired eyes up to meet mine. He sighed and went back to the paper.

Right. The only person excited about divulging our family secrets was Mom, and no one wanted to steal her joy, so we didn't talk about it. It was *the book that shall not be named.* I slipped through the French doors of the study, leaving Dad to his paper.

Tom was arranging hors d'oeuvres on pink and blue platters in the kitchen. "Want to try a little something while you wait?"

I poked a toothpick with pink and blue curlicues on top into a little meatball. "Why is Mom's publicist here? Where did she fly in from? Why does she have a publicist for a book she hasn't written?"

Tom's smile fell, but he quickly pulled it back together. "Your mom invited her. She's from New York. I have no idea." He lowered his voice. "Bree isn't thrilled."

I bit into the meat on my stick. "So we aren't talking about it."

He did a stage wink. "How's the meatball? I added a little grape jelly."

I moved closer, driven by curiosity and the common knowledge Tom was our weakest link. "Is this party going in the book? Should I watch what I say?"

He stepped back. "Bree!"

I munched another meatball.

Bree rolled into the kitchen, one hand on her back and the other on her belly. Her skin was glowing, but she looked like she could sleep until the baby arrived if we let her. "Yeah?"

Tom slid oven mitts over his hands and turned to the stove. "Mia's wondering about the guest list."

Bree's cheeks darkened. She was miffed. "Can we just…*not*…right now? This is my party. My big reveal." Her breaths came in short bursts as her temper tried to surface. I'd seen the look countless times before.

"Breathe," Tom suggested.

She shook her head and shoulders, as if she could

physically throw off the frustration. A bright smile spread over her face. "Mom asked if she could invite a friend. I assumed it would be an old babysitter of ours or someone special from our childhood, so I said yes."

"Duped," I groaned.

"Yes."

"What was that thing you just did before blowing up?"

She did it again. "I'm preparing for a natural childbirth. It takes concentration and centering, so I'm applying relaxation techniques to my life. Getting a jump start."

Grandma shuffled into the space beside Bree. "I could've used some relaxation techniques an hour ago. Traffic at the airport is ridiculous."

Marvin squeezed in behind Grandma, looking wildly happy. He removed his little cap. "I didn't mind the traffic, but I must've worked up an appetite. Everything smells delicious."

"Thanks." Tom pulled trays off the island and lined them on his arm. "Time to eat."

Mom and the lady headed for the table.

The doorbell rang again. I went to see who else Mom might've invited. Local news crew? Fashion police? Probably the latter since I was wearing a red sleeveless jumper and knee socks I'd had since undergrad.

I pulled the door open and my heart skipped. "Jake!"

His lips twitched. "It's too bad everyone I visit isn't this happy to see me."

"Rough day?"

He stepped inside and leaned into my space. The gentle scents of his shampoo and cologne weakened my knees. No one had ever smelled as amazing as Jake. "Would it be okay if I...?" He didn't finish the question.

I nodded. However he'd planned to finish the request, my answer was unequivocally yes.

He brushed a swath of hair over my shoulder and stroked the length of it down my back. Something in his eyes said there were a number of ways he'd considered finishing the question.

"Boom!" Something nasty dashed against my legs. Gwen smiled up at us, arms open, fingers skyward. A spit-covered balloon rolled at my feet. "Up."

"May I?" Jake pulled her into his arms before I had a chance to collect my marbles and answer.

I followed them down the hall, plucking the dress away from my overheated skin. "You started to ask me something back there." I pointed out. "You didn't finish."

He turned the corner toward the dining room hoopla, allowing me a brief look at his handsome face. He'd hitched one cheek into a crooked smile.

"Jake!" Mom exclaimed. She rose to her feet and hustled to get her hands on him.

Dad puttered out of the study. "Jake?"

My family pulled him around the room, shaking his hand and crowning him King of Everything. Dad poured him a drink.

"Careful," I called. "They suck you in and never let go." My laugh was cut short when the thin woman at Mom's side gave me a worried look. I sucked air. "That was a joke. A stupid one. We don't abduct people. I'm not funny." I shot a hand in her direction. "I'm Mia."

She folded her fingertips over mine, avoiding my palm completely and releasing me a heartbeat later. "Lydia Laurent."

Mom clapped her hands to her face like the kid in *Home Alone.* "Heavens! I am so sorry. Mia, this is my literary agent, Lydia Laurent. She's helping me with the book about our family. Lydia, this is Mia, my youngest." She gave me a funny look. "Where were you when she arrived? I could've sworn you were right behind me at the door."

I eyeballed Dad. He told me the lady was her publicist. I understood publicists. I dealt with them all the time for Guinevere's Golden Beauty and now for REIGN. I hadn't the foggiest clue what a literary agent was or did. Hopefully Mom wasn't paying her.

Dad tugged a bushy eyebrow, uncaring. It was all the same to him. All the nonsense that accompanied *the book that shall not be named*.

The table was packed. Tom had wisely added all the extra leaves, extending it to maximum capacity, and rounding up another chair from somewhere. Bree took a seat at the table's head. Dad, Mom and her agent took the three chairs on Bree's left. Tom sat opposite Bree, in the chair nearest the kitchen. He pulled Gwen's highchair in beside him at the corner. Jake dropped her in and patted her head. Grandma, Marvin, Jake and I crammed ourselves along the last side of the table. Lucky me. I was at Bree's right hand. My chair didn't match the rest, and my knee knocked against hers under the table.

"So," Lydia piped up. "Anyone have a fun story to share about life in this family?"

Mom beamed. She sought our faces, one by one, looking for who would go first. Dad, Grandma and Tom examined their plates as if the meaning of life was hidden in the delicate trim.

Bree and I exchanged a long look. For once I thought I really could read her mind. This was *her* party and *her* big deal. It wasn't about our past. It was about *her* future.

Mom's smile crumpled. "Well, don't all talk at once." Embarrassment colored her cheeks. She flicked a look in Lydia's direction.

I jumped up. "Oh, no! We forgot the drinks. Tom, tell them about the fun drinks." I ran to the kitchen for the colored punch in martini glasses. I returned with the big white tray.

Bree mouthed *Thank you*.

I winked. "What'll it be, Mama?" I started with Bree. "You're first."

She grabbed a pink drink without hesitation.

I followed suit. "Who am I to argue with the mama?" Jake also took pink.

Grandma and Marvin went blue. So did Dad and Tom. Hey, the guys in our family had to hope, right? They were sorely outnumbered. Lydia and Mom went pink.

The meal began with strawberry soup and a tiny bowl of blueberries on the side. From there, it was Cornish hens and salad with pecans and feta. Our group was un-usually quiet, but I had no idea what to say in front of Mom's guest, and it seemed I wasn't alone.

Bree stole continuous glances at Mom until her plate was empty. She pulled her napkin from her lap and dot-ted the corners of her mouth. "So, Mom, how's the book going?"

Mom lifted her head slowly. "Okay." She forced a smile. "We don't have to talk about it right now. This is your party. Everything is absolutely perfect."

Lydia nodded. "Do you get together often?"

"Yes." We answered in unison, even Jake chimed in.

"Are you always so creative?" she asked Tom.

Another big yes.

Dad wiped his mouth and leaned back in his chair. "I like that you said creative and not cuckoo."

"If I thought you were cuckoo, I wouldn't be so excited about this book. Your family is one I've followed for many years. My mother used Guinevere's Golden Bath Salts. I remember them on the edge of the tub when I was growing up. They came in a glass jar back then with a rose-colored lid and rhinestones along the top. Her bath time was a big deal. I used to open all her products and smell them one by one and think of how one day I'd be a proper lady who had bath salts of her own. Sometimes Mom would allow me to sit in the room and read while she soaked in a tub full of bubbles. The bubbles were yours as well."

I gave Lydia another look. Maybe she wasn't the devil, bent on humiliating our family for money.

Mom patted Lydia's hand. "Lydia believes in this project. She says we have the American Dream and others will relate to us and feel inspired."

"It's true," Lydia added. "I've garnered significant interest from several publishing houses and bent the ear of an exec looking for movie material."

"Movie?" Bree perked up.

"That's getting ahead of ourselves, of course," Lydia admitted, "but it's very telling of what your story has to offer. You have something rather special here."

My eyes inexplicably burned.

Jake's warm palm covered my knee.

Bree sniffled. "We really do." She wiped her eyes on a napkin. "Sorry. Hormones."

Tom cleared the table. Jake excused himself to help.

Thirty seconds later, Grandma thumped her giant

wedding planner in front of Mom and Lydia. "We're doing a Vegas Magic Show theme."

I slipped away and made a run to my car for something I'd meant to bring in. I moved at full speed as if the devil was chasing me. I stopped at Gwen's highchair and curtsied deeply. "I brought you something, milady."

She clapped.

I tucked both hands behind my back. "First, you must choose a hand."

Gwen tugged my right arm. I shifted the gift into my left hand and presented her an empty right hand. She went left and I repeated the process with my other hand.

Gwen tipped her head back and screamed.

"Yikes!" I whipped the box onto her tray. "Shh."

"Mia's teasing the baby," Dad narced.

I shook a silent fist in his direction. "I gave her a gift." I lifted the box lid and carefully removed the motion sensor monkey.

He crashed his tiny cymbals together.

Gwen clapped.

The more she clapped, the more Monkey clapped.

Mom frowned. "How nice of you."

"I'm always thinking of my sweet niece."

I headed back to my seat. Jake returned from the kitchen with Tom.

Tom carried a beautiful cake. "Now, the reason we're all here." He set the masterpiece in front of Bree. The two-tier dessert was covered in smooth blue frosting. Tiny yellow stars were sprinkled over the top. Words from a nursery rhyme were scribed along the edge. *Twinkle, twinkle, little star, how I wonder what you are.*

Mom leaned in for a closer look. "I still don't know

how you've kept this from her. I can barely stand the anticipation."

Tom slid his patient gaze to Bree. "It wasn't always easy, but this moment is about to make the secret-keeping worthwhile."

Bree lifted the crystal-handled knife used on her wedding cake and closed her eyes. "I can't do it."

Tom took the utensils and kissed her head. He lifted his eyes to ours. "Pink cake means we're having a girl. Blue cake means we're having a boy. Both colors are almond flavored."

Bree closed her eyes.

Tom placed a slice onto Bree's plate and lifted it into the air.

We gasped.

Bree peeked. One eye, then the other. "A girl!" She gaped at the bright pink slice of cake. "I knew it was a girl!" She pushed onto her feet and slung both arms around Tom's neck. "I love you."

"I love you, too." He nuzzled her neck.

I took over slicing and delivering cake to the guests.

Bree wiped her eyes and sobbed at her slice. "I'm sorry. I'm just so happy."

Tom kissed her head and went to the kitchen. He returned with another cake.

Silence fell over the room. I stared at the remaining half-cake in the table's center. Did that new cake mean what I thought it meant?

Bree covered her mouth.

Tom shoved her plate away and handed her the knife again.

She bawled.

He took the knife back and cut again. He spun the slice slowly, so we all had a good look. More pink.

Dad made the sign of the cross.

Jake lifted his strawberry-fizz faux martini. "Hear, hear! To Bree and Tom."

"Bree and Tom!" The room cheered.

Gwen squealed in delight.

The monkey banged its cymbals.

AN HOUR LATER, we walked Lydia to the door. She opted to call a car to take her to the airport. Whether she hated to break up the party or feared Marvin's driving, I couldn't say.

She hugged Mom. "I've had a lovely and insightful time, Gwendolyn. I was a fan of this concept from day one, but living it for an evening was better even than I imagined. I'm going to get to work on the plane and make magic happen."

Mom waved goodbye to the car and shut the door with a deep exhale. "I don't think I can write the story anymore. I changed my mind."

"What?" I looped my arm under hers and pulled her toward the wine. "Of course you can write the story. It's your story. You're the perfect one to write it, and you've already said this was your dream. Aren't you always telling us to chase our dreams?"

She accepted a tall glass of pinot from Tom. "I don't know. Fact checking has been such a nuisance. My memory isn't what it used to be, and none of you have been very forthcoming. Fiction would be so much easier."

I doubted that.

Grandma tipped her glass to Mom's. "Get back to us at the end of that glass and see if you still feel that way."

She pointed her glass at Jake next. "Mr. Marshal. How's the fugitive apprehension business going?"

Jake leaned his backside against the counter. He cast me a look. "We've got one pinned in. It won't be long now."

"Good." She moseyed to his side and squeezed his middle. "I'm glad you came tonight." Her head fell somewhere north of his navel and significantly south of his shoulders.

"I'm glad to be here. I have to say, I agree with Lydia. Your family is pretty amazing. You should tell your story, Mrs. Connors." He fixed Mom with soulful blue eyes.

Good luck resisting that.

Mom drained her drink.

Jake groaned. He pulled his phone into one hand and rubbed his face with the other. "I've got to go." He said his goodbyes in a hurry.

I followed him to the door. "Everything okay?"

"Yep." He kissed my cheek.

Lies. "Anything you want to share?"

"Nope." He jogged down the front steps.

My heart sank. Why wouldn't he open up to me? What if he was going to do something dangerous?

Jake turned to face me and took a few backward steps down the driveway. "Are you free for lunch tomorrow?"

Four days in a row? We were on a roll. "Are we official?" The juvenile words were out before I could stop them. I let my eyes shut briefly, squared my shoulders and reopened my eyes with my chin held high. I was a professional blurter, and it wasn't all bad. Worst case scenario, I didn't get the answer I wanted, but at least I knew the truth. "A couple-couple."

Jake drew his eyebrows together and marched back to me.

"Say something."

"I'm thinking."

I crossed my arms and prepared a rebuttal.

"Mia, to me, we were official long before I ever asked you out."

"Why'd you hesitate before you answered?"

He barked a laugh. "Are you kidding? I thought you were setting me up for one of your feminist rants."

I scowled.

He laughed and uncrossed my arms with big warm hands. "I've been part of a couple before. This is something else. You're something else."

"I don't like the way you said the last part."

He kissed my pouty lips. "See? Now, lunch tomorrow?"

"I have to meet Nate tomorrow. We're interviewing another project management company."

"All right. Another time, then." He headed back to his truck and drove away.

I shut the door and waited several minutes, watching to see if anyone tailed him.

# TWENTY

I ARRIVED AT my desk early the next morning, ready to contact the cab companies to see if they could tell me why two drivers were dodging my calls. I hoped it was because they were sick or fired and not because they were somehow in cahoots with the killer. I smoothed the paper with two cabbies' numbers on my desk. If they worked nights, which they must if they picked up the killer after nine, and I wanted to catch them on duty, then I had to waste a little time before calling.

The clubhouse was eerily still at this hour, but it was better than the a-killer's-in-your-closet quiet I had at my place. I kept my eyes on the time as I sorted email from my inbox, and secretly hoped Fifi would come to work early again. Footfalls pounded on the carpet outside my door. And stopped. My body went rigid. My mind on high alert. I searched the desk for something to use as a weapon if needed. "Hello?" I called.

The doorknob wiggled and my door swung open.

I squeaked. "Holy Mary!"

Mr. Peters held his palms up. "Sorry!"

I sipped sweet air and thanked the heavens he wasn't there to kill me or pelt me with dead mice. "Mr. Peters! What's going on?"

"Raccoons." He smiled. "The gamekeepers caught a half dozen raccoons."

I shifted onto my feet. That was good news. "Really?"

"Yes, and they asked my advice on planting food for the squirrels. I'm going out with them today to find the best locations for new squirrel boxes and food."

"That's great. Thank you."

He stepped into my office and pulled the door closed behind him. "I want you to know I'm removing the camera in the willow today. Do you think it will be all right if I install small cameras inside the squirrel boxes? I'd like to continue monitoring their activity without breaking any rules. I can tuck the cameras inside the boxes." He mimed the action. "The result will be much less intrusive. For humans," he added. "I don't think the squirrels mind."

"I think that would be fine." Cameras hidden intentionally inside the boxes? *Good luck replacing your wiring every day.*

He hitched a thumb over one shoulder and moved away from me. "I'm going to go make a big show of removing the willow's camera. I want to be sure word gets around that I've complied with your request."

"I can send an email."

"Excellent."

Fifi passed him in the doorway. "Hi, Mr. Peters. Bye, Mr. Peters."

I dropped into my seat. "Good morning, Fifi. Thanks for the party invitation last weekend. We had a great time."

She dropped her bags under her desk. "It looked like you were having a great time."

"I just said that."

She crossed the small space between us and took a seat on the edge of my desk. "Did you get the information you wanted from the senator?"

"No, but I left him my card."

She nodded. "That's something, right? Is there anything I can do to help with the investigation?"

"Not yet." I picked up the scrap of paper where I'd scratched a couple of phone numbers. "I want to touch base with two cab companies this morning." I dialed the first headquarters. "I only have two cabbies left to contact. One at each of these numbers. They might not be on duty this early, but maybe I can get some information from their managers."

"Gimme one."

I ripped the paper in half and passed her the second set of information while I spoke with the manager at Yellow Cab. My call was short and frustrating. I rested my forehead on my desk and tried to make sense of Fifi's conversation.

"Thank you so much," she trilled. Fifi covered the phone with her palm and turned to me. "I'm being transferred."

I lifted my head. "Transferred where? To the cabbie? Do you mean you get to talk to the guy?"

She hung her mouth open and nodded. Her eyes were wide with victory.

"Tell him you need a ride." I sprang to my feet. "Have him pick you up here. I'll call Bernie to tell her we're expecting him."

"Yes?" She uncovered her phone and turned away from me. "Yes. That's right. I'd like to arrange a ride to the airport."

Boo. The airport was twenty minutes away. We'd be gone an hour by the time we made the round trip, and I already had a full schedule.

She spun back to face me. "He's on his way."

Hope rose in my chest. Maybe this cabbie was the key to locating Dante's killer. "Thank you."

She looked at my phone and wrinkled her brows. "What about your guy? Any luck?"

I tipped my head side to side. "Turns out the other cabbie, Sammie Houts, is a woman, and she probably hasn't returned my call because she took a leave of absence. To have a baby."

Fifi clucked her tongue. "People and their weirdo priorities."

"Right?"

"Well, if this guy—" she scanned the slip of paper in her hand "—Calvin Besk, doesn't pan out, at least we know where we can find Sammie. I'm not above taking balloons to the maternity ward if it gets us some answers."

I chuckled. Why not?

I checked my watch. Two hours before I needed to meet Nate. I dialed Bernie to let her know about the cab, then opened my personal email on the off chance Josh Chan had a change of heart, dropped his lawsuit against Dante and decided to take my interview.

My phone rang, and Jake's face appeared on the little screen. "It's Jake," I told Fifi. "Why isn't he texting?"

She pointed a pen at my phone. "Ask him."

I lifted the device to my ear and pressed the green button to accept his call. "Why are you calling and not texting? Are you hurt? Is anyone hurt? Am I in danger? Do you have another lead?"

"Mia?"

"Yes." Panic seized me. "Can you hear me?"

"I can hear you, but I can't answer all those questions

at once. You're supposed to say Hello when the phone rings. Maybe you should cut back on texting."

"Maybe you should cut back," I retorted stupidly and trailed off with no idea how to finish. "Are you okay?"

"Yes. Are you?"

A smile cracked my worried thoughts. "Yes."

"Still too busy for lunch?"

"Yeah."

"Okay, I thought I'd take a chance. I'm heading to a hotel near Cleveland in a few hours. We had an unconfirmed sighting on Horton, then someone checked into the Downtown Renaissance under an alias Horton's used in the past. In case that's not a coincidence, we put a man on stakeout for a few nights. We think he's holed up inside somewhere. He hasn't left. Food is always delivered."

"So, what are you going to do? What's the plan?"

"I'm doing a little role-playing tonight. I'm intercepting Horton's dinner on the way up the elevator, then I'm going to knock on the door, deliver the meal and see who's really in that hotel room."

I couldn't see how this plan would work. "You aren't believable as a pizza boy."

"Why? Some like Taco Tuesdays. Maybe tonight's Country Man Monday."

"Can I get a menu for that?"

He laughed. "I'll see what I can do. Meanwhile take care of yourself and stick with a buddy when you go out. I haven't tied those dead mice to Horton, but they're definitely a threat. Be vigilant."

Bernie's voice burst through the speaker on Fifi's desk phone. "Ladies, your cab's here."

Fifi pushed the intercom button. "Send him to the clubhouse."

"Cab?" Jake asked. "What are you doing?"

Fifi hiked her hobo bag onto one shoulder and leaned her face near my phone. "See ya, Jake. We're taking a ride to the airport. Hopefully my dad's flight is on time."

"Oh," he whispered. Probably detecting her lie and wondering how much I could be trusted. "Mia?"

"Hmm?"

"I'm going to drop your blueberries off at Congress Lake on my way."

Oh my goodness, I'd almost forgotten about the stupid blueberries. "Thank you!"

"It's no problem. Remember what I said."

"I will. Be careful in Cleveland."

I dropped the phone into my bag and followed Fifi down the employee hallway to the double glass front doors. "Is your dad really coming in on a plane today?" Wherever he went, he'd have had to leave after I saw him Saturday night, and it was only Monday morning.

She held the final door open with her hip. "He's en route to Portland for a week, but we can still look at the boards and see if his flight's on time."

"I don't like lying to Jake."

"We aren't lying. We're creating a cover story." She climbed into the waiting taxi and scooted to the center of the backseat.

I slid in beside her and shut the door. "Pew." I pressed my fingers against my nose.

Fifi popped her head between the front seats. "Airport."

"Yes, ma'am." The cabbie pushed some buttons on his

dashboard and little green numbers flashed. The photo ID checked out. This was Calvin Besk.

His cab smelled like incense and cigarette smoke, despite the abundance of No Smoking stickers on the doors and seat backs. Whatever he'd eaten for breakfast mingled with the other scents until my eyes watered. The low and repetitive beat of house music pumped softly though rear speakers. Calvin was a disheveled mess. His eyes were rimmed in red. His clothes were wrinkled. He wasn't a man I'd have willingly gotten in a car with under normal circumstances, and here I was, paying him for the stinky experience. Hopefully Calvin took more care behind the wheel than he had on his personal hygiene.

We rolled slowly through Horseshoe Falls, stopping fully at the sign and waiting for a woman on horseback to pass. I waved to Bernie at the gate.

Fifi looked utterly at ease. "Thanks for coming on such short notice. Horseshoe Falls must be out of your way."

"Not really."

"Do you come here often?" She giggled.

He turned for a look at her over the seatback and busted out an all-teeth smile. "You're funny and good-looking. Must be my lucky day."

"Must be," I muttered.

He cast me a wayward gaze before pulling onto the main road away from our community.

"So, do you?" Fifi repeated. "Come here often? Out to Horseshoe Falls, I mean."

"Sometimes." His eager smile, understandably, lost its oomph. Only a real dodo wouldn't see she was up to something.

I leaned my shoulder against Fifi's, forcing my face

into the reflection of his rearview mirror. "Did you pick anyone up near Horseshoe Falls eleven days ago? On a Friday night? Around nine o'clock. He was dressed like a jogger and wearing all black. He would've been out of place, walking along the street. No car."

He swung an elbow over his armrest and angled back toward us.

"Eyes on the road," I ordered.

He faced forward until the next red light. "You're the lady who left those messages for me. I recognize your voice now." He made a disgusted face. "What do you want, lady? Is your dude cheating on you? Are you doing some crazy-chick maneuver, trying to bust someone for breaking your heart? 'Cause I don't get involved in messes like that. I pick up. I drop off. That's all." He gave Fifi another long look. "You can call me any time."

"Stop." I lifted my hand. "Did you or didn't you?"

He huffed again. "Look, maybe he's just not that into you."

"This has nothing to do with a broken heart. I'm investigating a murder."

"Murder?" The light turned green and he swiveled slowly in his seat.

Fifi edged me out of the way. "Did you pick up a guy like the one she described? Someone like that wouldn't be hard to remember. No one walks around here. There aren't even any sidewalks. We don't know how far he went before calling, but probably less than a mile. He'd want to get off the street as soon as possible without being picked up at the gate."

Calvin considered his answer so long I thought he might've decided on giving us the silent treatment for the remainder of our ride. "Nah."

"Nah?" Fifi echoed.

"No dudes. There was a lady dressed fancy, crying about a cheating boyfriend and trying to walk to the airport, but that's all. She wasn't too far from your place."

"She was walking to the airport?" I scoffed. "She must've been mad."

"She was. She flew in to surprise him, but he was with someone else, so she was catching the next flight home. She looked like a nice business lady. Cried all the way to Delta's drop-off."

Another dead end.

Fifi patted his shoulder. "Calvin, can you just take us back to the clubhouse? We don't really need to go to the airport."

Bernie made a face when we arrived at her gate ten minutes later.

I waved.

Fifi paid for the ride. I gave him a hefty tip for his time and the information.

She held the clubhouse door for me. "Looks like we're going to visit some newborn babies."

"Maybe Bree will have her girls soon and we can visit them all at the same time. Streamline this sucker." I stopped at the concierge desk to pour a consolation coffee. "I wonder if Sammie will care if we ambush her in the maternity ward to ask her about someone she picked up for a fare. It's the kind of thing that Bree would injure us for trying."

Fifi stroked her long blond ponytail over one shoulder. "Murder. Investigation."

"We can be extra nice and quick." I added a hefty dose of French vanilla creamer to my coffee and stirred it with a tiny wooden paddle. "I can bring a gift. Maybe cash."

"Everyone loves cash," she agreed.

Marcella appeared at the end of the employee hallway and jogged toward us with a severe look of constipation. Her hands were up by her shoulders. No one was chasing her.

"Why is she running?" Fifi asked.

"Um." I scanned the area for reasons to panic, angry residents, wild animals, the community's founder.

When she was within a few feet, Marcella began waving us closer.

We stayed put, although I set my coffee aside in preparation for a fast escape.

"Everything all right?" Fifi asked.

Marcella took my free hands in hers and dragged me in the direction she'd come. "There's someone here to see you," she whispered. "I am not allowed to tell you who he is and you are not allowed to tell anyone he is here. Is that okay?"

I dug my heels in. "No. Not okay. What if he's here to kill me?"

She latched both hands on to my wrist, turned to face me and leaned back. "No one is killing you right now."

"That doesn't make me feel better." I wiggled my wrists in her strangely viselike grip. "How are you so strong?"

"I raised five boys. I can do things you wouldn't imagine."

We padded over the soft carpet lining our employee hall and rounded the corner toward clubhouse storage and a set of unused rooms.

A big meathead-looking guy stood beside an unused office door. His suit clung to his unnatural biceps. His jaw was chiseled from stone. He nodded at Marcella.

She released me.

I rubbed my red wrists. "I know you," I told the guy. Who could forget that jawline? "How do I know you? Why'd you make her abduct me like that? What's this about?"

"Sorry," Marcella said. "He made it sound like this was really important."

And she wanted to know what it was about.

He ignored my questions. He stood straight as an arrow, or in his case a telephone pole. He clasped his hands behind his back like a soldier standing at ease.

What did this guy want with me? Why the big secret?

"Has Ms. Connors been informed of the terms of this visit?" he asked Marcella.

"Yes. I explained all the rules."

I gave her an angry face.

He dipped his chin sharply in acceptance and turned emotionless eyes to me. "Do you agree to the terms of this visit? Do you understand this is off the books, unofficial, and for all intents and purposes, this meeting is not taking place and never will?"

My mind raced with confusion.

"I need your answer now, ma'am."

Could I phone a friend? Ask the audience? Something? I lifted my shoulders to my ears. "I'm sorry, but no to all that. I think. I don't know what is happening. Can you repeat the questions?"

"Excuse me." Fifi's voice sounded behind me.

I turned toward the sound.

She leaned her head and shoulders around the corner. "Hello."

"Miss," the suit addressed her. "Come here, please."

She strode to my side. "Hi."

"Miss," he began again, "I need you to proceed to your office or wherever you normally are at this time. I must also ask that you do not speak of my presence here to anyone now or in the future."

Fifi smiled. "Of course." She stepped between the man and me, positioning her back to him and her face to mine. "Do you remember this guy from Saturday night?" She broke Saturday into three distinct sounds. "I believe you met him on your way in."

I looked past her to the man's remarkable jaw and deep-set eyes. "Yes!" He was a member of the security team outside the fundraiser.

Fifi squeezed my shoulder and left with a skip in her step. "Good luck."

"I agree to all the stuff," I told him. "Yes, to all that."

He opened the door for me to enter.

Marcella leaned around him for a look inside, but he pressed her back with one big palm.

I slid inside, trying not to focus on why he'd called Fifi "miss," but I was "ma'am." I was only two years older than her. I gave my outfit a serious look. I liked it.

"Ms. Connors?" Senator Vince Adams sat in one of two chairs in the little abandoned office. "I believe you requested my presence." He slid my business card across the desk in my direction. "Very slick. I didn't find it until this morning when my maid was collecting the dry cleaning."

I lowered myself onto the other chair. "Thank you for coming. Call me Mia."

He shifted his weight and gave me a cold smile. "I didn't get the impression there was a way to avoid you, and I don't want the bad press you'd bring."

"I only have a few questions."

"As you are aware," he interrupted, "Dante Weiss and I go way back. He's been a long-term proponent of my campaigns and positions. We've worked well together for decades, and he was greatly influential in getting me to where I am today, especially early on when I had no track record or contacts and he seemed to know everyone that mattered. All the right people. All the time."

"Not *all* the right people."

He laughed humorlessly. "So it appears."

"Did you know Dante maintained a relationship with a federal fugitive?"

"I knew he had the connections I needed and he was always decent and fair to me."

"That wasn't what I asked." I leaned forward in my chair, trying to recall how my body language should be if I wanted to really connect with him, get him to open up. I couldn't mimic his current posture or we'd both look disinterested and marginally annoyed. "This isn't a good turn for you. You're up for reelection this fall and you've lost your moneyman, plus he turned out to be on the wrong side of the law, so that's a double whammy if anyone finds out."

"Do you plan to tell them?" Anger flushed his cheeks. "Is that what this is? Blackmail?"

"Of course not. I told you Dante was a friend of my grandmother's. I want to know who killed him."

The muscles in his jaw relaxed. "So you want to know if I killed Dante, or if I had him killed. You think I'd kill to stop his bad press from tainting all the good I've done. You think my hard work will seem irrelevant in the face of questionable funding. Or maybe you think I killed him because I was pissed off he'd kept something so important from me for so long, dragged me unwittingly into his shit storm and potentially tarnished my legacy, when I've been nothing but upstanding and dedicated to my state and country every day of my life?"

"That was well thought out. Any of it how you truly feel?"

"All of it." He rapped a fist against the arm of his chair. "I'm mad as hell and I can't even yell at him about it. He didn't have the decency to tell me what an asshole he was before he got himself killed." Frustration burned in his eyes. "He could've cost me everything, and I had no idea. I considered him a great man."

I appreciated his honesty. The senator had a lot to lose by telling me anything at all about his respect and friendship with a man whose lifestyle probably got him murdered. Definitely not the sort of thing he'd want popping up during the next election. I watched the color drain from his face as his temper cooled. Adams had a reputation for good. For defending the defenseless. He funded battered women's shelters, after-school programs to keep kids out of gangs, and volunteered regularly at soup kitchens. He insisted his staff volunteer too, so they never forgot why their jobs existed. He wanted a better quality of life for everybody in our state.

Still, there was the little detail of where the funding came from and if the programs could legally keep it. "How much of Dante's money was used for your projects?"

He pulled polished brows low over his eyes. "Don't you dare."

"I'm just asking. If your connection to Dante gets out, people are going to ask."

"I'm well aware. The funds were mostly his. He was my biggest supporter. I poured every cent, not wasted on the campaign trail, back into those projects. If that money is determined to be dirty, the projects end. The people lose. It won't hurt me or my family. I'd be heart-broken but I'd survive. Closing every one of my projects won't do a damn thing to hurt my quality of life, but it will lead to untold deaths across this state. Hundreds of women and children will have nowhere to go except back to the monsters they fled from. Kids who spent their evenings in my after-school programs will be back on the streets until their moms get home from third shift at their second jobs. They'll be beat up until they agree to join local gangs for protection, fall into a life of drugs, crime and statistically premature death or early-adult in-carceration. I don't know with any certainty where the money Dante contributed to my causes originated, and I don't want to know. What if we learn it was dirty? Is it better to close those shelters and end those programs than continue to put the money to work for community betterment? So we can feel good about turning away a criminal's money?"

He posed the kinds of questions Nate and I spent hours debating over pizza and ruffled chips with dip. There wasn't a perfect answer. Sometimes everyone lost. And it sucked.

Senator Adams stood and buttoned his navy suit jacket. "I didn't kill my friend, Mia, though I would certainly like to give him a piece of my mind. If I'd had any idea he was in this kind of trouble, maybe I could've helped him for a change, returned one of the many fa-vors he's done for me."

I followed Senator Adams to the closed office door, with one final question on my tongue. "Where were you the night Dante died?"

His lips angled down on both sides.

"Sorry. I have to ask."

"I attended an alumni dinner at my old fraternity. I'm sure they'd lie for me if I wasn't there, but I was. Check YouTube. We try to keep these dinners quiet, but technology works against us."

"It might have worked in your favor this time."

He gripped the knob and swung the door open. His guard dog turned to look at us.

Senator Adams straightened his tie. "Please lose my number, Mia, and if we meet again, let's pretend it's a first." He stepped through the threshold.

"Wait!"

He gave me a dirty look.

"Sorry. Do you have access to mice? Not computer mice." I wiggled my fingers beside my nose, hoping they looked like whiskers. "Like pet mice."

Senator Adams stared for several beats at my wiggling nose and fingers. He turned on his heel and pulled the door shut in my face.

I dropped my hands to my sides and slunk back to the empty chair, alone with my thoughts and no closer to finding Dante's killer.

# TWENTY-ONE

NATE DROVE ME downtown for a lunch meeting with another project manager. He stopped at a historic building, completely the opposite of our last interview location, and checked the navigation app. "I guess this is it."

The bricks were ancient, crumbling at the corners and piled only three stories high. He took a spot right outside the front door and fed the meter two hours' worth of coins.

Nate turned slowly to take in our surroundings. "Is it a bad sign that no one else is here? Do you think the lack of cars means they're hard up for clients?"

I looked up and down the quiet street. "It might mean your Navigator isn't safe here."

He gave his beloved truck a worried look. "I'm sure it's fine. There's probably a surveillance system on the building." He shaded his eyes with one hand and checked the building for cameras.

"No cameras. Do you still want to park here?"

"Yeah." He nodded. "Wes is a friend. I promised to hear his proposal. If he's any good, we should hire him on the spot. We could get a deep discount if he's in need of work."

"Hose your friend? Nice. Smart, too. Let's see what he has to say."

An ancient security guard nodded as we entered the

lobby. He struggled to get onto his feet before we reached him but failed to accomplish the goal.

"We have a twelve o'clock appointment at Delecorte," Nate said.

The guard settled back on his barstool perch. "Third floor." His voice was an appropriate warble.

"Thanks." I took the lead to the elevator. "Excellent security. No cameras and someone's great-grandfather standing guard."

"Give this company a chance," Nate said.

"I could've outrun that guy in four-inch Via Spigas. I think he came with the building. He might've helped build it." I pressed the button and absorbed the surroundings. "You know, there was no one outside because this is a terrible neighborhood, and this building is in worse shape than the Ghostbusters' firehouse." The marble flooring was cracked down the center wide enough to wedge my heel in. "Does Delecorte own the building or are they renting?" I leaned back for a look at the numbers over the elevator. "Is this out of order?"

Nate hefted a tablet from his bag and tapped the screen to life. "Wi-Fi's good." He chuckled. "Delecorte must not have any squirrels."

"Ha. Ha."

My phone rang. "It's the caterer." I rolled my eyes and declined the call. "Jake dropped blueberries off for Bree's blessed rainbow fruit skewers. I'm sure they're just thanking me."

The elevator bell rang and the doors struggled apart. The car was a full inch below our floor. The ceiling was yellowed with decades of legal indoor smoking. "Oh dear."

Nate climbed aboard and jumped. He ducked before

bumping his big head on the ceiling and landed with an unhealthy creak of the car. "See? Sturdy. Come on."

I stuck my head in and appraised the buttons and emergency telephone.

"According to my master research techniques, this building was one of a dozen historic sites purchased last spring from a Restore Downtown benefit auction. Delecorte Resource Management bought it outright and has filed for several permits with the county zoning office."

"You probably found all that information in one article." I stepped gently aboard, wishing I'd had a lighter breakfast.

Hopefully one of the permits was for a new elevator.

Nate put away his tablet. "We could've taken the stairs."

I lifted one foot for his inspection. "Sure. I'll slip on your comfy leather dress shoes and let you climb three flights in these."

"Why do you wear them if they're so uncomfortable?"

I closed my eyes and counted to ten. "Do not get me started on that again." I reopened my eyes. "Why aren't we moving? Did you push the button?"

He poked a finger against the number three. "I thought you did."

"I did not."

"You always push the button."

The aged security guard stared at us from across the empty lobby until the shiny doors rumbled shut.

The car rattled around us, dragging its cargo painfully upward while I calculated our odds of survival.

"Hey." Nate dug something from his jacket pocket. He opened his big palm to reveal a small white satin jewelry box topped with a matching bow.

"What's that?"

He gripped the lid with his thumb and first finger. "Are you ready to see?"

"Obviously." I gave the elevator buttons another look. Second floor. One more to go.

He pulled the lid back and shoved the box in my direction. A two-carat cushion-cut diamond winked at me in the fluorescent overhead lighting. It was nestled in a plush satin bed that begged me to touch. The diamond-encrusted band probably raised the cost another thousand. "What do you think?"

"What do you mean?"

He snapped the lid shut and pushed the box into his pocket. "You know what I mean. Will she like it? Do not ask who or I'm leaving you here when we're done."

I processed the ring. His expression. The fact he'd told me this day was coming. "You're really doing this?" Fear hitched my voice a few octaves. When she hadn't shown up with a ring at work after he'd texted me a picture of a ring, I assumed he'd decided to wait before making another life-altering decision. Taking on REIGN and quitting his comfy job last fall were big adjustments. Adding a wife seemed like more than poor timing, possibly an act of lunacy. "When?"

"I don't know. Soon. We're having dinner at her new apartment tonight."

She said she wanted to ask him to move in. Had she asked? "Her place is finished already?"

"No. We're picnicking. Going over floor plans and details. I thought, maybe, while we're already thinking about the future—" he raised his eyebrows "—that might be a romantic time to ask her to be my wife."

My tummy dropped. Everything was changing. I

hated change. I wasn't good at adapting. I'd have been weeded out early in a Darwinian society. I took a long cleansing breath. "She'll love it."

The elevator stopped and the doors wobbled open.

"Really?" His expression was pure exhilaration.

"Yeah. Really. She'll go nuts. It's perfect."

He stepped off the elevator and managed to look taller. "You should come over tonight. It'd be fun having you there."

I jumped to safety and breathed easier. "I can't. I'm working at the Faire, then working on some things that fell behind because of my investigation."

"Arranging your books or Blu-ray collections again?"

The third floor of the ancient building was caught in a beautiful time warp. Everything from the high polished floors to the over-lacquered benches screamed of the nineteen twenties. The chandelier over the stairs had to have been original, but was completely restored.

Nate whistled. "I guess we know those building permits were put to good use. Looks like they started on the floor they use most. This is fantastic."

Framed posters from the early twentieth century lined the walls. Ads for cigarettes and liquor were displayed beside others for dish soaps and coffee brands I'd never heard of. "I guess this is pretty cool."

"You guess?" Nate barked a laugh that echoed around us. "You live for this retro stuff."

"Well, don't tell your friend or he'll jack his price up on us."

Nate flipped through files on his phone and handed it to me. "For example, what do you think of this old thing?"

I gasped. A snapshot of the most beautiful antique

diamond ring graced the screen. The braided band was delicate and painfully feminine. The stone was a simple round solitaire, from a world where the promise mattered, not the size of the jewel, and I was in love.

"I thought so." Nate leaned over the railing, admiring the regal staircase. "Why don't we make buildings like this anymore?"

I returned his phone with a punch of jealousy for the woman who'd worn that ring. It wasn't right for Fifi, but someone would fall in love all over when she put that on her finger. I joined Nate at the railing. "Times have changed, I guess. The craftsmanship here is beautiful," I admitted, "but we've learned a lot in the last century. Architects build for efficiency now. Cost savings. Best use of space. There are lighter, cheaper, more durable materials to work with and stringent building codes."

"It was a rhetorical question."

"Nothing's really rhetorical."

He tapped out a text before putting his phone away. "Time to meet the man." He led me through an arching doorway with a Delecorte plaque attached.

The interior room boasted more of the same furniture and décor from the hallway. Black-and-white photos of the building over the years hung across the waiting room walls. Newspaper articles featuring the building were pressed under glass on the tables.

"Hey, Nate!" A man in brightly colored golf gear waved from a nearby office. "I'm just wrapping up. Make yourself at home."

Nate waved. "That's Wes Kennedy."

"He founded Delecorte, right? How do you know him?"

"We met at a gamer convention two years ago. We talked about REIGN over drinks and wings. He couldn't believe it when I called last month and told him I bought the game and could use some help."

Wes and another man emerged from a small office.

I grabbed Nate's arm. "That's Josh Chan. The other guy is Josh Chan."

Nate whipped his head around for a look. "Oh snap."

"Don't say that." Adrenaline ignited fire in my veins. I needed to talk to him, but he'd already threatened to sue me for harassment if I tried.

Unless I lied about who I was. I chewed my lip. Fifi said lying on an investigation was called using a cover. I was a terrible liar. Could I pull off a cover?

The men moseyed past us to the door.

Nate gripped me back. "What do we do?"

*Oh, what the hell.*

"Josh?" I called. "Josh Chan, is that you?"

Nate swore and ducked back a few steps. "What are you doing? Is that a British accent?"

"Shut up, I'm nervous." And British, apparently.

Josh's smile fell. "Yeah." He moved closer, scrutinizing me. "Have we met?"

Behind him, Wes crossed his arms and smiled wildly. "What a small world."

I stole Nate's story. "We met at a convention, I think." I snapped my fingers and pretended to dig through memories. "Vegas? No. Chicago? I can't recall the venue, but I'd never forget that face. That was such a fun night. I probably could've done with one less chardonnay." I did my best to imitate Fifi's charming smile. "You founded Luminatti, right?"

He moved closer, unconvinced. "Yeah."

I lifted and dropped my hands. "I love paper lanterns."

He backed away, not taking the bait. "Nice to see you again. Best of luck."

"Wait!" I lifted onto my toes. I couldn't let him get away. "You were working on a deal with a television show?" I frowned. "I'm sorry I don't remember the details. How'd that work out?"

Wes clapped Josh on the back. "That deal with Shop At Home made this guy a millionaire. Lucky for me, he needed some project management advice." Wes showed a full set of used-car-salesman teeth. "He's entrusted me with a major project." He shook Josh's shoulder. "These guys will be in good hands if they follow your path. Am I right?"

Josh contorted his face. "I've got to get going. It was nice to see you again, Ms.…." He gave me a distinctly challenging look.

I did my best to look sad and rejected. "Spiga."

Nate choked.

"Right." Josh Chan exited with no less than three looks over his shoulder.

Wes and Nate headed toward the office where Josh had been. I hustled after them and took the seat beside Nate and across from Wes. I'd taken a big risk and got no reward.

Wes looked puzzled. "I thought your partner was joining you today. Ms. Connors?"

Nate struggled to get comfortable in his seat. We were no Bonnie and Clyde. "Mia was held up in another meeting. Ms. Spiga took her place."

Short. Sweet.

We watched Wes's face.

"Well, it's nice meeting you." He smiled at me.

"Thank you."

"I'm sure I'll have another opportunity to meet the yin to your yang, Nate."

I took notes during the interview and kept my mouth shut when I had questions. Playing the secretary was bollocks. It was hard to think about REIGN when I'd been close enough to tackle Josh Chan and demand answers, but he got away.

Soon, Nate stood and shook Wes's hand. "Thank you very much for meeting with us. We'll get back with you as soon as we make a decision."

I ghosted into the waiting area, imagining scenarios with Josh that ended differently. Sadly, they all came with harassment charges.

"Ms. Spiga." Wes extended his hand to me. "I'm sorry your reunion with Josh didn't go better. He's normally a more pleasant fellow. I suppose that went downhill when you mentioned his Shop At Home deal, but you wouldn't have known."

I doubted he was ever more pleasant. Jake had warned me of Josh's prior arrests for stalking behaviors. Maybe this wasn't over. Wes had mistaken my quietness for dejection. I put my big owl eyes to work, looking as heartbroken and embarrassed as possible. "He was so happy about it when I met him. I thought he might want to talk about it some more. Maybe over tea."

Wes cleared his throat and rubbed his palms together. "I probably shouldn't say anything, but that deal was a real kick in the pants for him. He'd worked with the Shop At Home people for months with no offers. Eventually, he gave up and turned to a local entrepreneur for advice, funding, connections, whatever it took to get his product into consumers' hands. Well, it was only a few days after he signed on with the new guy that Shop At Home called and made an offer for his product."

"I'm afraid I still don't understand."

"The new guy, the investor or whatever you'd call him—" Wes lowered his head and voice "—held Josh to their contract, which specifically stated that the investor was entitled to a chunk of all monies made on Josh's product beginning the day it was signed. Not just a portion of the advance, but part of the revenue forever. Josh hadn't even had time to use the investor's funds or connections, and the guy was already laying claim to the Shop At Home advance. He refused to let Josh break the deal with him. He threatened to sue for breach of contract. When Shop At Home heard about a potential lawsuit, they told Josh to work it out or they'd be forced to pull the products. Shoppers don't want to buy products with bad juju."

I rolled the new information around. "So, the Shop At Home contract was a bad thing because it came too late. He'd already signed with Dante, and Dante got part of the money, so Josh ended up making a lot less on a deal he'd personally arranged." That was dirty.

Wes straightened with a snap. "You know Dante Weiss?" Panic ran over his face.

"I won't say anything," I told him, momentarily forgetting the British accent.

"Thanks again," Nate said, shoving me toward the elevator. "We'll be in touch."

I FINISHED THE workday in a haze. All I could think about was Josh Chan. What Dante had done to him was slimy and unfair. No wonder Josh was mad. Maybe even mad enough to kill. He had millions of motives, but figuring out where he was on the night Dante died wouldn't be easy. He had no interest in talking to me by phone or email, and he'd seen my face playing the role of Ms. Spiga, his British stalker.

Overall, the meeting had been a disaster. Nate liked Wes's plan for REIGN, but we couldn't hire him. He thought I was Ms. Spiga the secretarial stand-in.

I parted ways with Fifi in the clubhouse lot after work. She had big plans with Nate. I owed my family some hours at the Guinevere's Golden Beauty booth.

The sun was high in the sky and baking hot. Suffering from heat stroke at the Ren Faire wasn't on my bucket list. I considered canceling due to a sincere lack of enthusiasm but knew I'd feel better once I got there. The Faire always cheered me up.

I hastened to my apartment, kicked my shoes off and grabbed a pale blue Queen Guinevere gown in the thinnest material available. According to my phone, I had eight messages. At least six of those were likely from my family members. I shimmied out of my work clothes and skipped through voice mails like a multitasking champion. Two from Mom. Three from Bree. One from Grandma. The swing band confirmed for the shower. Score!

I pinned my hair up. Grabbed my purse and locked up behind me. I'd see Mom, Grandma and Bree at the Faire.

I played the last message in the elevator on my way out.

"Ms. Connors, this is Congress Lake Catering. If you could please give us a call back, we need to talk to you about a delivery of unmarked blueberries we received. I'm afraid we can't use unvetted berries. We'd like to return them to you, if possible, and move forward without blueberries on the skewers."

"No, no, no." I activated the callback feature and rushed across the lot to Stella. "This is Mia Connors, I'm returning a call about blueberries."

"Thank you for returning the call so quickly," an overly perky voice replied. "I'm afraid we can't use the blueberries you had delivered. They aren't from one of our approved vendors."

"So what?" I gunned my little car through the Horseshoe Falls gate and headed for the highway. "Your vendors didn't have what you need. This is when you're supposed to outsource. That's what I did. I outsourced."

"No, ma'am."

"Yes." I nodded at the windshield. "Just put the blueberries on the skewers, after the kiwi and before the blackberries." I mentally checked the order. "Or before the raspberries. I left an assembly diagram when we chose skewers as the fruit option."

"I'm sorry. We can't use your blueberries."

I pounded one palm against the steering wheel as I eased into traffic going seventy on the highway. "Fine. I'll make them myself. I'll come by tomorrow and pick up all the fruits you have, assemble the skewers at home and bring them back for the shower."

"No. I'm afraid we can't allow any foods to be removed from the building and returned. It's a basic safety precaution that allows us to retain control for quality. We could become liable, if, for example, the food was removed, contaminated and returned."

I pulled the phone away to glare at it as I inched down the off-ramp nearest the Faire. "Why would I poison people at a party I'm hostessing?"

"I'm sorry. Just precautions. You understand."

"No. I do not." I couldn't help but wonder if any portion of this particular rule stemmed from a baseless allegation against my family last fall. We hadn't poisoned that guy either. "How about this? Can I come and assemble the skewers myself? Then, you aren't using the unvetted berries, and I'm not removing food from the venue. My sister really needs these rainbow fruit skewers. They're on her list, and they're part of her Noah's Ark theme, which is super important now because she just learned that she's having twins," I babbled. "It's extra meaningful because she's a twin. She's my twin, actually, and that makes this important to me too. Please let me do this. I don't mind at all. Honestly."

"Once again, I'm very sorry for the inconvenience, but only Congress Lake employees can work in the kitchen. Insurance reasons. What if you cut yourself?"

"Then hire me."

"Ms. Connors." She huffed, apparently fresh out of perk. "Our fruits can't mingle with your berries. Period."

I rolled my head against the seat. *Story of my life.* I showed my pass to the parking attendant outside the Faire and followed a long line of vehicles into the field for parking. "Fine. I'll make them myself. I'll buy all new fruit, prepare them at home and bring them with me. That's allowed, isn't it?"

"Yes. As long as you sign an outside food waiver relieving us from liability. We'll still have to charge you for the fruit we've already purchased. We can't take it back or use it for another event because it was purchased under the agreement you signed."

I gripped the wheel until my fingers turned white. "Fine. Goodbye." I poked the disconnect button hard enough to break my finger. I missed the satisfaction of slamming my phone down. Now, I needed to buy a carload of fruit on my way home, peel, slice and assemble two hundred rainbow fruit skewers before her shower.

A guy in coveralls was waving orange sticks up ahead. Parking was full and I was routed into the overflow area. I followed an unprecedented number of SUVs and minivans into no man's land and parked with a mild curse. I beeped the doors locked, hiked up my skirts and trudged toward the faux castle gates with my chin held high. I was Queen Guinevere of Camelot and this was my domain. I remained vigilant as I moved. No lurking lunatics, but dozens of women wearing babies in pouches and pushing double strollers puttered between parked cars, moving toward the replica castle gates. Lots of pregnant women, too. Weird.

I passed a pack of mommies-to-be and darted into the Faire on the scent of dumplings and turkey legs. Memories of sweet and flaky pastries moved my legs into high gear. Miles of twinkle lights blinked to life, outlining shops, booths and trees. Another day nearly gone. I got in line behind a woman with a double stroller at Treetop Tavern and prepared my dinner order.

Fifteen minutes later, I sat behind the Guinevere's Golden Beauty booth with a box full of everything that sounded good from the foodie section of the Faire. I texted Nate and asked him to please pick up my berries from Congress Lake and leave them outside my apartment door.

Grandma took my phone, then helped herself to a dumpling. "How's it going with REIGN? Have you found a project manager yet?"

I coaxed chocolate malt up a straw until my head hurt. "No. Not yet."

She sucked the tip of her finger. "I was thinking, when you find a winner, maybe talk to him or her about taking on some of your work for our company."

I released the straw and gawked. "What? Why?" I was slacking on my duties, but not so much that it mattered. I normally worked nonstop on Grandma's company, but I'd had to divert some energy to finding Dante's killer. Was she disappointed I couldn't keep up the pace? Was I a bad CIO? "I know I haven't been here as much as I usually am, but I stay on top of everything from my laptop. I promise."

She pressed a soft palm to my cheek. "You're misunderstanding me. The company is growing like gangbusters thanks to all your hard work. We all know it. The family sees what you consistently put into this business. You give it one hundred and ten percent, every day, just like everything you do."

"Then why?"

"We want you to have time to enjoy your life. It's a blessed life, Mia. Don't squander it working yourself to death. You're a millionaire, for crying out loud. You've got a family who adores you. A thriving business. Health. Great friends. A handsome beau, and a lovely figure. Enjoy it all. Take a minute to love your thirty-year-old life because before you know it, you're old and your best years are behind you. That's if you're lucky. Plenty of people don't get the chance to be old. Believe me, when you're my age, you'll wish you'd really lived right now."

"I like helping you."

She squeezed my hands. "We know you do, and we're guilty of taking advantage."

I didn't have to ask her to define "we." My family was "we" and I'd never stop making time for whatever they needed, no matter how overwhelming or bonkers.

Tom and Dad strutted down the dusty path between booths, rolling a massive wooden circle. They stopped at the front of our booth and wiped their brows with their sleeves. Dad's face was bright red from sun and exertion.

I uncapped a bottle of water from Grandma's cooler and handed it over. "What is that thing?" I stepped outside the booth with another bottle for Tom.

The big wooden sign rested against our counter. It was a lovely rendering of my eighteen-year-old face with curly golden script announcing, *Pampered Womb Products Sold Here*.

The mob of pregnant women and stroller-pushers suddenly made sense. "Bree's doing a demonstration tonight."

Tom handed me his freshly drained water bottle. "Actually, she's holding a Love Your Body Rally. We're expecting an incredible turnout. She's been blogging and promoting across the county at obstetrician and pediatrician offices. She's given samples to maternity wards and visited mommy and Lamaze groups. There was a mass mailing and flyer distribution. She's really gotten into this, and the turnout is fantastic."

He was right. The crowd was nearly double that of a normal weeknight and most of the faces were glowing with a double dose of hormones.

Grandma loaded the counter with products from Bree's new line. "See? It's no problem for you to take some time off. Everyone will assume Bree is you. We can order her a maternity version of your gown if you want."

I laughed. "Definitely not. I like being Queen Guinevere. I like being here." I leaned my head on her shoulder. "With all of you."

"Yes, but it's okay to love being with someone else, too."

Wild applause broke out around us. The women and strollers drew nearer.

Bree arrived in a golf cart decked out to look like a carriage with no horses. I laughed and clapped with the crowd. How could I miss this?

Then, she got out.

My jaw dropped. I gripped the counter to stop myself from covering her with the Love Your Body banner Dad had just hung overhead. "Where are her clothes?" Bree loved to show some skin, but this was ridiculous. She currently had way too much skin to show, and people could see it.

Grandma fluffed tissue paper in gift bags. "She's supposed to look like a fertility goddess or something. Isn't she beautiful?"

"Uh, no. She's naked."

Tom chuckled his way into the booth beside Grandma. "She's Aphrodite, the goddess of love, beauty and sexual passion. I think she looks amazing."

Bree twirled through the crowd wearing nothing but strategically placed flesh-colored wrappings. The gauzy material flowed behind her arms as she spun. Her tube top was rolled into a literal tube covering her giant pregnancy boobs and bunching at the top of her baby bump, which I now thought of as my forthcoming nieces.

Tom smiled proudly. "She's fully clothed, except her belly. We chose material as close to her natural skin tone as possible and commissioned the outfit from a local designer. Her belly has to be exposed as proof of her products' legitimacy. If her skin wasn't so flawless, who would want the creams?"

"Right." I crept away from the booth for a better look at my sister. Her belly was definitely bare, and the outfit was scanty no matter what he called it. The way she'd arranged her hair, with little white flowers and pins, was cute. It worked well with the costume. Bree made a pretty Aphrodite. Maybe I could take one night off.

I snuck past Grandma and collected my cell phone from the basket where she put it when she caught me texting. "I might go home and lie in a hot bubble bath until I can't recognize my pruny toes."

She smiled and pushed a forkful of dumpling into her mouth. "Atta girl, but leave the food."

I curtsied. "Yes, of course, milady."

I sauntered away from the booth feeling lighter and free. The sun had almost set and the sky was lined in spectacular hues of apricot, crimson and gold. I tilted my head back to soak in the moment. It was an unbelievable high not to be expected anywhere. No one was counting every minute I ran late. I couldn't be late. I had nowhere I had to be. When was the last time that was true?

I texted Jake before the euphoria wore off. Good luck tonight. I bit my lip and headed for my car. I wanted to tell him to come over later, if he wasn't staying in Cleveland, but I wasn't sure how. I checked the distance to my car and decided on one more text. A smaller risk, but a risk nonetheless. I miss you.

I stared at the phone, hoping I hadn't said something stupid as I stomped through the overgrown grasses in overflow parking. No response.

I shouldn't have told him I missed him. That was too

needy. I definitely wasn't needy. Neurotic? Yes. Nerdy? Every day. Needy? No.

I had to text again and clarify I wasn't needy.

I beeped my doors unlocked and groaned at my stupidity for texting while high on endorphins. It had to be the equivalent of drunk dialing.

I lifted my gaze to Stella, and a scream lurched through my lips. Dozens of dead-eyed mice covered my windshield. It was too far to run back to the Faire, especially in my gown. I jumped inside the car and locked the doors. Beady, unseeing eyes stared through my windshield. I snapped pictures and texted the shots to Dan. I'd promised myself to keep a specimen for research if the mice deliverer struck again. Calling Dan seemed like a better choice. Crime Scene workers had access to labs I'd never get into. They'd have answers in half the time, leaving me free to have that nervous breakdown I needed. A shudder rushed through me. I rubbed my arms and checked myself for any live specimens potentially clinging to my gown.

Memories of Dante's abandoned car came to mind.

I screamed again and twisted for a look in my backseat. Hallelujah—no unwanted, dagger-wielding passengers.

My phone buzzed with a text.

Dan replied to the photos. I'm en route. Don't move the car and don't touch the mice. Crime Scene is on the way as well.

Yep. So much for a relaxing night in the tub.

# TWENTY-TWO

I TEXTED NATE while I waited for Dan.

Nate and Fifi arrived seconds later, bouncing recklessly through the bumpy overflow-field in his Navigator. The truck had barely stopped before Fifi jumped out and ran to my car. She pounded her palms against my window. Fear and distress marred her beautiful face.

I powered the window down. "How are you here?" I'd barely hit Send on the text and they appeared.

"We were here when you texted. Stuck in a line of minivans at the entrance."

Tears sprang to my eyes. "Why?"

"I think there's some kind of mom rally going on tonight."

I choked on a laugh. "Not the minivans. You. Why are you here? What about your picnic?"

She frowned. "We knew you had a terrible day. We wanted to check on you."

"Get in." I unlocked the doors and Fifi took the passenger seat.

Nate fed a picnic basket through my open window. "Have you eaten?"

I tried to shove it back. "Yes. Keep this. Why do you have a picnic basket?"

He tipped his head.

*His proposal picnic.*

"Oh, no. No. No. No. You eat. In fact, you should

leave. Enjoy a romantic dinner. It's okay. Dan's almost here."

Nate bore down on my tiny car, flames of anger in his usually soft eyes. "Mia, there's a pile of dead mice on your windshield. The police are on their way. Do you truly believe I'm leaving you alone here under any circumstances?"

"He won't," Fifi said. "We won't."

I pressed the heels of my hands against stinging eyes. "Thanks."

Nate set the rejected picnic onto my roof and turned his back to me. He crossed his arms and put his massive size to use, looking dangerous as he stood guard.

Fifi leaned on the dash, examining the mice from inside the window. "They're all wet."

"I think whoever drowned Dante is taunting me by drowning mice."

She sat back. "A real-life game of cat and mouse."

"I think I'm the mouse."

Dan's big black truck rolled slowly up the beaten path, leading an ominous procession of cruisers and one nondescript sedan.

Dan approached with a sad smile. "Hey, Nate, Mia."

Nate nodded.

"Hey," I said.

"I'm glad you called this time." He squatted to look past me. "Fifi. It's nice to see you again."

A pair of women in navy Crime Scene jackets bagged and labeled the mice. Uniformed officers checked the immediate area, kicking the tall grass and inspecting the ground with flashlights. They split off as they moved away, in a wide sweeping arch, checking the tree line, nearby cars and interviewing people in the field.

Nate turned defensively at Dan's side. "Who do you think did this, Archer?"

"I don't know, but now that we've got evidence to test, I'll have him in custody by the end of the week."

I didn't see how that was possible. "That's a big promise."

Dan leaned his forearms on my open window. "How many times has this happened with the mice?"

"Four." I swallowed a lump in my throat, unable to project my voice above a whisper. "The pile keeps growing."

He nodded. "That's why we'll find him. Whoever is doing this has gotten away with it three times. He's getting braver with each contact. Braver means sloppier for criminals, plus, you finally called me, so we have evidence to work with now."

I tried not to translate *braver* as *escalating*.

"Do you think this is the work of the same person who killed Dante?" Nate asked. "Is there any chance whoever did this is mad about something else? Maybe some stalker from the Faire or someone who knows her online?"

I'd been nearly killed by men fitting both of those categories last year. The possibility it could happen again squeezed my insides painfully.

Dan ignored the questions and kept his attention on me. "Does Jake know about this?" He tipped his head to my freshly harvested windshield.

"No. He's working on something important tonight, and I don't want to be a distraction." Distractions could be deadly for someone in Jake's position, marching himself stupidly into harm's way every day. Trying to save the world. Facing off with society's worst criminals. What was he thinking? *If anything happened to him...*

A small sob escaped me.

"I know this is hard," Dan said, drawing me back to the moment, "but can you tell me about anyone you've spoken to lately who might want to frighten you?"

I took a steadying breath and kneaded my shaking hands. "I talked to Joshua Chan today. He's not my biggest fan."

Dan rubbed his stubbled neck. "The Joshua Chan who's suing Dante and threatened to sue you if you contacted him again?"

Jeez. Jake had a big mouth. "Yeah. I ran into him downtown, but I pretended to be someone else."

"Who did you pretend to be?"

"Ms. Spiga, a woman he met at a convention but rudely forgot."

Dan tented his brows. "Do you think he knows who you really are?"

"No, I was British."

Dan swung his wary gaze to Nate and back. "Okay, I'll talk to Chan." He stood and rolled his shoulders for a stretch.

I pushed my head through the window. "I talked to another cabbie today. I went for a quick ride to ask if he'd picked anyone up outside Horseshoe Falls the night Dante died."

Dan zipped back into view, regaining his squat. "You did what?"

Fifi filled him in on my cab theory and our ride around the block with Calvin Besk.

He made notes in the little flip pad he kept inside his

jacket. "I hate to ask, but is there anything else I should know?"

I dropped my head against the headrest until Fifi came into view. "What about my visitor?" I whispered.

"What visitor?" Nate and Dan asked in near unison.

She looked past me for several beats, presumably at the men outside my window. Indecision played her pretty face. "I think you have to."

"Mia?" Dan pressed. "I can't help you if I don't have all the information."

I turned slowly back to him, hating the way this was going. Would there be retaliation if I told Dan about my secret meeting? If so, who would receive the brunt of it? And in what format would the retaliation arrive? "Off the record."

"On the record."

We had a short staring contest.

"Fine." I caved. "I spoke privately with someone today who had motive to get rid of Dante, but I don't think he did it." The mice seemed beneath Senator Adams, unless that had been his plan all along—to throw me off. Could he have had someone watching me from the start, trying to scare me away with rodents? "The agreement was that I'd never tell anyone he came to see me."

"Who was he?" He wiggled his pen over the paper. "I need a name."

Warnings from Marcella, the security guy and the senator rang in my mind. "Vince Adams."

"Senator Vince Adams?"

"He made it clear I wasn't to tell anyone that we spoke, so tread lightly, okay? If he's connected to the killing, I don't want to tick him off or give him a reason to target you."

"Adams is on my list already. I've gone to his office twice and his home once looking for him. He's constantly on the move, it's like trying to nail Jell-O to the wall."

"He's on your list?"

Dan tapped a finger to his detective shield. "You can go home. Get some rest. I'll get a message to Jake about this. I'm sure he'll call you as soon as he can."

Nate shook Dan's hand. "Fifi and I will follow her home and stay with her tonight."

Dan clapped him on the shoulder before joining the Crime Scene women at their car. "You're a good man, Nathan Green."

I blinked back a fresh flood of emotion. He really was.

Fifi buckled her seat belt. "I'll ride with Mia."

I gunned Stella to life and flipped on my windshield wipers. I violently jammed the lever on my steering console until a river of blue washer fluid flooded the glass. Stella and I had been through a lot this year. She'd had her interior defaced, notes tied to her antenna, dead mice piled on her windshield. How much could one Mini Cooper take? "I might need a new car."

Nate followed me onto the highway in his SUV, careful to stay behind my little car in streaming traffic.

Fifi made a chipper sound. "I love car shopping. Do you have something in mind?"

"Yeah. A tank."

THE HAPPY COUPLE accompanied me to Congress Lake to pick up my blueberries, then to three all-night grocers where I collected enough fruit to star in a high school algebra word problem. They refused to leave me when we got back to my place, so they spent the night in my guest room.

I walked to work with Fifi in the morning. We left Nate snoring and grabbed lattes at Dream Bean before moving slowly into the day.

"How are you holding up?" she asked. "You're really quiet."

"Just thinking." I treaded the familiar path to the clubhouse with a grand idea percolating in my overburdened mind. Maybe Grandma was right. Maybe it was time for me to streamline my life. She was definitely wrong about where I'd make cuts. I watched Fifi sip her coffee and smile and wave to a family on horseback. What if I passed the community IT torch to Fifi? I loved Horseshoe Falls, but I lived here now, so quitting as the IT manager wouldn't keep me away.

"Mia?" she nudged, a hint of worry in her soft soprano.

"Nothing. Just thinking."

"Tell me later?"

"Definitely."

I walked home alone at five with the same idea floating in my head. I could streamline my life.

It'd been twenty-four hours since CSI collected mice from my windshield, and I hadn't heard from Jake or Dan. My brain was in some sort of protection mode and anytime I tried to rehash the dead mice situation, my thoughts jumped to nonsense or scenes from my favorite movies. So I succumbed to the mental pressure, donned my favorite LOTR pajamas and set up to make two hundred rainbow fruit skewers.

I peeled, sliced and piled the fruits in the correct order on my counter, then began an assembly line, and stacked completed sticks on cookie sheets lined with foil. When my fingertips grew raw from one too many pokes with a sharp wooden skewer, I stopped to send email reminders to the shower guests, per Bree's request. Bring a favorite children's book for my new nieces' library or make donations to St. Jude's in lieu of gifts. Tomorrow's shower wasn't about acquiring everything a new mom needed. This time we were celebrating the miracle of life and the blessing of family, blood related or otherwise.

I tightened the strings of my gray Gandalf robe around my middle and padded into my living room to start another *Lord of the Rings* movie. I had a new appreciation for Bilbo Baggins. I, too, was on an unexpected journey. My life was also filled with orcs and trials and second breakfasts.

The phone rang, and I paused the show. I went back to assembling rainbows. "Hello?"

"Mia? This is Dan Archer. I have some lab results on the mice from your windshield."

I fell onto the couch and focused on breathing. "Okay."

"They weren't drowned."

"But they were dripping wet," I reminded him. "Someone dunked dead mice in something before delivering them to me?" That didn't make sense. "Did you test the liquid?"

"The mice were frozen. They were wet from melting. Defrosting is more accurate, I guess. The good news is there's no longer a reason to think the person who drowned Dante is drowning innocent mice for the purpose of inciting terror."

This was what my life had come to. The dead mice weren't drowned, and that was considered good news. "Great." I couldn't find enthusiasm for the word.

"Another thing."

Oh, goodie. "Yeah?"

"We've also got fibers from the backseat of Dante's car. We're tracing them now. Hope to have definitive news on their origins soon. Could be nothing. Could be what we need. I thought you'd want the information as soon as I had it. I'll let you get back to your evening."

"Thanks." Another autonomic response. I disconnected and dropped my phone on the cushion beside me. Someone was hounding me with frozen mice. Hopefully the fiber from Dante's backseat would lead to an arrest before I had to drive anywhere else.

My doorbell rang and I groaned. I didn't want any more coddling from Nate and Fifi or surprises from anyone. I wanted to finish the skewers, throw popcorn at Gollum and go to bed. I shoved myself upright and headed to the door. No one got inside my building without a key code, so Fifi and Nate were clearly checking on me again. As if they didn't have anything better to do. When had I become the third wheel? An aged marm for them to worry over?

I peeked through the hole.

Jake stood outside with a grim expression. His left eye was swollen, and the corresponding brow was pinched together with butterfly bandages. His jaw was red with abrasions. His navy shirt was torn at the shoulder.

I yanked the door open and pulled him inside. "What happened to you?"

The door across the hall shut on Nate's heels.

"Rough night. Saw Nate in the parking lot and rode up with him." Jake gave my jammies a look. He winced when he smiled. "Movie night?"

"Do you like *Lord of the Rings*?"

"Yeah. I also like whiskey."

I locked the door behind him. "Fresh out of whiskey,

but how about one of Nate's beers and an ice pack for your face?"

"Deal." Jake hobbled to my couch and collapsed in the space I'd just vacated. "I heard about the mice. I'm sorry I wasn't there."

I wrapped ice in a dish towel and uncapped a bottle of ale from the Great Lakes Brewing Company. I delivered both to Jake.

"Thanks." He pressed the towel to his cheekbone and sucked air. "That hurts." He swigged the beer with his free hand. "I got here as soon as I could. I'd have been here last night if it was humanly possible."

I fell into the space beside him. "You look awful. You should stay here tonight. You can't drive like this. Start again tomorrow."

He made a grouchy face. "You aren't supposed to feel sorry for me. I came to check on you. You're stealing my thunder."

"Well, you should've thought about that before you let someone beat up your face."

He smiled, then quickly winced. "Funny."

"Really. Stay." My chest warmed as I spoke the word. "It's crazy to drive another hour to Stone Creek when you're clearly exhausted and hurting. I've got everything you need. A hot shower. Fluffy towels. Comfy couch. Spare bedroom." I stopped talking before I said anything to scare him away.

He held my gaze long enough to give me goose bumps.

"If you're nice, I might even make breakfast."

He laced his bruised fingers with mine. "I got Terrance Horton. He's in custody."

"He is?"

He nodded. "I had to chase him down and tackle him.

His goons did their best to separate us, but I was highly motivated after hearing about those mice."

"Did he kill Dante?"

"My team's questioning him now. So far, he's admitted to hearing the rumor Dante was an informant. Couple that with the fact he made his way to a hotel less than an hour from Dante's home the same week Dante was killed, and we've got a solid case. Odds are that Dante got wind his gig was up and packed his bags. He tried to run, but someone stopped him. If not Terrance, personally, then an associate."

I leaned my head on his shoulder, relief flooding my heart. "I'm glad you're okay."

"Back at ya." He nudged me back an inch and caught me in his steely blue gaze. "Are you sure you want me to stay here tonight?" There was yearning in his voice and intent in his eyes. For once, I didn't need a human-to-human translator.

"Yes."

He leaned closer. The intoxicating scents of him muddled my thoughts. "When Dan called me, I couldn't get here fast enough. I cut some corners to get Horton in cuffs so I could leave. I hated not being here for you." He placed a palm on my cheek.

I released a quick breath and hungrily breathed him in again.

"Mia?" He raised his brows in question.

I took the liberty of kissing him thoroughly in response.

Maybe some alone time with Jake wasn't the worst suggestion Bree had ever had.

# TWENTY-THREE

THE LODGE AT Congress Lake was packed with happy women. Despite Bree's request for donations in lieu of gifts, there was a wall of elaborately wrapped boxes stacked four deep near the windows. My rainbow of baby clothes hung adorably over the gift table, and the fruit skewers were flying off the buffet. Bree's white-on-white décor punctuated with a careful selection of rainbows was both cheery and breathtaking. She had a definite knack for stage setting.

In fact, the sister who drove me bonkers on a regular and ongoing basis for thirty years was beloved for multiple reasons and clearly at home in the controlled chaos of a mammoth country club baby shower. She was dressed ironically in white and wearing a pink paper crown that said Mama. The event was full swank, but I'd chosen a silver sleeveless tunic over black leggings so I could bend, lift and hostess all day without any fear of showing dirt or my backside.

In short, Bree was engaging and beautiful. I was trying to blend with the waitstaff. Mostly because I'd told seven strangers no, I wasn't married, and no, I didn't want to meet their son, grandson, neighbor or friend, before hors d'oeuvres. Seriously. Was this a baby shower or a meat market?

Grandma had the crowd's attention, regaling them from center stage with tales of Bree as a child. Comparison stories of Bree and her daughter Gwen and ways our mother was like both of them or different. Grandma was a gifted storyteller.

I moved table to table, delivering trays of puffy paints and white onesies. I did my best to relax, but fear and panic pressed on my lungs, standing the fine hairs on my neck and arms at attention. I lifted my face slowly and scanned the room. Clearly, I'd had a rough week and my anxiety was high, but it felt as if I was being watched.

Applause rang out. I joined in the clapping, clueless about what I'd missed.

Two hundred women smiled at me. I guessed I was being watched. Onstage, my mother, grandmother and sister extended their arms in my direction. When had they all gathered up there?

I'd ask them after the party. Right before I killed them.

"Come on," Bree insisted. "Let them see what I used to look like."

The mob laughed.

I moved on autopilot to their sides and gazed timidly on the sea of welcoming faces.

The room had turned out beautifully, dripping with white linens and twinkle lights. Taper candles flickered in natural lighting from a wall of windows. Little fans twirled slowly at the peak of a twenty-foot ceiling. If not for the brightly colored gifts and hugely pregnant woman beside me, we could've been at any high-class event from a fancy gala to a wedding reception. As requested, all the elegant décor was set in twos and anchored in pairs of baby animals. Her Noah's Ark theme was more than fitting, given the double pink cakes at her gender reveal.

"It's beautiful," Bree whispered against my hair. "You gave me the perfect shower."

My mouth had dried out beyond the ability to speak. Nerves coiled in my gut. Being in the spotlight felt a lot like being in the crosshairs.

Grandma's voice echoed through the room and everyone clapped once more. She replaced the mic on the stand.

The crowd turned to chat amongst themselves. Some pawed eagerly at the trays I'd delivered to their tables.

The four of us walked offstage, arm-in-arm like the Monkees, and took our seats.

Bree sipped her ice water. "How are things with Jake?"

"Good. He apprehended the fugitive."

Grandma released a long breath. "Praise Zeus. So, we can all rest now? You're safe again?"

I rubbed the gooseflesh on my arms. "That's the assumption." No need to point out that Terrance Horton was only one possible suspect and we had no idea if he even knew Dante was dead. Only that he came to Ohio after hearing Dante was an informant. I avoided their curious stares and changed the subject. "How did things go making the belly mold?"

Mom pressed a hand to her mouth.

Grandma barked a laugh. "Awful. We ruined two kits and the last one looked like a giant's boob."

Bree touched the upturned belly button poking through her dress like an awkward nipple. "Total bust, but I was able to reach your friend Tennille, and we set an appointment for next week. I'll get pregnancy pictures now and newborn pictures when these two arrive." She rested interlaced fingers on her bump.

I was surprised at how much I enjoyed having my worlds collide. It had been a long time since anyone other than Nate knew my family. Lately, the circle was growing. Nate, Fifi, Jake, Dan, Tennille. My friends and my family were blending into a pretty amazing and eclectic mix, from lawmen to magicians.

*Speaking of magicians.*

"How are the wedding plans coming along, Grandma?"

She beamed. "I think we've got the most important details hammered out. I hired a professional coordinator, so you can attend as a guest instead of unpaid help."

Mixed emotions coursed through me. I was fired? "You didn't need to do that, Grandma. I would've helped."

Bree slid one hand off her bump and used it to cover mine. "I'm sorry I sometimes treat you like a slave. I max out all your time, and then I complain that you haven't started a family. When are you supposed to meet someone if you're busy running my errands all the time? Plus working at Horseshoe Falls and with our company. It's stupid of me, and I'm sorry."

I turned my hand over and gave her fingers a squeeze. "I don't mind. I like being useful."

Mom grabbed my other hand. "You're useful to us without doing anything at all."

THREE HOURS LATER, the reception hall was empty and the outdoor topiaries were covered in confused Monarch butterflies, recently released from weird see-through envelopes. Bree seemed more disturbed by the sight of the flattened Monarchs in their travel packs than she was about the color scheme disruption. So, Nate would live to see another day.

I loaded gifts, centerpieces and luncheon leftovers into our family vehicles. I filled Tom's truck first, then Dad's, then Marvin's trunk. I worked with the three men until everything I'd brought to the event was safely packed away for a trip home, along with plenty of new things and fifty pounds of paid-for, unused fruits.

My phone rang and the clubhouse number appeared on the screen. My day had been going so well. I could only imagine what catastrophe needed my attention back at Horseshoe Falls. I rejected the call.

Ding! Voice mail. I hung my head and keyed in my password to replay the message.

"Mia, this is Marcella. Some residents saw a squirrel enter the boathouse attic and they want to set a trap before the Wi-Fi is ruined again. They brought a cage to the field, but Mr. Peters climbed their ladder and won't come down. My heart can't take this drama. Isn't there some way to have the Wi-Fi and the squirrels? Can you come and talk to them?"

I cut the message short and pressed my fingers to my temples. Fifi would help me. I sent her a quick text asking her to call Marcella and deal with the situation until I could get home.

I received an immediate thumbs-up emoticon response and nearly hugged the phone.

"Everything okay?" Dad asked, dusting his palms as he approached.

"I hate squirrels." I shoved the last box of vases and lilies into Marvin's trunk.

Dad laughed, but he didn't ask.

My phone rang again. This time Jake's face appeared on my screen. I tossed my car keys to Dad. "Everything else should fit in my car. This is Jake. I'm going to take the call."

"Hi." I walked away from the guys and found a shaded

bench alongside the building. Warm, misty air blew over me as a breeze hit the nearby fountain.

"How was the shower?" Jake asked.

"Really good." Seeing my family members getting married, having babies and writing books made me insanely happy. I wanted to do anything I could to help them and to be a part of their joy. Who knew? Maybe one day, it'd be me in one of those scenarios. If it was me, I knew they'd be at my side too.

"You sound good. I hear baby showers have that effect on women."

"I'm going to ignore that because I think you're goading me." Also because it was a little true.

"Never." The jovial sound of his voice widened my smile. "I'm glad it worked out. You sound happy."

"I think Bree's crazy enthusiasm finally got to me. She makes starting a family sound like fun."

"Are you busy later?"

"Why?" I smiled, hoping I knew the answer.

He laughed. "I just want to see you. Don't worry, I'm not planning to talk you into starting a family after dinner or anything."

Good. In the frame of mind he usually put me in, I'd have probably agreed.

"I have a stack of paperwork that I could probably do anywhere I found a pen."

"I have pens."

He chuckled quietly on the other end. "Yeah?"

"Would you like to do your paperwork at my place?"

"Only if you supply the pen."

"Deal." I smiled against the receiver.

Dad stopped his truck in front of Tom's and waved through the open window. "We've got it all, and we're headed home. Marvin's driving the ladies. Your car's filled to the gills."

"Thanks." I waved back.

Each vehicle in the Connors processional beeped at me as they motored away.

"I guess I'm heading home," I told Jake. "See you in an hour?"

"Thirty minutes," he drawled.

I headed back to my car with a little bounce in my step, grabbed the keys from my seat and went inside for a final sweep of the venue. The caterers were running vacuums and Swiffer vacs over the carpet and hardwood floors. The chairs and tables were broken down and stacked on carts to be rolled away. It was almost unbelievable that a party had been going on here an hour before.

I moved into the kitchen with a stack of envelopes from my bag.

A woman piling dishes into an industrial washer smiled in my direction. "Hello." Bubbles floated over her head, mingling with the scents of bleach and baked chicken. A Wonder Woman travel mug sat beside a cell phone and set of keys.

I forced myself not to start a conversation about the mug. When I'd attempted similar conversations in the past, the item that motivated me to speak always turned out to be a gift, it didn't belong to them, or the person I'd asked had no idea what I was talking about. I pried my gaze away from the mug. "I'd like to leave these here for the staff. I've marked them individually: chef, waitstaff, setup/cleanup and venue coordinator."

She rubbed her hands against her apron and accepted

the envelopes. "Of course. Is there anything else we can do for you before you go?"

Not unless she could tell me if Terrance Horton had killed Dante.

"No thank you. It was a lovely event. Have a nice night."

I drifted toward the front doors thinking of Wonder Woman. Wonder Woman would know what to tell my three nieces when little boys flipped their skirts up in elementary school and later when male peers told them to smile or made other ignorant comments. She'd know how to explain that knowledge was power and physical strength wasn't exclusive to those with a less stable XY chromosomal makeup. Wonder Woman made feminism cool and obvious. I didn't want to botch those lessons. My nieces were too important.

Women could be anything. I slowed my pace.

*They could even be killers.*

Ideas exploded in my mind like Fourth of July fireworks. If a woman had hidden in the backseat of Dante's car and stabbed him from behind, there would be no need to overpower him. Even a tiny person could be lethal in that situation, and it certainly didn't take any amount of physical strength to drown a bleeding man who couldn't swim.

I forced the grainy images from Mr. Peters's hidden camera to mind. Could the other figure in the footage have been a woman? A tall woman? The killer had a hood over his or her head when the pack jogged by me that night. I'd paid no attention. I hadn't known it was important. I pinched the bridge of my nose beneath my glasses. *Think, Mia.*

Dante's crazy ex-wife was tall and angry. Could she

have been behind this all along, and I'd discounted her at the start? Why had I done that? What was her alibi? She was working? That could've been faked. She could've left her phone at her desk. Why hadn't I looked at her more closely? Was it because she was a woman and I was a hypocrite?

My head pounded with frustration. The weight of my investigation came crashing over me. Details presented themselves at will, as if I'd known them all along but hadn't understood. The cabbie had picked up a professionally dressed woman. She'd had a story about a cheating lover, but that was smart, right? She'd even taken a ride to the airport to make it more real. She had a cover. The airport was the excuse Fifi had used when we needed a cover. Angelina was a professional. She was smart. She had a temper and openly loathed her ex-husband. She could've easily killed him from his backseat. The dagger was probably already in his car, a gift from Mr. Plotz.

I opened an internet browser on my phone. I needed a picture of Angelina that I could text to Calvin Besk. He might be able to identify her as the woman he'd picked up that night. I needed to call Jake, too, and tell him to forget his paperwork and get to my place fast. I knew who killed Dante, or I would as soon as I sent the text to Calvin.

A quick search of Angelina's name brought up dozens of web articles about Happy Farmer. I scrolled through the results, seeking a clear photo of her face. An article on A-Res Labs stopped me short. Why did that sound so familiar? I tapped the phone to my forehead, willing the information to the forefront.

Fresh adrenaline flooded my system, and a curse popped out of my mouth. I jogged in place while I read the article at warp speed. I didn't need to wait for confirmation from Calvin. I had her.

I dialed Jake.

"Archer."

"Angelina killed Dante," I nearly screamed. "She had a file on her desk from A-Res Labs when I visited her. A-Res Labs is a facility that breeds and distributes mice for testing. She had access to lab mice for her job at Happy Farmer. The mice started appearing after I questioned her. If she didn't kill Dante, then why try to scare me? Dante was our only connection."

"Slow down. Start again." The carefree voice that had answered the call was gone, replaced by the business-voice of a Deputy US Marshal. "I'm on my way, but keep talking."

"Okay." I made a dash for my car and switched the call to hands-free. "According to an article I found online, Angelina partnered with Dante on a veggie-wash venture. She'd created a formula that consumers could spray onto vegetable plants to repel bugs and wildlife. The spray was supposed to wash away with water and leave the veggies safe for consumption. She parted ways with A-Res and Dante after they had a dispute about the test mice. I think the mice on my car were lab mice from A-Res Labs. More specifically, I think they were lab mice Angelina had preserved to support her side of the dispute." I hit the highway and pressed the gas pedal to the floor.

"I'll contact Dan." Pride oozed through the phone to my heart. "We'll have Angelina picked up. Test the fiber from Dante's backseat against her. We've got some DNA from the dagger that didn't match the victim. If it's hers, she'll have a tough time explaining her way out of it. I'll be at your place in ten minutes. Stay put and lock the door. Call me if you need anything."

The world blurred past my window at more than seventy miles per hour. "Got it."

A round of clanging and banging rose from my backseat.

"What was that?" Jake asked.

Ice fingers slid down my spine. "My motion sensor monkeys." I'd left the opened box in my backseat.

I raised my eyes to the rearview mirror.

Angelina Weiss stared back at me with seething unfettered hate. "Hang up the phone."

# TWENTY-FOUR

"MIA!" JAKE DEMANDED. "Tell me what's going on and where you are."

I held Angelina's heated gaze. I'd been down the hostage road twice before. In both instances, I'd had no choice but to cooperate with my captor. This time I was in control. I flicked my attention back to the road and repositioned my hands on the wheel in sheer defiance. "Angelina Weiss is in my backseat telling me to give up my phone. We're approaching exit ninety-nine." I shot her a look and arched my brow. She'd gotten into the wrong car.

Angelina's eyes went wide before narrowing to slits. "You stupid cow!" she barked. She raised a Taser over the seat and pointed it at my head. "Pull over. Now!"

I glared at her in the mirror. "She has a Taser," I tattled. "I'm not sure how she thinks incapacitating her driver on the highway is going to end well for her."

"Mia," Jake snapped. "Do not provoke her. It's okay to pull over. I'm not far from ninety-nine. I'll be there in minutes with backup. Don't let her tase you while you're driving."

Anger spread through me. There weren't enough words to explain how tired I was of being a victim. I steadied the car and caught her gaze once more. "My car is the size of a roller skate and you aren't wearing your seat belt." I yanked the wheel to prove a point and veered onto the rural exit.

Angelina nearly fell over sideways.

I slowed to adjust for the curved ramp and turned my focus back to Jake. "I'm getting off here. I'll meet you at the police station."

I disconnected. The overwhelming sensation of euphoria and satisfaction warmed my bones. I lifted my cocky eyes to Angelina. "I'm turning you in myself."

She pressed the button on her Taser. "We aren't on the highway anymore."

Electricity jolted through my body. Pain pulsated like a thousand muscle cramps. My arms drew in. My legs flexed out. We peeled rubber through the intersection at the bottom of the off-ramp. My world went dark.

"WAKE UP!" a woman's voice screeched in my ear.

My face hurt. My body hurt. I dragged my eyes open.

Angelina stood outside my open car door, wild-eyed and spitting mad. Her hand whipped out and cracked my cheek. "Wake up!"

I opened my mouth to complain, but drool coursed over my chin instead. My wrists ached and burned. My thoughts were fuzzy. My heart banged painfully.

She fisted her hand in my tunic. "Not so smart now, are you? Wrecked your little car. Smashed your face. I knew I hated you the minute you walked into my office. Get up. Come on."

I forced rubbery legs out the door. She'd untethered my seat belt and bound my wrists with a zip tie while I was unconscious. "What are you doing?" The words slurred. My tongue was too big. I stretched and curled my fingers, taking a physical inventory. "I think you broke my pinky finger." Sore muscles. Confusion. Fatigue.

"Shut up and move it." She hoisted me to my feet and shoved me toward the tree line. "We aren't going to a police station."

Cornfields and country roads stretched in both directions. "What are we doing? Where are we going?"

She wiped frosting off her face with the back of one hand. Her fancy jeans and blouse were ruined. "I'm covered in cake. How am I supposed to explain that at the airport?"

"Bree's going to be pissed about her cake." Dad must've trusted me to bring the leftover foodstuffs from the shower. That was an unfortunate move.

*Where was my dad? Where was my phone?*

I blinked my swollen eyes, searching for clarity. "We're nowhere near the airport. You made me wreck my car. What are we doing?"

"Your car probably had a tracking system. We had to ditch it. Keep walking." She pressed the Taser against my back and shoved me forward. "I'm calling an Uber."

My heels stuck in the ground with every step. The car grew smaller and smaller in the distance over my shoulder. Tree cover thickened overhead. "I can't keep walking out here. My shoes are sinking. We need to walk on the road."

"Yeah, right. Then take off the shoes. I'm not an idiot. We're not walking along the road." She made a hacking sound in her throat and muttered under her breath.

I hopped on one foot, then the other, removing my favorite black patent leathers.

"Hurry up," she complained. "I'm on a schedule."

I dropped one shoe immediately and held the other

to my chest as we moved. The ground was bumpy and hot under my feet. I assessed my limbs once more. I didn't like the disconnect between my thoughts and actions. The crash might have rattled my brain. I could have a concussion or worse. I needed to pull myself together. Jake would find the car, but we'd made good time through the woods, all things considered. She could get away if I wasn't careful. I couldn't outrun her, barefoot, in the forest, but maybe I could slow us down until help arrived. Maybe I could take her out. I ran my finger along the stiff spine of my last shoe. If I tried and failed, she might not let up on the Taser trigger next time. It was risky, but I had to try. As soon as I could hold my thoughts together.

"Put it down, Mia." She jammed her weapon against my spine. The Taser dug into the tender skin at the back of my neck.

I flinched and stumbled. "What?"

"I know you still have one shoe in your hands. Don't even think of using it to attack me. Drop it!"

I obeyed. I'd lost one weapon, but we were surrounded by more. Rocks. Sticks. Trees. Besides, if Jake found the first shoe and stayed on our trail, he'd find the next, and hopefully me. My beautiful patent leathers had become modern-day bread crumbs. Images of pet store mice chowing on food pellets came to mind. "Why were you sending me dead mice from your lab?"

She stepped wide, appearing in my peripheral vision. Following a half step behind and to my right. "You were supposed to be afraid, assume you'd upset a killer, and stop poking around, but you didn't. I left more and more mice because you couldn't seem to get the obvious message."

"So, you just followed me around, leaving mice?"

"Yes!" she screamed. "I thought you were a cop, but the handsome one came to see me after you left, and he told me you weren't who you said you were. You tricked me. I knew you were going to be trouble."

I lifted my adjoined hands. "I never said I was a cop. You inferred that."

"You let me believe it!" She made maniac eyes at me. "I looked you up after I got rid of him and do you know what I found? I found Mia Connors the little millionaire. A tech nerd. A hardhead who'd chased down two other killers in a year. Considering my whole alibi was the fact I left my phone in my office, I needed you to buzz off."

I shuffled my tender feet, looking for safe places to step on the bumpy, stick-laden ground. "Yeah, well, I'm not easily diverted, and leaving the mice was dumb. The mice were what gave you away. I saw the A-Res file on your desk, and eventually I connected the mice on my car to mice from that lab."

"Why wouldn't you just stop snooping?"

An excellent question. "It's not in my nature. Why'd you keep following me? Why leave more and more mice instead of fleeing the country?"

She held the Taser inches from my head. Madness darkened her eyes. "I like my life! I didn't want to leave. I wanted you to stop poking around. Stop visiting Dante's clients and office and friends." Her voice screeched higher as her temper flared. "Everyone you talked to knew me. They knew how much Dante hated me. I imagined them all pointing at me. Every interview ending in my name. And all I had as a defense was a cell phone left on my desk all night."

The scent of burnt skin stung my nose. My vision blurred. "Are you going to kill me?"

She shook fisted hands in front of her, waving the Taser wildly. "I'm not a killer, or you'd be dead."

"Then can I sit down?"

She clicked the Taser trigger. Zzzz. Zzzz. "What do you think?"

I thought we were way too far from the car. I patted my pockets, recalling the phone call I'd been on when she'd appeared in my backseat.

"I took your phone. I pulled the SIM card, too, so there's no tracing us."

An old cemetery came into view at the crest of the hill.

Angelina laughed. "This is exactly what we need." She shoved me in the direction of an old mausoleum. The stone slabs were covered in moss and dirt. Shards of light filtered through leafy treetops, flickering and dancing on stones and the forest floor. The words once etched in the mausoleum dormers were long gone, eroded by age and weather. A rotting iron gate stood guard over the small dank interior. "Get in."

I grimaced. "I can't. It's locked." Something ran over my bare foot and I kicked spastically.

She shoved a loose rock in my direction with her foot. "Use this to break the lock."

Jeez, her feet had to be size ten. I blinked up at her face. Where did she find clothes? Where could she get shoes for those feet?

"Open it!" she screamed.

"I can't." I lifted my bound hands as evidence. My right pinkie finger was swollen like a sausage. "You'll have to untie me."

She rested her hands on her hips and examined the gate.

There was zero chance I was going willingly into a mausoleum this side of a personal invitation from my maker. "Why are you doing this?" I forced my marbles into order. The haze had lifted a bit, and my mind grew sharper by the minute. "Why are you abducting me? Why aren't you already in another country? This is a huge waste of time, and you're making everything worse."

She seemed to consider the words a moment. "Never mind. Just sit over there." She pointed to a large flat slab outside the rotting gate.

"You can leave. I won't follow you."

"Sit!"

I hobbled over broken twigs and discarded acorn shells, snagging the soft bottoms of my feet with every step and thoroughly ruining my pedicure.

She clicked the Taser trigger a few more times.

I sat.

Angelina lifted my joined wrists to the gate and liberated another zip tie from her back pocket. She connected the tie binding my hands with the new one on the gate and gave the connection a tug.

"Good enough." She produced a cheap-looking flip phone from her hip pocket and made a call. "Pick up at Orchard and Applegrove."

I jerked the ties, rattling the ancient gate. Reality sank in. She planned to leave me and make her getaway. No one would be looking for her at the airport. They'd be traipsing through the woods looking for *us*. "Why would someone as smart as you become a killer? Is it because you were jealous of Dante?" I braced for her retort. No self-respecting woman wanted to be accused of something as petty as jealousy, especially for an ex.

"Excuse me?" She cocked her head to one side and

stowed the flip phone in her pocket. "Do I look like the kind of woman who gets jealous? I could have any man I want. I've got more than any man could give me, and I did it all myself." Her eyes bulged. "Surely, you can see that."

I wiggled my ties, testing the gate. Flakes of rusted iron fell away. "I don't know. Stabbings are a crime of passion."

"That was an accident. The dagger was already back there and I was mad."

"You sure you weren't hiding in his car to see if he was with another woman?"

She snarled. "I hid in his car because the jerk wouldn't take my calls. He refused to see me," she seethed. "He'd once professed his love to me in front of our families and friends, but suddenly he couldn't be bothered to talk to me when my life was falling apart."

"Do you mean because of your failed plant wash?"

Her expression turned droll. She walked a few paces away for a look over the hill in every direction.

I worked at the bars with all my might, wearing away the decrepit material and finding hope in the rot.

"My wash didn't fail. He did. Dante promised to help me with the project, but all I needed from him was mice and a lab where I could run tests and document findings. He volunteered the mice. I thought it was a generous offer at first. I was wrong about him, as usual. Another client of his had a load of dying mice, already exposed to who-knows-what in a beauty supply lab. They offered the mice to Dante at a deep discount, so he bought them for me." Her face turned red. She looked to the sky. "I thought my product was killing the mice. It didn't make any sense, and I couldn't take it to the FDA when it killed every mouse I tested it on, so I ran physical tests on the mice and found they were all defective. When I confronted him, he told me he was sorry. Sorry. Can you believe that? I demanded retribution for what he'd put me through, the time I'd wasted. I never asked him to buy mice!" She shook her head. "He didn't have time to hear about the mess he'd made. He stopped taking my calls. I kept the mice as evidence. I wanted him to make it right."

I stilled when she turned back to me. The ancient bar was nearly broken. "You should've let it go. Now you're going to jail for murder."

"I told you that was an accident."

I nodded, mockingly. "Accidental stabbings happen all the time."

"I told him to stop the car so we could talk, but he wouldn't listen. He kept saying he had to go, and I had to get out, so I poked the blade through his seat to show him I meant business, but he did exactly what you did! He jammed the gas. Another car cut into our lane and Dante swerved. He got the car straightened out, but when he'd jammed the brakes to avoid the other car, the dagger…" She choked on the words. Tears sprang to her eyes. "I just wanted him to tell me he was sorry. Really sorry. Not shut-up-I'm-busy sorry. I wanted to hear that my product was worth more than half his attention and a bunch of sick mice. I begged his forgiveness when I saw all the blood, but he still wouldn't pull over and let me help him. Instead he called your grandmother." She made a wide-eyed, open-mouth, what-could-I-do expression. "I couldn't let him rat me out."

Sirens cut through the distance, delivered to my ears on warm summer wind. They grew quickly. I worked the binds faster.

Angelina turned in a circle, probably determining the best route for escape. "Tell them it was an accident."

"Sure thing."

She turned away and I lunged. The gate busted, throwing rust into my hair and face. Angelina ran.

My name echoed in the distance.

"Here!" I screamed, balancing my joined hands in front of me as I pounded through the forest behind Angelina. "We're here!"

"Stop that," she hissed. "Stop screaming. Go away."

Through the thinning trees on the south side of the hill, a yellow cab was visible on the corner of Orchard and Applegrove.

"Hurry!" I screamed. "Orchard and Applegrove! Orchard and Applegrove!"

"Shut up!" Angelina cursed. Her toe hit a half-buried limb and she lost her footing.

I grunted and dove for her, catching air for a moment as my flight and fall became one over the hill's edge. We collided in a tangle of hair and elbows, bouncing against the ground and rolling full speed toward the street below. The Taser flew from her grip and was swallowed by a pile of brush.

We wrecked into a set of saplings and young, bendy trees.

"Get off me!" She shoved hard, toppling me off her side.

I rose to my knees and gave chase as she crawled away, trying to find new footing. I hefted my arms into the air and brought them over her head and chest, securing her in a backward hug before she could stand.

"Where are you going?" She clawed my skin and

swore at the ties, forcing my arms higher as I lowered myself behind her.

She wasn't getting away. Not after what she'd put Dante and my grandma through.

She pulled me to my feet with her and flung us backward into the wide trunk of an old oak tree. Something cracked. Pain radiated down my spine.

I swung my short legs around her and locked bare, bleeding feet against her stomach. I was a tiny backpack on a giant woman.

We were only a few yards from her cab. I couldn't let her go.

Angelina bit my hand and slammed me into the tree again.

The sirens roared louder. Squad cars tore into view and surrounded the cab.

"We're here!" I yelled.

She tried to smash me into another tree, but I squeezed the air from her chest with my legs and three decades of horseback riding.

Fury roared through me. "Stop fighting! You're caught. Where are you going? They have your getaway cab." I adjusted myself on her back and angled the crook of my elbow around her throat. "Stop fighting." I squeezed. "Go to sleep."

She flailed, tossing blind slaps over her head and whacking me weakly.

"We're here," I cried out again.

Quiet sobs rocked my chest as I waited for her fight to slip away.

Her knees finally buckled, and we fell again. Not as far this time. My limbs were too numb from the last thumping to feel this one. We landed in a gulley beside the road. Years of dried-up leaves skated down the incline behind us and rained over our heads.

"Mia!" My name lifted on a dozen voices. "Mia!"

I thrashed my legs in the bug-infested leaves. "Here." I choked the word, eating dirt and who-knew-what else with each inhalation. "Here."

A shadow fell over us. Jake peered down with a look of humor or relief. I wasn't sure which. "Whatcha doin'?"

Hot tears slid over my burning cheeks. My teeth began to chatter. "I think I killed her. I wanted her to pass out before she broke my spine, but then we rolled again and her head's bleeding. She's not moving."

He crouched over us with a pocketknife and cut the ties binding my wrists.

I fell away, scrambling backward against the hill, putting distance between Angelina and me.

"We need a bus over here," Jake called.

A group of men I hadn't noticed before stood a few feet away with mixed expressions from confusion to elation.

I wiped trembling fingers under my eyes. "Is she dead?"

Jake lifted his fingers from her pulse. "Nope. How'd you learn to do that?"

"Standard dating-prep." I rubbed my battered wrists and winced when my right arm didn't appreciate the effort. "Dad was a beat cop with two daughters, remember?" He'd taught us self-defense from the moment we could comprehend it. The lessons got scarier when we wanted to date. "Angelina confessed."

Jake passed Angelina off to a pair of EMTs and reached for me. "Come on. You, too." He slid an arm around my back, the other under my legs and counted to three. A moment later, he cradled me to his chest and headed for the ambulances. "You're bleeding from your head, wrists and feet. Your clothes are torn and bloody. Your car is totaled." He settled me on a gurney. "These guys are going to take care of you. I've got my truck. I'll follow you to the hospital."

"I don't need a hospital."

An EMT wrapped my neck in a big cone. "I have to disagree." He slid a pressure cuff around my arm and pumped. "Burn marks on the neck."

"I was tasered."

He looked at Jake. "Probably how she wrecked the car."

"I'll get her official statement once you've got her stabilized and bandaged up."

A second medic pulled wide Velcro strips over my arms and chest. "There are multiple abrasions and contusions. Significant head trauma." He prodded the hot wet place at the back of my head. "This is going to need staples."

The first man hung a bag of clear liquid on a metal pole and prepped my hand for an IV.

"See you on the other side." Jake shut the doors and patted the side of the bus twice.

The vehicle rumbled to life.

Something warm crawled up my arm.

"Hey," I slurred. "What's in that baah?"

# TWENTY-FIVE

I CLIMBED OUT of Jake's truck and inhaled the sweet mountain air.

He grabbed our bags from the back and tossed them onto the porch at my family's cabin. "You were quiet on the way here. How are you doing?" He wound strong arms around my middle.

I unlocked the door and turned the knob, letting stale air out and fresh air in. "Good." Better now that his arms were around me and a long weekend lay before us.

The family cabin stood sentinel over a wide and marvelous gorge in the Blue Ridge Mountains. Mom and Dad had brought us here regularly as children, but I hadn't been back since high school.

I'd never looked forward to the trip the way I had this time. This getaway felt different, somehow. Pivotal. "I'm glad you finished your Terrance Horton case in time to join me."

"Wasn't too hard. Horton sang like a bird when we offered him a plea deal. Threatening a guy like that with a maximum-security prison usually does the trick."

"What about Angelina?" I forced the word from my lips. It was the first time I'd said her name aloud since giving my statement to the police ten times that night.

He tucked me against him, wrapping his arms tighter and resting his head on mine, as if he could secure me in an Archer cocoon and keep me safe forever. "She kept her mouth shut a while longer. Her attorneys are bartering a deal, but we matched her DNA to the DNA on the dagger, and the fibers in Dante's backseat were from her lab coat, probably stuck to her clothes then left behind at the crime scene. The medical examiner found her hair on Dante's jacket and her skin cells under his fingernails."

"From their tumble outside the lake."

He released me on a sigh. Big hands dug into the back of his neck. Frustration lined his forehead. "I should've gotten to her before she got to you."

"It's not your fault," I whispered.

"I'll decide that. Now, answer truthfully. How are you doing?"

In the two weeks since I'd tumbled down a hill with Angelina Weiss, I'd healed physically. The staples in my head were removed ten days later. Most of my bruises were gone, others were in the pale golden stage, and I didn't mind them as much. My pinky finger was splinted and covered in white gauze, but all things considered, I was lucky. Really lucky. I lifted the small cast on my left wrist. "By the time my fracture heals, the whole mess will be long forgotten."

Emotional healing would take time.

Jake stroked flyaway hair from my cheek. "How about the anxiety? You were still recovering from the last psychopath and it happened again." A storm brewed in his eyes.

"This wasn't your fault," I repeated. "Besides, at least Angelina didn't try to hurt me. She just wanted to get away. I was supposed to be a distraction." I placed a palm against his stubble-covered cheek. "I'm okay. Okay?"

He raised his eyes to mine. "Okay." He pulled me closer, his gaze sweeping the beautiful mountain views around us. "Now tell me something else. Does a girl like you have any idea what to do on a mountaintop for four days?"

I glanced at the cabin. "There's cable and cell service. Town's not far. Cooter's is a pretty good honkytonk, if you like those. And don't get me started on your assumption I can't have fun out here, or the fact you called me a girl. I am not a girl. I'm a woman."

He lowered his lips to my nose and planted a tiny kiss. "Yes, you are."

I smiled. "Don't forget it."

"Yes, ma'am."

I smiled at his sexy Southern drawl. "Did you know my mom's putting you in her book? She's portraying you as some kind of hero." I rolled my eyes.

Jake grinned. "I see she's done her homework."

"Yeah, and her literary agent was right about the interest in our family story. They signed a contract last week for a jaw-dropping advance. Mom's planning a kitchen remodel."

"Of course." He lowered his hands from my waist to my hips and hauled me against him. "We should invite the crew up here in a day or two. Nate, Fifi, maybe Dan and Reese."

"I'd like that. Grandma told me to invite you to her Vegas wedding. As if my family isn't crazy enough in Ohio, we're heading to Vegas."

"Has Nate proposed yet?" he asked. "Maybe they can have a double wedding. Streamline the whole thing."

I laughed. "You might be my soul mate."

"Sounds like a good gig." He lowered his lips to mine and kissed me slowly. He stopped far too soon and pulled back to look into my eyes. "I think this place would make a great place for a wedding."

I stroked the soft fabric over his broad shoulders. "Me, too."

His grouchy face appeared. "You'd like that?"

"Yeah." The thing I'd realized most over the past few weeks was that I'd marry Jake anywhere. I wasn't afraid of anything with him at my side, and losing him was something I feared more than any amount of embarrassment caused by saying so. "Were you thinking that I should get married up here?"

He made a shocked face. "Was that a proposal?"

"No." I laughed. "That would've been the world's worst."

"I thought so too. Besides—" he kicked up a crooked smile "—the man's supposed to ask."

I pulled in a long audible breath. "You and I have some work to do, Archer. And speaking of work…" I smiled. I'd saved the big news for our arrival. "I took Grandma's advice and offloaded some of mine."

"You and Nate finally chose a project manager?"

"Yep, me. I gave my notice at the Horseshoe Falls Clubhouse and suggested Fifi as my replacement. She'd be great in that role, and I'm sure the manager will gladly move her up. Everyone loves her."

"And you hired yourself as project manager?"

"Sort of. Nate and I hired his friend from Delecorte to assist on some big picture stuff at REIGN, but I'll be overseeing everything. We liked his company so much, I signed him on to help with some similar things at Guinevere's Golden Beauty. Now that I don't have anywhere to be from nine to five, I manage the project manager.

I'm still the boss, but now I'm a boss with minions and time to kiss her boyfriend."

"Well, I like how that sounds." He kissed my lips, my temple, my forehead.

I relaxed against him, arching my back for a better view of those smoldering blue eyes. "I've got a little more time than that."

He turned his black ball cap around backward and lowered his lips to mine.

I sank into his kiss and reveled in the taste of his lips. I fantasized about all the things we could do, alone on a mountain for four days. The crew could join us some other time.

His pant leg vibrated against me. Jake broke the kiss by a fraction, pulling his lips only a centimeter from mine. "Ignore it."

I wiggled and laughed. "I can't. It tickles."

He peeled himself away with a sigh and fished the phone from his pocket. "Archer."

My phone dinged on the seat of his truck. I crossed the short yard and stretched an arm inside the open window to retrieve my phone.

"Who's that?" Jake stood behind me frowning.

I read the screen aloud. "Bree thinks she's in labor." I tossed the phone back onto the seat. "Grandma started the phone tree. Who called you?"

"The team's got a lead on a fugitive near Lake Erie." He pushed the device back into his pocket.

"So, we're leaving?" I gave the cabin a long, sad look.

"I guess," he said, clearly disappointed. "Do you think we can get back before she has the babies?"

I wrinkled my nose. "We're not leaving for that."

"We aren't?"

"If I left a romantic weekend with you to watch Bree give birth again, she'd kill me."

He matched my crazy expression. "You were going to watch?"

"Well, yeah. We all…" I drifted off. "My family's…" I couldn't finish that sentence either. "What about you and the fugitive? I thought that was why we were leaving."

He lifted and dropped a shoulder, color rushing to his cheeks. "I told them I'm unavailable."

"Unavailable?" I liked the sound of that. As in off the market, spoken for. Mine.

"I explained how I'm in the middle of a very important operation at the moment and couldn't be disturbed."

My heart fluttered. I was important enough to him that he skipped the chance to chase a fugitive. Important enough that he wanted to play operation. Oh boy!

He towed me back against him. "Are you sure Bree won't mind if you aren't there to meet her new daughters?"

"No, Bree won't mind." I pulled his handsome face down to mine. "I think I love you."

His lips parted. Excitement flitted over his furrowed brows. "I know I love you."

Adrenaline and something else coursed through me. "You want to go inside and turn off our phones for a few days?"

Jake scooped me into his arms.

I kissed his face as he carried me inside. "Now that I've got all this free time, maybe I'll write a book like Mom."

"Oh, yeah?" He kicked the door shut behind us. "What are you calling your book?"

I kissed him slow and deep as he lowered me onto my feet. "How about *Geek Girl Gets the Guy*."

Jake lowered himself to one knee as I regained my footing. "That might be the perfect title. I'll let you know in a minute." He fished a little box from his pocket and popped it open.

I covered my mouth with one hand and pointed with the other. "That's the vintage ring Nate considered for Fifi."

"Nope."

"Yes, it is. He showed me a picture. He asked me if I liked it."

"Yes." Jake's bright eyes twinkled. "This ring belonged to my nana. She and Papa were married sixty-two years, and now I have a question to ask you."

Tears brimmed in my eyes as the most beautiful words I'd ever heard were spoken.

And I said yes.

\* \* \* \* \*

# ACKNOWLEDGMENTS

I'M SUPPORTED BY an incredible team of women who deserve a big thank-you. My critique partner, Jennifer Anderson. My best friend, Melinda Crown. My editor, Deb Nemeth. Additionally, my family, husband and children. Without them, I'd still be telling my stories to strangers in line at the market. And of course, I must thank my readers. Without you, there'd be no point. No inspiration. No motivation. No joy in the process. So, thank you, readers, for making it all worthwhile.

# ABOUT THE AUTHOR

JULIE ANNE LINDSEY is a multi-genre author who writes the stories that keep her up at night. She's a self-proclaimed nerd with a penchant for words and proclivity for fun. Julie lives in rural Ohio with her husband and three small children. Today, she hopes to make someone smile. One day she plans to change the world. Julie is a member of the International Thriller Writers (ITW) and Sisters in Crime (SinC). She is represented by Jill Marsal of Marsal Lyons Literary Agency. Julie sometimes writes as Julie Chase. Learn more about Julie Anne Lindsey at julieannelindsey.com.

# Get 4 FREE REWARDS!

## We'll send you 2 FREE Books <u>plus</u> 2 FREE Mystery Gifts.

**Love Inspired® Suspense** books feature Christian characters facing challenges to their faith... and lives.

FREE Value Over **$20**

# READERSERVICE.COM

## Manage your account online!

- Review your order history
- Manage your payments
- Update your address

> ### *We've designed the Reader Service website just for you.*

## Enjoy all the features!

- Discover new series available to you, and read excerpts from any series.
- Respond to mailings and special monthly offers.
- Browse the Bonus Bucks catalog and online-only exculsives.
- Share your feedback.

*Visit us at:*

# ReaderService.com